INTRODUCTION

Grandma is relocating from her house in the Wyoming country-side to a retirement home in the city and allows each of her four granddaughters to pick a favorite item from the attic.

Grandma's Doll by Wanda E. Brunstetter
When Sheila Nickels is offered something from her grandmother's attic, she chooses Grandma's doll. The trouble is, the doll isn't there anymore. Determined to find it, Sheila enlists the help of Dwaine Woods, a local antique dealer. Throughout the search Sheila fights her feelings for Dwaine and wonders if her trip to Casper, Wyoming, has been in vain. Will Sheila's desire to have a coveted childhood treasure interfere with God's will for her life?

Fishing for Love by Tammy Shuttlesworth
Kimber Wilson picks a box of old fishing tackle from her grand-mother's attic unaware it will lead her to the one man who can show her the true value of love. Jake Evans knows some of the antique lures are worth a lot and he believes Kimber should keep them, but will the call of money tempt her to throw away a chance at God-given happiness?

This Prairie by Janet Spaeth
Lauren Fielding and her husband, Bob, trade their high-powered careers in Chicago for the Nebraska farm where he'd spent many happy childhood hours. A christening dress from Lauren's grand-mother's attic, an unexpected litter of kittens, and a country church bring Lauren and Bob closer. Will returning to their heritage bring them back to God?

Seeking the Lost by Pamela Kaye Tracy
On further inspection of the intricately designed wooden box Jessica Fleming chose as a keepsake from her grandmother's attic, she finds some old photographs that lead her down a disturbing path. Her past is not as she'd always believed it to be, and now a man is asking questions that could lead to an even worse discovery. Does Jessica have the strength to go down this road?

ATTIC
Treasures

*Out of the Dust Came Memories of Yesterday
that Initiate Four Romances of Today*

WANDA E.
BRUNSTETTER

TAMMY
SHUTTLESWORTH

JANET
SPAETH

PAMELA KAYE
TRACY

BARBOUR
PUBLISHING

ISBN 1-59310-273-9

Cover image © GettyOne and Corbis

Illustrations by Cheryl Miller

Published by Barbour Publishing, Inc., P.O. Box 719, Uhrichsville, Ohio 44683, www.barbourbooks.com

Our mission is to publish and distribute inspirational products offering exceptional value and biblical encouragement to the masses.

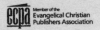
Member of the
Evangelical Christian
Publishers Association

Printed in the United States of America.
5

ATTIC
Treasures

Grandma's Doll

by Wanda E. Brunstetter

Dedication

To Aunt Margaret, who gave me her Bye-Lo baby doll
many years ago. Thank you for the special treasure
I will someday give to one of my granddaughters.

Chapter 1

S heila Nickels shivered as a blast of chilly March air pushed against her body. She slipped the tarnished key into the lock and opened the door. This was Grandma's house—the place throughout her childhood where Sheila had come for holidays, special occasions, and everything in between. She'd felt warmth, love, and joy whenever she visited this Victorian home on the north side of Casper, Wyoming.

Sheila stepped into the dark entryway and felt for the light switch on the wall closest to the door. "At least the electricity hasn't been turned off yet," she murmured.

An eerie sense of aloneness settled over her as she moved to the living room. Everything looked so strange. Much of Grandma's furniture was missing, and the pieces left had been draped with white sheets, including the upright piano Sheila and her cousins used to plunk on. Several cardboard boxes sat in one corner of the room, waiting to be hauled away. It was a dreary sight.

A sigh stuck in Sheila's throat, and she swallowed it down. She'd just come from visiting her grandmother at Mountain Springs Retirement Center on the other side of town. Grandma's one-bedroom apartment looked like a fishbowl compared to this grand home where Grandma and Grandpa Dunmore had lived for over fifty years. Grandpa passed away two years ago, but Grandma had continued to stay here until she finally decided taking care of the house was too much for her. She'd moved to the retirement center a few weeks ago.

Grandma's old house didn't look the same without the clutter of her antique furniture. It didn't sound the same without Grandma's cheerful voice calling from the kitchen, "Girls, come have some chocolate chip cookies and a glass of milk."

Sheila slipped off her coat and draped it across the arm of an overstuffed chair. She then placed her purse on the oak end table and turned toward the stairs. She was here at her grandmother's request and needed to follow through with what she'd set out to do.

As a feeling of nostalgia washed over her, Sheila climbed the steps leading to the second floor. Another flight of stairs took her to the attic, filled with so many wonderful treasures. A chain dangled from the light fixture overhead, and Sheila gave it a yank.

"Kimber, Lauren, Jessica, and I used to play here," she whispered into the dusty, unfinished room. She lowered herself to the lid of an antique trunk and closed her eyes, allowing the memories of days gone by to wash over her.

❧❦❀❦❧

"Look at me, Sheila. Aren't I beautiful?"

Sheila giggled as her cousin Lauren pranced in front of her wearing a pair of black patent leather heels that were much too big for her seven-year-old feet. Wrapped in a multicolored

10

crocheted shawl with a crazy-looking green hat on her head, Lauren continued to swagger back and forth.

"You can play dress-up if you want to, but I'm gonna get the Bye-Lo baby and take her for a ride." Sheila scrambled over to the wicker carriage, where the bisque-headed doll was nestled beneath a tiny patchwork quilt. Grandma had told her she'd made the covering many years ago when she was a little girl.

Of all the treasures in her grandmother's attic, the Bye-Lo baby was Sheila's favorite. She could play with it for hours while her three girl cousins found other things to do.

Sheila leaned over and scooped the precious doll into her arms. "Bye-Lo, I wish you could be mine forever."

❦

Sheila's eyes snapped open as she returned to the present. Since Grandma had already moved, her house would soon be put up for sale. She'd called Sheila at her home in Fresno, California, and invited her to choose something from the attic that was special to her. Sheila knew right away what that *something* would be—the Bye-Lo baby doll. Some might think it was silly, but when she was a child, Sheila had prayed she could own the doll someday, and her prayers were finally being answered. Now all she had to do was find her treasure.

Sheila scanned the perimeter of the attic. An old dresser sat near the trunk, and an intricately designed wooden container was a few feet away. Her gaze came to rest on the small wicker doll carriage, which Bye-Lo used to lie in. It was empty.

"How odd. The doll always sat in that baby carriage." She stood and lifted the lid of the trunk. "Maybe it's in here." Near the bottom she found several pieces of clothing that had

11

belonged to the doll. There was even a photograph of young Sheila holding her favorite attic treasure. The dolls she had owned as a child hadn't been nearly as special as Bye-Lo. The church her father had pastored then was small and didn't pay much. Sheila had learned early in life to accept secondhand items and be grateful, but she'd always wished for more.

She grabbed the picture and placed it in the pocket of her blue jeans, then slammed the trunk lid. "That doll has to be in this house someplace, and I'm not leaving until I find it!"

The telephone jingled, and Dwaine Woods picked it up on the second ring. "The Older the Better," he said into the receiver. "May I help you?"

"Is Bill Summers there?" a woman's gravelly voice questioned.

"Sorry, but Bill's not here. He sold his business to me a few months ago."

"Oh, I see. Well, this is Lydia Dunmore, and I did some business with The Older the Better Antique Shop when Bill owned it."

"Is there something I can help you with, Mrs. Dunmore?" Dwaine asked.

"As a matter of fact, there is. I'd like to see about having my old piano appraised. I've recently moved and will need to sell it."

"Sure. No problem. When would you like to have the appraisal done?"

"How about this afternoon? One of my granddaughters is at the house right now, and she could let you in."

Dwaine reached for a notepad and pen. "If you'll give me the address, I'll run over there and take a look. Would you like me to call you with my estimate, or should I give it to your granddaughter?"

"Just give it to Sheila. She'll be coming back to the retirement center where I live to return my house key sometime before she leaves Casper."

Dwaine wrote down the particulars, and a few minutes later he hung up the phone. Lydia Dunmore's house was on the other side of town, but he could be there in ten minutes. He put the CLOSED sign in the store's front window, grabbed his jacket off the antique coat tree, and headed out the door. Things had been slow at The Older the Better this week, but it looked like business might be picking up.

≈✦≈

With an exasperated groan, Sheila shut the lid on the cedar chest—the last place she had searched for Grandma's old doll. For the past couple of hours, she'd looked through countless boxes and trunks, organizing each one as she went. Except for the room being much cleaner now, her trip to the attic had been fruitless. There was no doll to be found.

"Grandma would probably tell me to choose something else," Sheila muttered, "but nothing here matters to me except the Bye-Lo baby."

Once more, Sheila thought about her grandmother's recent move and consoled herself with the fact that if Grandma hadn't left this rambling old house, Sheila and her girl cousins wouldn't have been asked to choose something special from the attic. The boy cousins had been invited to check out the basement for an item they would like to have.

"Too bad I can't find what's special to me," she grumbled.

13

Maybe the doll had been removed from the attic and was in one of the boxes downstairs. Sheila decided it was worth the time to take a look. She yanked on the chain to turn off the light and headed for the stairs. If she didn't find Bye-Lo in the next hour or so, she planned to head back to the retirement center. Maybe Grandma could shed some light on the doll's disappearance.

Sheila entered the living room and was about to kneel in front of a cardboard box when the doorbell rang. "I wonder who that could be."

She went to the front door and looked through the peephole. A man stood on the porch—an attractive man with sandy-blond hair and brown eyes. Sheila didn't recognize him, but then she hadn't lived in Casper for twelve years and didn't get back for visits that often. The man could be one of Grandma's neighbors for all she knew. He could even be a salesman, a Realtor, or. . .

The bell rang again, and Sheila jumped. Should she open the door? She sent up a quick prayer. *Protect me, Lord, if this man's a criminal.*

She slipped the security chain in place and opened the door the few inches it would go. "May I help you?"

"Hi, I'm Dwaine Woods from The Older the Better Antique Shop across town. I got a call to come here and take a look at an old piano."

Sheila's gaze darted to the living room. Grandma obviously had left the piano behind because there wasn't enough room in her apartment at the retirement center. How sad that Grandma felt forced to sell something she'd dearly loved for so many years.

14

"I have my business card right here if you'd like to see it," Dwaine said, as if sensing her reservations about opening the door. He reached into his jacket pocket, pulled out a leather wallet, and withdrew a card. "I bought the place from Bill Summers not long ago." He slipped it through the small opening, and Sheila clasped the card between her thumb and index finger. She studied it a few seconds and decided it looked legitimate.

"Who asked you to look at the piano?" she asked with hesitation.

"Lydia Dunmore. She called awhile ago and said she'd like an estimate. Told me her granddaughter Sheila was here and would let me in." He shuffled his feet across the wooden planks on the porch. "I presume that would be you?"

Sheila opened her mouth to reply, but the sharp ringing of the telephone halted her words. "I'd better get that. Be right back." She shut the door before Dwaine had a chance to say anything more.

❧

Not knowing how long he might be expected to wait, Dwaine flopped into the wicker chair near the door. He couldn't believe how nervous the young woman seemed. She acted like she didn't believe Lydia Dunmore had called and asked him to give an estimate on the piano.

She must not be from around here. Most everyone I know is pretty trusting. Dwaine hadn't been able to get a good look at her face through the small opening in the doorway, but he had seen her eyes. They were blue, like a cloudless sky, and they'd revealed obvious fear.

Sure hope she comes back soon and lets me in. Now that the sun's going down, it's getting cold out here. Dwaine stuffed his hands inside his jacket pockets while he tapped his foot impatiently. Finally, he heard the door creak open. A young woman with jet-black hair curling around her face in soft waves stared at him.

"Sorry for making you wait so long," she said. "That was my grandmother on the phone. She called to let me know you were coming to look at the piano."

Dwaine stood. "Does that mean I can come in?"

She nodded, and her cheeks turned pink as a sunset. "I'm Sheila Nickels."

Dwaine stuck out his hand and was relieved when she shook it. Maybe now that her grandmother had confirmed the reason for his visit, Sheila wouldn't be so wary.

"It's nice to meet you. I take it you're not from around here?"

She motioned him to follow as she led the way to the living room. "I grew up in Casper, but twelve years ago my folks moved to Fresno, California. My father's a minister and was offered a job at a church there. I was fourteen at the time."

"So you're a Christian then?"

She smiled. "I have been since I was twelve and went to Bible camp. That's when I acknowledged my sins and accepted Christ as my personal Savior."

Dwaine grinned back at her. "I'm a Christian, too, and it's always nice to meet others who have put their faith in the Lord."

She nodded. "I agree."

"What brings you to this part of the country?" he asked.

Sheila motioned to the array of boxes stacked in one corner of the room. "Grandma recently moved to Mountain Springs

Retirement Center, and she'll be putting this old house on the market soon."

"Which is why she wants to sell the piano?"

"Right. Grandma called me a few weeks ago and asked that I come here. She said she'd like me to choose an item from the attic—something I felt was special. Since she needed it done before the house sold, I decided to take a week's vacation and fly here before everything's been gone through." Sheila sucked in her lower lip. "She asked each of her granddaughters to come, and I'm the first to arrive."

"Have you found what you wanted yet?" he questioned.

She shook her head. "It's an old doll I'm looking for, but there was no sign of it in the attic."

Dwaine massaged the bridge of his nose. "Hmm. . .did you ask your grandmother about it? Maybe she moved the doll to some other part of the house."

Sheila pulled out the wooden piano bench and sat down. "I would have asked her when we were on the phone a few minutes ago, but I didn't want to leave you on the porch in the cold."

"If you'd like to call her back, you two can talk about the missing doll while I take a look at this old relic," he said, motioning to the piano. "I should have an estimate by the time you get off the phone."

"That sounds fine." Sheila turned and walked out of the room.

Dwaine moved over to uncover the piano and smiled. *She's sure cute. Guess I'll have to wait 'til she comes back to find out if she's married or not.*

Chapter 2

Sheila returned to the living room ten minutes later, a feeling of defeat threatening to weigh her down. She'd come all the way to Casper for nothing.

She tossed aside the white sheet on the aging, olive-green sofa and groaned. "I can't believe it!"

Dwaine sat on the piano bench, writing something on a notepad, but he looked up when she made her comment. "Bad news?"

She nodded, not trusting her voice and afraid she might break into tears if she related her conversation with Grandma.

Dwaine's forehead wrinkled. "What'd your grandmother say about the doll?"

"It's gone." She paused and drew in a deep breath. "Grandma said she sold it to you."

He shook his head. "I've never met Lydia Dunmore. The first contact I've had with her was today, when she asked me to appraise this." He motioned toward the piano with his elbow.

"She said she took the Bye-Lo doll to The Older the Better Antique Shop last fall and sold it."

"That may be, but I wasn't the owner back then. I bought

the place from Bill Summers two months ago."

Sheila sniffed. "Guess I'd better talk to him then. Do you have his home phone number or address?"

Dwaine fingered the small dimple in the middle of his chin. That, along with his sandy-blond hair and dark brown eyes, made him the most attractive man Sheila had met in a long time. *Of course, looks aren't everything,* she reminded herself. *Kevin Carlson was good-looking, too, and he broke my heart.*

"Bill moved to Canada right after he sold the store. I'm sorry to tell you this, but he's in the early stages of Alzheimer's, so his daughter and son-in-law came to Casper and moved him up there to be near them."

Sheila tapped her fingernails along the edge of the couch. "Are you saying he probably wouldn't remember what became of my grandmother's doll, even if I could contact him?"

"Exactly. The poor man wouldn't have been able to handle the details of selling the store if his family hadn't taken over and done all the paperwork." Dwaine shook his head. "It's sad to see an older person forced to give everything up when some unexpected illness overtakes his body or mind."

Sheila nodded and swallowed around the lump in her throat, feeling sad for Bill Summers and thankful Grandma was still fairly healthy. Then her thoughts went to the doll she would never have, and unable to control her emotions, she covered her face and let the tears flow.

Dwaine stayed on the piano bench a few seconds, unsure of what to say or do. He didn't want Sheila to misread his intentions if he offered comfort. He wrestled with his thoughts a moment longer and finally realized he couldn't remain seated and do nothing but watch her cry.

He hurried across the room and took a seat beside her on the couch. "Would you like me to call someone—your husband, grandmother, or some other relative?"

"I–I'm not married," she said with a sniffle. "And I don't want to bother Grandma. She's got enough problems of her own right now." Sheila lifted her head and looked at him through dark, heavy lashes. Her blue eyes were luminous behind the tears that filled them, and her chin trembled as she made a feeble attempt at smiling. "Sorry for blubbering like that. I don't know what came over me."

"I'm not married either, and I may not know a lot about women, but I do have a sister who can get pretty emotional at times, so I try to be understanding when someone's in tears."

When Sheila offered him another half smile, Dwaine fought the urge to wipe away the remaining moisture on her cheeks. He couldn't explain the reason this dark-haired beauty made him feel protective. He'd just met the woman, so it made no sense at all.

"I'd like to help you find that doll," Dwaine announced.

Her eyes brightened some. "How?"

"The first place I want to look is my antique shop. Even though I haven't seen any Bye-Lo dolls lying around, she could still be there hidden away in some drawer, a box, or a closet."

Sheila's dark eyebrows disappeared under her curly bangs. "You think so?"

"It's worth checking. At the very least we ought to find a receipt showing the doll was brought into the shop, and if it was sold again, there should be a receipt for that, too." Dwaine returned to the piano bench, where he retrieved the notepad. He ripped off the top page, moved back to the sofa, and handed the paper to Sheila. "Here's the estimate on the piano. If you want to give me the phone number of the place where you're staying, I'll call you if and when I locate the doll."

She frowned. "I was hoping, before I return Grandma's house key, that I might go over to your shop and see what you can find out."

"I haven't been all that busy today, so I guess we could head over there now and take a look."

"I'd appreciate that." Sheila reached into her jeans pocket and withdrew a picture. "This is me as a child, holding the Bye-Lo, in case you're wondering what the doll looks like."

He nodded. "Yep. About the same as the ones I've seen advertised in doll collector's magazines."

"I'm only here on a week's vacation, which means I won't be in Casper long. So if we could go to your shop now, that would be great."

It was obvious that Sheila was desperate to find her grandmother's doll, and Dwaine didn't have the heart to tell her it could take days or even weeks to go through everything in his store. Bill Summers hadn't been much of an organizer, not to mention the fact that he'd become forgetful toward the end. Dwaine had already discovered this was the reason so many things seemed to be missing or were found in some obscure places. Of course, Dwaine couldn't say much about being disorganized. Tidiness was not his best trait, either.

"If you have your own car, you can follow me over to the shop. If not, I'll be happy to give you a lift," he offered.

"That won't be necessary. My rental's parked in the driveway."

21

"Sounds good. Are you ready to head out then?"

She nodded and grabbed her jacket from the arm of an overstuffed chair, then reached for her purse on the end table.

"Oh, and by the way," he said, turning back to the piano and lifting the sheet off the top, "I found this while I was doing my appraisal. It looks old, and I figured it might be a family treasure." He handed her a black Bible with frayed edges and several pages ready to fall out.

Sheila smiled. "Thanks. This must belong to Grandma. I'll take it to her when I return the house key. She probably didn't realize she'd left it on top of the piano."

Dwaine felt a sense of relief. At least Sheila was smiling again.

✦✦✦

Sheila had never been inside an antique store so full of clutter, but she remembered Dwaine saying the previous owner's memory had been fading. The poor man probably had struggled with keeping the shop going and hadn't been able to clean or organize things. For all she knew, Dwaine might not be any better at putting the place in order. He did seem to be kind and caring, though, if one could tell anything from first impressions.

Kind, caring, and cute, Sheila mused as she followed Dwaine to a long wooden counter in the center of the store. An antique cash register sat on one end, and a cordless phone was beside it. An odd contrast, to be sure.

"I'll start by looking through the receipt box," Dwaine said as he reached under the counter and retrieved a battered shoe box that looked like it belonged in the garbage.

Sheila stifled a groan. *That's where he keeps his receipts? I'd say this man's in need of a good secretary as well as some new office supplies.*

While Dwaine riffled through the papers, Sheila leaned against the front of the counter and reflected on her job back in Fresno. For the last two years, she'd worked as a receptionist in a chiropractor's office. The clinic had been in total disarray when she was hired, and it had taken nearly six months to get everything organized. She'd finally succeeded, and the office was running more smoothly and efficiently than ever before. Dr. Taylor often praised Sheila for her organizational skills.

"Do you miss living in Wyoming, or are you a bona fide California girl now?" Dwaine asked, breaking into Sheila's thoughts.

"I like my job working as a receptionist for a chiropractor," she replied, "but I miss some things about living here."

"Such as?"

"Grandma for one. I used to love going over to her house and playing in the attic with my girl cousins. There were so many wonderful treasures there." She wrinkled her nose. "The boy cousins preferred to play outside or in the basement where they could get dirty and look for creepy crawlers."

Dwaine chuckled. "Anything else you miss about living in Casper?"

"The cold, snowy winters, when we went sledding and ice-skating."

"Guess you don't get much snow in California, huh?"

"Not in Fresno."

Dwaine laid the stack of receipts he'd already gone through on the countertop. "Is Lydia Dunmore your only relative living here now?"

"My cousin Jessica is still in the area, and so is Aunt Marlene. Mom and Dad are missionaries in Brazil, my brother lives in San Diego, and the rest of my aunts, uncles, and cousins have moved to other parts of the country."

Dwaine scratched the side of his head. "Most of my family lives in Montana, and my sister lives in Seattle, Washington. We all keep in touch through phone calls and e-mail."

Sheila nodded and fought the urge to grab a handful of receipts and begin searching for anything that might help find her missing Bye-Lo baby. Her conversation with Dwaine was pleasant, but it wasn't accomplishing a lot.

A few minutes later, Dwaine laid the last piece of paper on top of the stack. "There's nothing here that would indicate a Bye-Lo doll was bought or sold last fall, and these receipts go clear back to the beginning of April that year."

Sheila resented his implication, and she bristled. "Are you suggesting my grandmother just *thought* she brought the doll here and sold it to Bill Summers?"

Dwaine's ears turned pink as he shoved the receipts back into the shoe box. "I'm not saying that at all. Since Bill was so forgetful, it's possible he either didn't write up a receipt or filed it someplace other than the shoe box."

Which is a dumb place to file anything. Sheila forced a smile. "Now what do we do?"

Dwaine patted his stomach. "I don't know about you, but I'm starving. How about we go to the café next door and get some grub? Then, if you have the time, we can come back here and check a few other places."

Sheila's stomach rumbled at the mention of food. She hadn't taken time for lunch this afternoon, and breakfast had consisted only of a cup of coffee and a bagel with cream cheese. A real meal might be just what she needed right now.

She slung her purse over her shoulder. "Dinner sounds good to me."

Dwaine lifted one eyebrow and tipped his head. "Around here it's called supper."

She grinned up at him. "Oh, right. How could I have forgotten something as important as that?"

Chapter 3

Casper's Café wasn't the least bit crowded, but this was Wednesday, and Sheila remembered that most people didn't go out to eat in the middle of the week. At least not around these parts.

Sheila studied the menu place mat in front of her, although she didn't know why. She and Dwaine had already placed their orders for sirloin steaks and baked potatoes. It was more than she normally ate, but for some reason Sheila felt ravenous. Maybe it was the company. She felt comfortable sitting here in a cozy booth, inside a quaint restaurant, with a man who had the most gorgeous brown eyes she'd ever seen.

Dwaine smiled from across the table. "You remind me of someone."

"Who?"

He fingered the dimple in his chin. "I'm not sure. Shirley Temple, maybe."

Sheila squinted her eyes. "Shirley Temple had blond hair, and mine's black as midnight."

"True, but her hair was a mass of curls, and so is yours."

She reached up to touch the uncontrollable tendrils framing

her face. Her hair had always been naturally curly, and when she was a child, she'd liked not having to do much with it. Now Sheila simply endured the nasty curls, envying others with straight, sleek hair.

He traced his fingers along the edge of the table. "Do you know what an original Shirley Temple doll is worth on today's market?"

She shook her head.

"Several hundred dollars."

"Wow. That's impressive."

"Your lost Bye-Lo baby's going for a tidy sum, too."

"Really?"

He nodded. "I saw an eighteen-inch Bye-Lo listed in a doll collector's magazine several weeks ago, and it cost a thousand dollars."

Sheila's mouth fell open. "That's a lot of money. I had no idea the doll was so valuable."

"Actually, the eight-inch version, like your grandmother had, is only selling for five hundred dollars."

"Only?"

"You see that as a bad thing?"

"It is for me, since I don't have the doll or that kind of money lying around."

"We're going to find it," Dwaine said with the voice of assurance, "and it might not cost as much as you think. If the doll's still at my shop, I can sell her back to you for whatever Bill Summers paid your grandmother, which I'm sure wasn't nearly as much as the doll is worth."

Sheila's heart hammered. Why should she be forced to buy something she was told she could have? Of course, Grandma hadn't actually said Sheila could have the doll. It had been sold several months ago, and Grandma probably figured there were lots of other things in the attic Sheila could pick from.

She squeezed her eyes shut, hoping to ward off the threatening tears. It might be childish, but she wanted that doll and nothing else.

"You okay?"

Sheila felt Dwaine's hand cover hers, and her eyes snapped open. "I—I'm fine. If you can find the doll, I'll pay you whatever you think it's worth."

"I'll do my best."

Sheila studied Dwaine's features—the prominent nose, velvet brown eyes, sandy-blond hair, and heavy dark eyebrows. He looked so sincere when he smiled. Hopefully, he meant what he said about helping find the precious Bye-Lo baby. Maybe he wasn't like Kevin, who'd offered her nothing but lies and broken promises.

"You mentioned earlier that your folks are missionaries in Brazil."

"Yes. They've been living there for the past year."

"That sounds exciting. My church sent a work and witness team to Argentina last summer. The group said it was a worthwhile experience."

"Are you active in your church?" Sheila questioned.

He reached for his glass of water and grinned at her. "I teach a teen Sunday school class. Ever since I accepted the Lord as my Savior, I've wanted to work with young people." He chuckled. "I was only fourteen at the time of my conversion, so I had to grow up and become an adult before they'd let me teach."

Sheila relaxed against her seat. *Why couldn't I meet someone as nice as you in Fresno?* She shook her head, hoping to get herself thinking straight again. Her vacation would be over in a week, and then she'd be going back to California. It might be some time before she returned to Casper for another visit. Dwaine Woods could be married by then.

"So if your folks live in Brazil and your brother lives in San Diego, what's keeping you in Fresno?" Dwaine asked.

"My job, I guess." Sheila fingered her napkin. What was taking their order so long?

"That's all? Just a job?"

She nodded. "As I said earlier, I work as a receptionist at a chiropractor's office."

Dwaine leaned his elbows on the table and looked at her intently. "You're so pretty, I figure there must be a man in your life."

Sheila felt her face heat up. Was Dwaine flirting with her? He couldn't be; they barely knew each other. "There is no man in my life." *Not anymore.*

She was relieved when their waitress showed up. The last thing she wanted to talk about was her broken engagement to Kevin. She was trying to put the past to rest.

"Sorry it took so long," the middle-aged woman said as she set plates in front of them. "We're short-handed in the kitchen tonight, and I'm doing double duty." There were dark circles under her eyes, and several strands of gray hair crept out of the bun she wore at the back of her neck.

"We didn't mind the wait," Dwaine said. He smiled at Sheila and winked. "It gave me a chance to get better acquainted with this beautiful young woman."

His comment made her cheeks feel warm, and she reached for her glass of water, hoping it might cool her down.

"Would you mind if I prayed before we eat?" he asked when the waitress walked away.

"Not at all." Sheila bowed her head as Dwaine's deep voice sought the Lord's blessing on their meal and beseeched God for His help in finding her grandmother's doll.

Maybe everything would work out all right after all.

❧❦❧

Dwaine became more frustrated by the minute. They'd been back at his shop for more than an hour and had looked through every drawer and cubbyhole he could think of. There was no sign of any Bye-Lo doll or even a receipt to show there ever had been one.

"Maybe your grandmother took the doll to another antique shop," he said to Sheila, who was searching through a manila envelope Dwaine had found in the bottom of his desk.

"She said she brought it here."

"Maybe she forgot."

Sheila sighed. "I suppose she could have. Grandma recently turned seventy-five, and her memory might be starting to fade."

Dwaine looked at the antique clock on the wall across the room and grimaced. "It's after nine. Maybe we should call it a night."

She nodded and slipped the envelope back in the drawer. "You're right. It is getting late, and I've taken up enough of your time."

30

"I don't mind," Dwaine was quick to say. "This whole missing doll thing has piqued my interest. I'm in it 'til the end."

"If there is an end." Sheila scooted her chair away from the desk and stood. "Since you have no record of the doll ever being here, and we don't know for sure if Grandma even brought it into this shop, I fear my Bye-Lo baby might never be found."

The look of defeat on Sheila's face tore at Dwaine's heartstrings. She'd come all the way from California and used vacation time, and he hated to see her go home empty-handed. He took hold of her hand. "I'm not ready to give up yet. I can check with the other antique shops in town and see if they know anything about the doll."

Her blue eyes brightened, although he noticed a few tears on her lashes. "You'd take that much time away from your business to look for my doll?"

"Searching for treasures is my job."

"Oh, that's right."

He squeezed her fingers. "Why don't you go back to your grandmother's and get a good night's sleep? In the morning, you can come back here, and we'll search some more."

She drew in a deep breath. "I'd like that, but I'm not staying with Grandma. I'm staying at a hotel."

"How come?"

"Her apartment at the retirement center is too small. She only has one bedroom."

"But you have other relatives in town, right?"

She nodded. "Jessica and Aunt Marlene. Jessica's painting her kitchen right now, and I'm allergic to paint. And Aunt Marlene is out of town on a cruise."

"Guess a hotel is the best bet for you then, huh?"

"Yes, and since I'll only be here a short time and got a good deal on the room, I'm fine with it."

He grinned at her. "Great. I'll look forward to seeing you tomorrow then, Sheila."

"Yes. Tomorrow."

Chapter 4

S heila stood at her second-floor hotel window, staring at the parking lot. She'd slept better last night than she thought she would, going to bed with confidence that her doll would be found. Dwaine had assured her he would locate the missing doll, and for some reason, she believed him. The new owner of The Older the Better seemed honest and genuinely interested in helping her.

Sheila crammed her hands into the pockets of her fuzzy pink robe. *Of course, he could just be in it for the money. Dwaine did tell me the Bye-Lo baby is worth several hundred dollars.*

The telephone rang, and she jumped. Who would be calling her at nine o'clock in the morning? She grabbed the receiver on the next ring. "Hello."

"Sheila, honey, it's Grandma."

"Oh, hi."

"I didn't wake you, did I?"

"No, I was up. Sorry I didn't get by your place last night to drop off the house key. I'll come by later today, okay?"

"No hurry, dear. You'll be here a week and might want to visit the old place again."

Sheila's gaze went to the Bible Dwaine had found. She'd set it on the nightstand by her bed. "Grandma, Dwaine found a Bible on top of the piano yesterday. Would you like me to bring that by when I drop off the key?"

"An *old* Bible?"

"Yes, it's black and kind of tattered."

"That belonged to your grandpa. Guess it didn't get packed. Would you like to have it, Sheila?"

"Don't you want to keep it?"

"Since you haven't been able to locate the Bye-Lo doll, I'd like you to have the Bible."

"I'd be honored to have Grandpa's Bible, but I'm still going to keep looking for the doll."

"That's fine, dear. Speaking of the doll. . . What did you and that nice young man find out yesterday?" Grandma asked. "Did you find a receipt?"

Sheila blanched. How did Grandma know she and Dwaine had spent time together searching for anything that might give some clue as to what had happened to her Bye-Lo baby?

"Sheila, are you still there?"

"Yes, I'm here." Sheila licked her lips. "How did you know I was looking for the doll with the owner of The Older the Better?"

"He called me yesterday afternoon. Said the two of you were going through some papers in his shop."

"It must have been while he was in the back room," Sheila said. "I never heard him call you."

Grandma sneezed and coughed a few times, and Sheila felt immediate concern. "Are you okay? You aren't coming down with a cold, I hope."

She could hear Grandma blowing her nose. "I'm fine. Just my allergies acting up. I think I'm allergic to the new carpet in my apartment here."

Sheila's heart twisted. Grandma shouldn't have been forced to leave the home she loved and move to some cold apartment in a retirement center where the carpet made her sneeze.

"Why don't you come back to Fresno with me for a while?" Sheila suggested. "I live all alone in Mom and Dad's big old house, and if you like it there, you can stay permanently."

"Oh, no! I could never move from Casper." There was a pause. "It's kind of you to offer, though."

Sheila understood why Grandma had declined. Her roots went deep, as she'd been born and raised in Casper, Wyoming. She had married and brought her children up here as well. Besides, Grandma probably wouldn't be able to adjust to the heat in California, especially during the summer months.

"I understand," Sheila said, "but please feel free to come visit anytime you like."

"Yes, I will." Another pause. "Now back to that young man who's helping you look for my old doll. . ."

"What did Dwaine want when he called you?" Sheila asked.

"Dwaine?"

"The new owner of The Older the Better."

"Oh. I think he did tell me his name, but I must have forgotten it."

Sheila dropped to the bed. So Grandma *was* getting forgetful. Maybe she had taken the doll to some other place. Or maybe Bye-Lo was still in her grandmother's possession.

"How come Dwaine phoned you?" Sheila asked again.

Grandma cleared her throat. "He said you and he were

going to eat supper together."

"He called to tell you that?"

"Where did you go, dear?"

"To Casper's Café. It's near his shop."

"How nice. I was hoping you would get out and have a little fun while you're here."

Sheila stifled a yawn. "Grandma, I didn't come back to Casper to have fun. I came to choose something from your attic, remember?"

"Yes, of course, but you're twenty-six years old and don't even have a serious boyfriend." Grandma clucked her tongue. "Why, when I was your age, I was already married and had three children."

"Grandma, I'm fine. I enjoy being single." *Liar. I almost married Kevin and was looking forward to raising a family someday.*

Sheila gripped the phone cord in her right hand. "I don't want to spend the rest of my life alone, but the Lord hasn't brought the right man into my life." *And maybe He never will.*

"You might be too fussy," Grandma said. "Did you ever think about that?"

Sheila swallowed hard. Maybe she was. She'd had many dates over the years, but except for Kevin, she'd had no serious relationships.

She shook her head, trying to clear away the troubling thoughts. "Grandma, why did Dwaine really phone? I'm sure it wasn't to inform you that he and I planned to grab a bite of dinner at Casper's Café."

"Supper, dear. We call it supper around here."

Sheila blew out her breath. "Supper then."

"Let's see. . . I believe he called to ask me some questions about the doll."

Sheila's hopes soared. "Did you remember something that might be helpful?" She didn't recall Dwaine saying anything about his call to Grandma. Surely if he'd discovered some helpful information, he would have told her.

Grandma released a sigh. "I'm afraid not, but he did say he was looking for a receipt."

Sheila jumped off the bed and strode back to the window as an idea popped into her head. "What about your copy of the receipt, Grandma? Didn't Bill Summers give you one when you took the doll in?"

"Hmm. . ." Sheila could almost see her grandmother's expression—dark eyebrows drawn together, forehead wrinkled under her gray bangs, and pink lips pursed in contemplation.

"I suppose I did get a receipt," Grandma admitted, "but I have no idea where I put it. With the mess of moving and all, it could be almost anywhere."

"I see." Sheila couldn't hide her disappointment.

"I've got a suggestion."

"What's that, Grandma?"

"Why don't you go over to The Older the Better again today? You're good at organizing and might be able to help find it."

"I doubt that." Sheila had already spent several hours in Dwaine's shop. The place was a disaster, with nothing organized or filed in the way she would have done had she been running the place.

"Besides," Grandma added, "it will give you a chance to get to know Dwaine better. He's single, you know. Told me so on the phone yesterday."

Sheila's gaze went to the ceiling. Grandma was such a romantic. She remembered how her grandmother used to talk about fixing candlelight dinners for her and Grandpa. Grandma delighted in telling her granddaughters how she believed love and romance were what kept a marriage alive. "That and having the good Lord in the center of your lives," she had said more than once.

Sheila reflected on a special day when Grandma had taken her, Kimber, Lauren, and Jessica shopping. The girls had just been starting into their teen years, and Grandma had bought them each a bottle of perfume, some nail polish, and a tube of lipstick. Then she'd told them how important it was to always look their best in public.

"You never know when you might meet Mr. Right," Grandma had said with a wink. As they drove home that day, Grandma had sung "Some Enchanted Evening."

"Sheila, are you still there?"

Grandma's question drove Sheila's musings to the back of her mind. "Yes, and I will go back to the antique shop today," she replied. "But please don't get any ideas about Dwaine Woods becoming my knight in shining armor."

"Of course not, dear. I'll let you make that decision."

⤞⋆⤝

Dwaine whistled as he polished a brass vase that had been brought in last week. It was an heirloom and would sell for a tidy sum if he could find the right buyer. He hoped it would be soon, because business had been slow the last few weeks, and he needed to make enough money to pay the bills that were due.

If I could find that Bye-Lo doll for Sheila, I might have the money I need.

A verse—1 Timothy 6:10—popped into Dwaine's head. *"For the love of money is a root of all kinds of evil."*

"I don't really love money, Lord. I just need enough to pay the bills."

Then *"My God will meet all your needs according to his glorious riches in Christ Jesus,"* from Philippians 4:19, came to mind.

Dwaine placed the vase on a shelf by the front door. He'd done the best he could with it and knew it would sell in God's time. And if he found Sheila's doll, it would be because he was trying to help, not trying to make a profit at her expense.

An image of the dark-haired beauty flashed into his head. Sheila fascinated him, and if she lived in Casper, he would probably make a move toward a relationship with her.

But she lives in California, he reminded himself. *She'll be leaving soon, so I shouldn't allow myself to get emotionally involved with a woman I may never see again.*

The silver bell above the front entrance jingled as the door swung open. Sheila stepped into the store, looking even more beautiful than she had the day before.

Dwaine's palms grew sweaty, and he swallowed hard. So much for his resolve.

"Hi, Sheila. It's good to see you again."

Chapter 5

S heila halted when she stepped through the door. Dwaine
stood beside a shelf a few feet away, holding a piece of
cloth and looking at her in a most peculiar way.

"Good morning," she said, trying to ignore his piercing gaze.
*Is my lipstick smudged? Could I have something caught between
my teeth?*

"You look well rested." He smiled, and she felt herself
begin to relax.

"The bed wasn't as comfortable as my own, but at least I
slept."

"That's usually the way it is. Hotel beds never measure up
to one's own mattress."

Dwaine's dark eyes held her captive, and Sheila had to look
away.

"Have you had breakfast yet?" he asked. "I've got some cinnamon rolls and coffee in the back room."

"Thanks, but the hotel served a continental breakfast." She
took a step forward. "I dropped by to see if you've had any luck
locating the Bye-Lo doll or at least a receipt."

"Sorry, but I haven't had time to look this morning." He

nodded toward a brass vase on the shelf. "I started my day by getting out some items I acquired a few weeks ago."

Sheila struggled to keep her disappointment from showing. "I suppose I could go visit Grandma or my cousin, Jessica, then check back with you later on." She turned toward the door, but Dwaine touched her shoulder.

"Why don't you stick around awhile? I'll give you more boxes to go through, and while you're doing that, I can finish up with what I'm doing here."

She turned around. "You wouldn't mind me snooping through your things?"

Dwaine leaned his head back and released a chuckle that vibrated against the knotty pine walls.

"What's so funny?"

"When you said, 'snooping through my things,' I had this vision of you dressed as Sherlock Holmes, scrutinizing every nook and cranny, while looking for clues that might incriminate me."

Sheila snickered. "Right. That's me—Miss Private Eye of the West."

"I know we covered quite an area yesterday," Dwaine said, "but there are a lot of boxes in the back room, not to mention two old steamer trunks. If you'd like to start there, I'll keep working in this room, trying to set out a few more things to sell."

"Sounds like a plan." Sheila shrugged out of her jacket and hung it on the coat tree near the front door.

Dwaine nodded toward the back room. "Don't forget about the coffee and cinnamon rolls, in case you change your mind and decide you're hungry."

"Thanks." Sheila headed to the other room as the bell rang,

indicating a customer had come in. She glanced over her shoulder and saw an elderly man holding a cardboard box in his hands.

❦

Here, let me help you with that." Dwaine took the box from the gray-haired man who'd entered his shop and placed it on the counter.

The man's bushy gray eyebrows drew together. "My wife died six months ago, and I've been going through her things." His blue eyes watered, and he sniffed as though trying to hold back tears.

"I'm sorry about your wife, Mr.—"

"Edwards. Sam Edwards." He thrust out his wrinkled hand, and Dwaine reached across the counter to shake it.

"My wife had a thing for old dolls," Sam went on to say. "I have no use for them, and I could use some extra money. If you think they're worth anything and want to buy 'em, that is."

Dwaine rummaged through the box, noting there were three dolls with composition heads and bodies, two wooden ball-jointed bodies with bisque heads, and an old rubber doll that looked like it was ready for burial. He was sure there was some value in the old dolls—all except the one made of rubber. He could probably make a nice profit if he had the dolls fixed, then sold them at the next doll show held in the area. Still, the dolls might be heirlooms, and he would hate to sell anything that should remain in someone's family.

"Don't you have children or grandchildren who might want your wife's dolls?" Dwaine asked.

Sam shook his head. "Wilma and I never had any kids, and

none of my nieces seemed interested when I asked them."

"How much are you needing for the dolls?" Dwaine asked, knowing there would be some cost for the repairs, and he might not get his money back if he paid too much for them.

"A hundred dollars would be fine—if you think that's not too high."

Dwaine shook his head. "Actually, I was thinking maybe two hundred."

Sam's eyebrows lifted. "You mean it?"

"Two hundred sounds fair to me."

"All right then."

Dwaine paid the man, escorted him to the front door, and went back to inspect the dolls now in his possession.

"How's it going?" Sheila asked as she entered the room an hour later. "Are you getting lots done?"

He shrugged. "Not really. A man brought in this box of dolls that belonged to his late wife. I've been trying to decide how much each is worth, which ones will need fixing before I can resell them, and which ones to pitch."

"You wouldn't throw out an old doll!" Sheila looked at him as though he'd pronounced a death sentence on someone.

She hurried over to the counter before Dwaine had a chance to respond. "May I see them?" she asked.

He stepped aside. "Be my guest."

❧❦❧

Sheila picked up the rubber doll first. It had seen better days, although she thought there might be some hope for it. The head was hard plastic and marred with dirt, but it wasn't broken. The rubber body was cracked in several places, and a couple of fingers and toes were missing. Sheila didn't know much about doll repairs, but it was obvious the rubber body could not be repaired.

"The ball-jointed dolls need restringing, and all the composition ones could use a new paint job," Dwaine said. "I don't see any hope for the rubber one, though."

"But the head's in good shape. Couldn't a new body be made to replace the rotting rubber?" Sheila loved dolls and hated the thought of this one ending up in the garbage.

"Replace it with another rubber body, you mean?"

She shook her head. "I was thinking maybe a cloth one. Even if you could find another rubber body, it would probably be in the same shape as this one."

"My sister lives in Seattle, and there's a doll hospital there. I could take these when I visit Eileen next month for Easter." Dwaine smiled. "Our family always gets together at Easter time to celebrate Christ's resurrection and share a meal together."

Sheila thought about all the Easter dinners she and her family had spent at Grandma and Grandpa Dunmore's over the years. She missed those times, and now that Mom and Dad were on the mission field, unless she went to San Diego to be with her brother, she'd be spending Easter alone.

Dwaine closed the lid on the cardboard box. "I'll worry about these later. Right now, let's see if we can locate your Bye-Lo baby. Unless you've already found something in the back room, that is."

She released a sigh. "Afraid not. I did manage to tidy up the place a bit, though."

"You organized?"

Was he irritated with her, or just surprised?

"A little. I took a marking pen and wrote a list of the contents on each box. Then I placed the boxes along one wall, in alphabetical order. I also went through the old trunks, but there was nothing in those except some ancient-looking clothes, which I hung on hangers I found in one of the boxes." She took a quick breath. "I hung the clothes on the wall pegs, and that might help take some of the wrinkles out."

Dwaine released a low whistle. "You've been one busy lady!"

She wondered if he was pleased with her organizational skills or perturbed with her meddling. "I hope you don't mind."

He shook his head. "What's to mind? Your offer to snoop has helped get me more structured. At least in the back room." He nodded toward the front of his shop. "This part still needs a lot of help."

"I'd be glad to come by any time during my stay in Casper and help you clean and organize."

Dwaine tipped his head to one side. "You're too good to be true, Sheila Nickels."

"I just like to organize."

"I'm glad someone does." He made a sweeping gesture with his hand. "As you can probably tell, neatness isn't my specialty. Guess I'm more comfortable in chaos."

She shrugged but made no comment.

"I think I'll check one more spot for a receipt," Dwaine said, "then I say we take a break for some lunch."

Sheila had to admit she was kind of hungry. "That sounds fine."

Dwaine marched across the room, pulled open the bottom drawer of a metal filing cabinet, and rummaged through its contents.

Sheila stood to one side, watching the proceedings and itching to start organizing the files alphabetically.

"Bingo!" Dwaine held up a receipt and smiled. "This has got to be it, Sheila."

She studied the piece of paper and read the scrawled words out loud. "Bye-Lo doll, in good condition: Sold to Weber's Antiques, 10 South Union Avenue, Casper, Wyoming." Sheila frowned. "There's no date, so we don't know when Bill Summers sold Grandma's doll."

Dwaine scratched the side of his head. "How about we take a ride over to Weber's? It's on the other side of town, and there's a good hamburger place nearby."

"Why not just phone them?"

He shook his head. "It'll be better if we go in person. That way, if Tom Weber doesn't still have the doll, you can show him the picture you have, and he'll know if that's the same doll we're looking for."

Sheila blew out an exasperated breath. "Of course it's the same doll." She pointed to the receipt in his hands. "It says right here that it's a Bye-Lo."

He nodded. "True, but it might not be the same one your grandmother sold to Bill Summers."

She shrugged. "Okay, let's go find out."

Chapter 6

Sheila leaned her elbows on the table and scowled at the menu in front of her. They'd paid a visit to Weber's Antique Shop but had come up empty-handed. After looking at the receipt Dwaine showed him and checking his own records, Tom Weber had informed them he'd received a Bye-Lo doll several months ago but had sold it to a doll collector in town. He'd been kind enough to give them the woman's address, and Dwaine had eagerly agreed to drive over to Mrs. Davis's place to see if she had the doll. After going there, Dwaine had suggested they stop for a bite to eat.

"I can see by the scowl on your face that you're fretting about the doll and the fact we still haven't found it."

Dwaine's statement jolted Sheila out of her contemplations. "I was just thinking we're no further ahead than when we first started."

He shook his head. "I don't see it that way. We found a receipt for a Bye-Lo doll, discovered it had been sold to Weber's Antiques, who in turn sold it to Mrs. Davis, who said she'd originally planned to make new clothes for it and then sell it at the next doll show she went to."

"Then she ended up giving it to her niece for her birthday, but the girl's in school right now so we can't even check on that lead." Sheila pursed her lips as she thought about how much Grandma's doll meant to her. However, she wasn't sure she could take the doll away from a child, even though she would be offering payment.

Dwaine reached for his glass of iced tea. "Let's eat lunch and get to know each other better, then we'll drive over to Amy Davis's house at three thirty, which is when her aunt said she should be home from school."

"I suppose we could do that, but it's only one now. What do we do between the time we finish eating and three thirty?"

"How about we return to my shop, where I can wait for potential customers and you can do more organizing?" He wiggled his eyebrows. "My place is such a mess, and you've done a great job so far in helping get things straightened out."

She smiled in spite of her disappointment over not yet finding Grandma's doll. She had made Dwaine's antique shop look better, and if given the chance, she probably could put the whole place in order.

❦

Dwaine whistled as he washed the front window of his store. It was more enjoyable to clean and organize when he had help. Sheila was at the back of the store, putting some old books in order according to the author's last names. Dwaine thought it was kind of silly, since this wasn't the public library, but if it made her happy, he was okay with the idea. Besides, it allowed him more time to be with her. He didn't think it was merely Sheila's dark, curly hair and luminous blue eyes that had sparked his interest, either. His attraction to Sheila went much deeper than her physical beauty. She was a Christian, which was the most important thing. Dwaine knew dating a nonbeliever was not in God's plan.

When he heard Sheila singing "Jesus Loves Me," Dwaine smiled and hummed along. When the song ended, he shook his head. *She and I are complete opposites. She likes to organize; I'm a slob. She says "dinner"; I say "supper". She's from sunny California; I'm from windy Wyoming. Still, during the time we've spent together, she has made me feel so complete.*

The grandfather clock struck three, and Dwaine set his roll of paper towels and bottle of cleaner aside. "I think we should head over to Amy Davis's place," he called to Sheila. "She should be home from school by the time we get there."

Sheila strolled across the room. "Are you sure you have time for this, Dwaine? If you keep closing your shop, you might lose all your customers."

He shook his head. "Nah, I'll leave a note saying what time I plan to return, and they'll come back if they were here for anything important."

She eyed him curiously. "Don't you worry about money?"

He shrugged. "It does help pay the bills, but I've come to realize money can't be my primary concern."

"Why are you in business for yourself then?"

"I like what I do." He smiled. "And if I can make a fairly decent living, that's all that matters."

"But you won't even do that if you keep closing your shop."

"Not to worry, Sheila. I'm enjoying the time spent with you."

She blushed. "At first I thought you were only helping me so you could make some money, but since the doll's not in your shop, if we do find her, there's really nothing in it for you."

He grabbed his jacket off the coat tree. "What can I say? I'm just a nice guy trying to help a damsel in distress."

⁂

Sheila climbed the steep steps leading to the home of Amy Davis. It was a grand old place and reminded her of Grandma's house. A small balcony protruded from the second floor, and Sheila couldn't help wondering if that might be Amy's room. *Any girl would love to have a balcony off her bedroom. I know I would.*

When Sheila heard a *thunk*, she glanced over her shoulder. To her shock, she discovered Dwaine lying on the bottom step, holding his leg. Her heart lurched, and she rushed to his side. "What happened?"

He groaned. "I was so intent on looking at Mrs. Davis's historical-looking house that I wasn't watching where I was going and missed a step. Fell flat, and I think I sprained my ankle."

Sheila felt immediate concern when she looked at his ankle, already starting to swell. "If you hadn't been traipsing all over town trying to help me find my grandmother's doll, this never would have happened. What if it's broken? What if you can't work because of the fall?"

Dwaine smiled, even though he was obviously in pain. "I'm sure it's not broken, and it's definitely not your fault." He winced as he tried to stand.

"Here, let me help you." Sheila offered her arm, and Dwaine locked his elbow around hers. "I'd better drive you to the hospital so you can have that ankle X-rayed."

He shook his head. "Not yet."

"What do you mean, not yet? In case it is broken, you need immediate care."

"Just help me to the car. I'll wait there while you speak to Amy Davis."

"Are you kidding me? I can't leave you alone while I go running off to see about a doll that might never be mine."

He hopped on one foot and opened the car door on the passenger's side. "We're here, it's three thirty, and you need to know once and for all if your grandmother's doll is still around."

"But Amy might not want to part with it, and I can't fault her for that."

Dwaine slid into the seat and grimaced. "Ouch."

"Are you sure you're going to be okay?"

"I'll be fine. Now please go knock on the door and find out if the doll's here or not."

Sheila looked up at the stately home, then back at Dwaine again, and sighed. "I'll only be a few minutes, and as soon as I'm done, we're going to the hospital."

He saluted her. "Whatever you say, ma'am."

Sheila closed the car door and made her way up the long flight of stairs. *I'm surprised it wasn't me who fell. I was studying this grand home, too, and it could have been my ankle that was injured instead of Dwaine's.*

A few seconds later, she stood on the front porch and rang the doorbell. While she waited, she glanced down at her rental car. At least Dwaine hadn't wasted his gasoline on this trip.

Finally, the door opened and a middle-aged woman with light brown hair greeted her with a smile. "May I help you?"

"I'm looking for Amy Davis."

"I don't believe I've met you before. Do you know my daughter?"

Sheila extended her hand. "I'm Sheila Nickels, and I'm in Casper visiting my grandmother who lives at Mountain Springs Retirement Center."

The woman shook Sheila's hand, but her wrinkled forehead revealed obvious confusion. "I'm not sure what that has to do with Amy."

Sheila quickly explained about her visit to Grandma's attic, the missing Bye-Lo doll, and how she and Dwaine had gotten Amy's name and address.

"Let me get this straight," Mrs. Davis said. "You believe the doll Amy's aunt gave her might actually be your grandmother's doll?"

"Yes, I think it's quite possible."

Mrs. Davis opened the door wider. "Please, come in."

Sheila took one last look at the car. She could see Dwaine leaning against the headrest, and a wave of guilt washed over her. She should be driving him to the hospital now, not taking time to see about a doll. *But I'm here,* she reminded herself, *and Dwaine insisted he was okay, so I may as well see what I can find out.*

"Have a seat in the living room and I'll get my daughter." Mrs. Davis ascended the stairs just off the hallway, while Sheila meandered into the other room and positioned herself on the couch. It was near the front window, so she could keep an eye on Dwaine. *I hope his leg's not broken, and I pray he isn't in much pain.* Sheila hated to admit it, but the carefree antique dealer was working his way into her heart, even though she'd only met him yesterday. It wasn't like her to have strong feelings for someone she barely knew. She, who had kept her heart well guarded since her broken engagement to Kevin.

Sheila heard the floor creak, and she snapped her attention away from the window, turning toward the noise. A teenaged girl with hazel-colored eyes and long blond hair gazed at her with a curious expression. "I'm Amy Davis. My mother said you wanted to speak to me and that you were interested in the doll my aunt gave me for my birthday."

Sheila nodded. "Yes, that's right."

"I hope you're not planning to take the Bye-Lo away, because I collect dolls, and she's special to me."

"I–I just want to see her. I need to know if she's the same doll my grandma used to have in her attic." Sheila didn't have the heart to tell Amy that if it was Grandma's doll, she planned to offer payment to get it back.

"Hang on a minute." Amy whirled around and hurried out of the room. A short time later, she was back, holding a small cardboard box in her hands. She set it on the coffee table in front of the couch and opened the lid. Carefully, almost reverently, she lifted the doll and cradled it in her arms as though it were a real baby.

Sheila's heart hammered. It sure looked like Grandma's doll. It was the same size and had the exact shade of brown painted on its pink porcelain head, and the doll's hands were made of celluloid. "May I have a closer look?"

With a reluctant expression, Amy handed Sheila the doll. "Be careful with her. She's breakable."

"Yes, I know." Sheila placed the Bye-Lo baby in her lap and lifted her white nightgown.

"What are you doing?" Amy's eyes were huge, and she looked horror-struck.

"I want to see if there's any writing on her tummy."

Amy dropped to the couch beside Sheila. "Why would there be writing? I never wrote anything on the doll."

"If this is my grandmother's, then my name should be on the stomach. I wrote it there when I was a little girl, hoping someday the doll would be mine." Sheila pulled the small flannel diaper aside, but there was no writing. Part of her felt a sense of relief. At least she wouldn't be faced with having to ask Amy to give up a doll she obviously cared about. Another part of her was sad. Since this wasn't Grandma's doll, then where was she?

Sheila smoothed the clothes back into place and handed the Bye-Lo to Amy. "It's not my grandmother's doll, and I apologize for having troubled you."

Amy's mother stepped into the room just then. "It was no bother." She walked Sheila to the door. "I hope you find your grandmother's doll. I suspect it meant a lot to you."

Sheila could only nod in reply, for she was afraid if she spoke she might break down in tears. It was clear she wasn't going to locate the missing doll, and now she had to take Dwaine to the hospital to have his ankle checked out. All she'd accomplished today was getting Dwaine hurt and making herself feel more depressed. *Maybe I never should have come back to Casper. Maybe I'm not supposed to have that doll.*

Chapter 7

For the next week, Sheila divided her time between Mountain Springs Retirement Center, to see Grandma, and The Older the Better Antique Shop, to help Dwaine. After his ankle had been X-rayed, the doctor determined that it wasn't broken but he'd sprained it badly. Dwaine would be hobbling around on crutches for a couple of weeks, which would make it difficult to wait on customers, much less stock shelves, clean, or organize things in his shop. Since Sheila felt responsible for the accident, she'd called her boss and asked if she could take her last two weeks of vacation now. Dr. Carlson agreed, saying the woman he'd hired in Sheila's absence was available to help awhile longer and telling Sheila to enjoy the rest of her time off. Since Sheila couldn't afford another week or two at a hotel, after speaking with Grandma, she decided to stay in her grandmother's old house until she felt ready to leave Casper. There was still enough furniture for her to get by, and since the power was on, she figured she could manage okay.

"This is so much fun," she muttered under her breath as she dumped another load of trash into the wastebasket near Dwaine's desk. Every day this week when she'd been helping

Dwaine, Sheila had continued to search for Grandma's doll or a receipt. No amount of cleaning or organizing revealed any evidence that the doll had ever been in Dwaine's store. Dwaine had phoned all the other antique shops in town, but no one had any record of her grandmother's doll. Sheila felt sure it was hopeless.

"I'd like to meet your grandmother in person and ask a few more questions about the doll," Dwaine said as he hobbled up to Sheila on his crutches.

"That's a great idea. Grandma's been wanting to meet you, and I happen to know she baked a batch of peanut butter cookies yesterday afternoon."

He wiggled his eyebrows. "One of my all-time favorites."

Sheila smiled at Dwaine's enthusiasm. He reminded her of a little boy. During the past week, she'd gotten to know him better. His lackadaisical attitude and disorganization bothered her some, but he had a certain charm that captivated her. Not only was Dwaine good-looking, but he seemed so kind and compassionate. Several times she'd seen him deal with customers, and always he'd been polite and fair in his business dealings. Even though Sheila knew little about antiques, she could tell by the customers' reactions how pleased they were with the prices he quoted.

"So when do we leave?"

Dwaine's question halted Sheila's musings, and she gazed up at him. "Oh, you mean go to Grandma's place?"

He nodded and grinned at her. "That's where the peanut butter cookies are, right?"

"Yes. I just didn't realize you wanted to go there this minute."

"Business has been slow this morning, so there's no time like the present."

Sheila was tempted to say something about Dwaine's overly casual manner, but she decided it was none of her business how he handled things at his shop.

He made his way across the room and reached for his jacket. In the process, the coat tree nearly fell over, and Sheila was afraid Dwaine might lose his balance, too. With one hand she grabbed the wobbly object; with the other she took hold of Dwaine's arm. "Better let me help you with your jacket."

As soon as they had their coats on, she opened the front door, stepped outside, and headed for her rental.

"I've always wondered how it would feel to have a chauffeur," Dwaine said in a teasing voice. "Since I sprained my ankle, it's been kind of nice having you drive me around."

꧁꧂

Dwaine had never been to Mountain Springs Retirement Center, but when they pulled into the parking lot, he was impressed with the facilities. The grounds were well cared for and included numerous picnic tables, wooden benches, bird feeders, and a couple of birdbaths.

When they entered the building, he noticed the foyer was decorated with several green plants, and a huge fish tank was built into one wall.

Sheila led the way, walking slowly down a long corridor and up the elevator to the third floor. Soon they were standing in front of a door with Lydia Dunmore's name engraved on a plaque.

A few minutes after Sheila knocked, the door opened. A slightly plump, elderly woman with her hair styled in a short bob greeted them with a smile. Her blue eyes sparkled, the same way Sheila's did, and she held out her arms. "Sheila, what a nice surprise!"

Sheila giggled and embraced the woman. "Grandma, you know I've dropped by here nearly every day since I came back to Casper. I don't see how my being here now can be such a surprise."

"Of course not, dear, but this is the first time you've shown up with a man at your side." She glanced over at Dwaine and smiled. "And such a nice-looking one, too."

Dwaine's ears burned from her scrutiny, and he noticed Sheila's face had turned crimson as well.

"Grandma, this is Dwaine Woods, the new owner of The Older the Better Antique Shop."

"It's nice to meet you in person. I'm Lydia Dunmore." She held out her hand.

Dwaine was surprised at the strength of Lydia's handshake. "It's good to meet you, Mrs. Dunmore."

"Lydia. Please call me Lydia."

He nodded in reply.

"Sheila told me about your ankle. How are you doing?"

"Getting along quite well, thanks to your granddaughter helping out at my shop."

"Glad to hear that. So now, to what do I owe the privilege of this visit?" she asked, motioning them inside her apartment.

"I heard you made some cookies," Dwaine blurted.

Sheila nudged him gently in the ribs. "I can't believe you said that."

"Me neither." Dwaine shook his head. "The words slipped out before I had time to think. Sorry about that, Mrs.—I mean, Lydia."

58

She chuckled and headed for the small kitchen area. "You remind me of my late husband. He always said exactly what was on his mind."

Sheila pulled out a wooden stool at the snack bar for Dwaine and took his crutches, placing them nearby. "Have a seat. Grandma loves to entertain, so I'm sure she can't wait to serve us."

⋘⋙

Sheila studied Dwaine's profile as he leaned his elbows on the counter and made easy conversation with Grandma.

"Yes, ma'am," he said in answer to Grandma's most recent question. "I've gone to church ever since I was a boy. Accepted the Lord as my Savior when I was a teenager, and now I teach a teen Sunday school class."

Grandma piled a plate high with peanut butter cookies and placed it in front of Dwaine. Then she poured a tall glass of milk and handed it to him.

"Hey, don't I get any?" Sheila stuck out her lower lip in an exasperated pout.

"Don't worry your pretty little head." Grandma put half as many cookies on another plate, poured a second glass of milk, and handed them to Sheila.

Before Sheila could voice the question, Grandma said, "What can I say? He's a growing boy with a sprained ankle and needs more cookies than you do."

Dwaine patted his stomach. "If I'm not careful, I'll be growing fat."

"You could use a little more meat on your bones." Grandma glanced at Sheila. "Don't you think so, dear?"

Sheila's face flamed. She thought Dwaine looked fine the way he was. A bit too fine, maybe. She sure wasn't going to admit that to her grandmother, though.

Searching for a change of subject, Sheila said, "Dwaine and I have looked high and low for anything that would show you took the Bye-Lo doll to his shop, but we haven't found a thing."

Grandma tipped her head to one side. "Guess you'd better make another trip to my attic."

"I appreciate the offer, but as I told you before, there's nothing else I want." Sheila took a bite of her cookie. "Umm. . .this is good."

"Thanks." Grandma grinned and snatched a cookie from Sheila's plate. "I'm glad you two stopped by so I didn't have to eat them all myself."

"I was wondering if you've had the chance to look at my appraisal of your piano," Dwaine said.

Grandma's forehead wrinkled. "Your offer sounds fair, Dwaine, but to tell you the truth, I'm having a hard time parting with that old relic. I've had it since I was a girl."

Dwaine swallowed the last of his milk. "Too bad there isn't room for it here."

Tears welled up in Grandma's eyes. "Even if I could have had it moved to this apartment, I don't think the others who live here would appreciate my playing it. These walls aren't soundproof, you know."

"There's a piano downstairs in the game room," Sheila said. "Grandma can play that whenever she wants."

"Maybe someone in your family would like to buy the piano," Dwaine said.

Grandma smiled. "I'll have to ask around."

Dwaine looked at Sheila. "One good thing has come from hunting for the missing doll."

"Oh, what's that?"

"I've gotten to know you."

"The man has a point," Grandma put in. "I can tell by the way you two look at each other that you're a match made in heaven."

"Grandma, please!" Sheila knew her face must be bright red, because she felt heat travel up the back of her neck and cascade onto her cheeks.

"You look a little flushed, dear. I hope you're not coming down with something."

"I think Sheila's embarrassed by your last statement," Dwaine said, coming to Sheila's rescue.

Grandma looked sheepish. "Sorry about that."

"Dwaine and I barely know each other," Sheila said. "I think you're a romantic at heart, Grandma."

Grandma grinned. "Your grandpa and I got married after knowing each other only one month, and we had a wonderful marriage. It's always been my desire that each of my children and grandchildren find a suitable mate and know the kind of happiness Grandpa and I had." She winked at Dwaine. "Sheila's more priceless than any of my attic treasures, so don't let her get away."

Chapter 8

Sheila and Dwaine drove back to his shop in silence. He was busy writing something in a notebook he'd taken from his jacket pocket, and she needed time to think. Was Grandma right about her and Dwaine? Were they a match made in heaven? Could it be that God had brought Sheila back to Casper to begin a relationship with Dwaine, not for the Bye-Lo baby?

Sheila gripped the steering wheel as a ball of anxiety rolled in the pit of her stomach. *No, it couldn't be. If I allow myself to fall for this man, one of us would have to move. A long-distance relationship won't work. Kevin proved that when he moved to Oregon and sent me a letter saying he'd met someone else.*

As though he sensed she was thinking about him, Dwaine looked over at her and smiled. "It's almost noon, and I'm getting kind of hungry. Should we stop for lunch somewhere?"

Sheila focused on the road ahead. "After all those cookies you ate at Grandma's, I wouldn't think you'd have any room for lunch."

"Aw, those only whetted my appetite."

She snickered. "Yeah, I could tell."

"Seriously, I would like to take you to lunch."

"How about I pay for the meal today? You bought me dinner—I mean, supper—a couple times last week and only let me leave the tip." She clucked her tongue. "And that was just because I threatened to make a scene if you didn't."

Dwaine tapped the notebook against his knee. "You really don't have to even things out. I enjoy your company, and while our meals aren't exactly dates, I find myself wishing they were."

Sheila's heart pounded, and her hands became sweaty. "You do?"

"Yep. In fact, I've been working up the nerve to ask if you'd go out with me."

"You mean something more than supper?"

"Right. A real date, where I come to your grandma's old place and pick you up."

"Where would we go?" Sheila hadn't meant to enjoy his company so much. She'd be leaving Casper soon, and then what?

"I thought maybe we could take in a show. A couple of good movies are playing right now, and tonight there shouldn't be a lot of people."

"But this is Monday—a weeknight," she reminded.

"And?"

"You'll need to get up early tomorrow for work." Sheila was an early to bed, early to rise kind of person, and it was a good thing. Dr. Carlson opened his chiropractic clinic at eight o'clock, five mornings a week, and Sheila had never been late to work.

"I own my own business, which means I can set my own hours," Dwaine replied.

"Still, maybe we should wait until Friday to go out."

"I don't want to wait that long. You'll be leaving for

California soon, and we shouldn't waste the time you have left."

Sheila's heart skipped a beat. "You've seen me nearly every day for the last two weeks."

"Those weren't dates. That was business." He touched her arm, and even through her jacket she felt warm tingles.

Sheila stared at the road ahead. She had to keep her focus on driving, not Dwaine. The truth was, except for his disorganization, he had all the attributes she was looking for in a man. Dwaine appeared to be kind, gentle, caring, humorous—and as a bonus, he was good-looking—but most important, he was a Christian.

"You haven't said if you'll go out with me tonight or not," he prompted.

Sheila took a deep breath and threw caution to the wind. "Sure, why not? Since we can't seem to find Grandma's doll, I may as well make good use of my time spent here."

A knock at the door let Sheila know her date had arrived. She took one last look in the hall mirror and hurried to answer it, hoping she looked okay. She'd decided to wear a long black skirt and a pale blue blouse, which she knew brought out the color of her eyes.

When she opened the door, Sheila's breath caught in her throat. Dwaine was dressed in a pair of beige slacks and a black leather jacket, and a bouquet of pink and white carnations was tucked under one arm. "The flowers are for you, pretty lady."

Since Dwaine's hands gripped his crutches, Sheila reached for the bouquet. "Thanks. They're beautiful." She scanned the room, looking for something to put the flowers in. "I'd better get a glass of water from the kitchen. I'm pretty sure Grandma's vases have all been packed away, because I haven't seen any in the kitchen cupboards."

When Sheila returned a few seconds later, she set the glass of water on the small table in the entryway and placed the flowers inside.

"You look beautiful tonight," Dwaine said, offering her a wide smile.

"You don't look so bad yourself."

"Ready to go?"

She nodded and grabbed her coat from the closet, but before she could put it on, Dwaine set his crutches aside and took it from her. "Here, let me help you with that."

"You're going to fall over if you're not careful."

"Nah. I'm gettin' good at doing things on one foot."

As Sheila slipped her arms inside the sleeves, she shivered.

"You cold?"

"No, not really." She buttoned the coat and opened the door. "What times does the show start?"

"Not until seven thirty. I thought we'd start with dinner at a nice restaurant, then follow it with the movies."

Sheila snickered. "You just said 'dinner' instead of 'supper.' "

He winked. "This is a date. Gentlemen take their ladies out to dinner, not supper."

❧

Sheila hated to see her date with Dwaine end. Dinner had been delicious, the show had been great, and she'd enjoyed every minute spent in his company. Now they stood on Grandma's front porch, about to say good night.

"I had a good time tonight. Thanks," Sheila said.

"Yeah, me, too." His voice was husky, and his dark eyes held her captive. "How about a drive to the country tomorrow during our lunch break? I can get chicken to go from Casper's Café."

She licked her lips. "That sounds good. I love fried chicken."

There was an awkward pause, then Dwaine lowered his head and his lips sought hers. The kiss was gentle and soft, lasting only a few seconds, but it took Sheila's breath away. Things were happening too fast, and her world was tilting precariously.

"Good night. See you tomorrow," Dwaine murmured before she had a chance to say anything. He hobbled down the steps, leaving Sheila with a racing heart and a head full of tangled emotions as she shut the door.

She'd been caught up in the enjoyment of the evening and had let him kiss her. "I've got to call a halt to this before one of us gets hurt," she mumbled at her reflection in the mirror. "Even though I enjoy Dwaine's company and believe he's a true Christian, a long-distance relationship will never work. I'll tell him in the morning that I'd rather not take a drive to the country."

Somewhere in the distance an annoying bell kept ringing. Pulling herself from the haze of sleep, Sheila slapped her hand on the clock by the antique bed in Grandma's guest room. "It can't be time to get up. It seems like I just went to bed."

The ringing continued, and she finally realized it was the

phone and not her alarm. She grabbed for the receiver. "Hello."

"Hi, Sheila, it's Dwaine. When you didn't show up at nine this morning, I started to worry. Are you okay?"

Sheila stifled a yawn and rolled out of bed. "I'm fine." She glanced at the clock and cringed when she realized it was almost ten o'clock. "Sorry, guess I overslept and must have forgotten to set the alarm."

"That's okay, but I've got some news to share when you get here."

"Can't you tell me now? I'm curious." Sheila stretched and reached for her fuzzy pink robe.

"I stayed up last night reading some doll collector's magazine I recently bought, and I think I may have found your missing doll."

She flopped onto the bed, draping the robe across her legs. "Really? What makes you think it's the one?"

"It fits the description you gave me, and there's some writing on the doll's cloth body. Could be your name, Sheila."

She sucked in her breath. *Maybe the trip to Casper hasn't been a waste of time after all.* Her conscience pricked. *How could I even think such a thing? Grandma's here, and I've enjoyed spending time with her—Dwaine, too, for that matter.*

"Sheila, are you still there?"

"Yes, yes. You really think you've found my grandma's doll?"

"There's no way to be sure until you take a look at the magazine." There was a brief pause, and Sheila thought she heard the bell above the door of Dwaine's store jingle. "A customer just walked in, so I'd better go," he said. "If you can come over as soon as possible, we'll have time to check out the doll information before we go for our drive."

Sheila clutched the folds in her robe. "About our picnic date—"

"Gotta go. See you soon, Sheila."

There was a click, and the telephone went dead. Sheila blew out her breath and placed the phone back on the table. Even though she was a bit put out with Dwaine for hanging up so abruptly, she felt a sense of elation over the possibility that he might have actually found Grandma's doll.

❧❧❧

For the next hour, when Dwaine wasn't waiting on customers, he watched the door, anxious for Sheila to arrive. He was excited to show her the information about the Bye-Lo doll in the magazine he'd found, but more than that, he looked forward to seeing Sheila again. After their date last night, he was convinced he wanted to begin a relationship with her.

Dwaine snapped the cash register drawer shut and shook his head. *This is ridiculous. I can't be falling for someone who lives three states away. Would Sheila be willing to relocate? I don't think I could live in California.*

The bell above the door jingled as one customer left the store and another entered. It was Sheila, wearing a pair of blue jeans with a matching jacket. "Have you got time to show me that doll magazine?" she asked.

"Sure. There's a lull between customers, so come on back." Dwaine motioned for Sheila to follow him over to his desk in one corner of the room. He leaned his crutches against the side of the desk and took a seat. She sat in the straight-backed oak chair nearby.

Dwaine pointed to the magazine. "Here's the Bye-Lo that

caught my attention. Don't you think she looks like your grandmother's old doll?"

Sheila jumped out of her chair and leaned over his shoulder. "That does look like her, but I can't be sure. I wish the writing on the doll's stomach was clearer."

Dwaine stared at the picture. "Guess I'd better contact the person who placed this ad and ask what the writing says."

"It might be good to find out how much they're asking for the doll, too." Sheila blew out her breath, and he shivered as it tickled his neck.

"I want that doll really bad, but if it's going to cost too much, I may have to pass."

"After all the searching we've done, you can't walk away if this is your grandmother's doll. I'm sure we can work something out."

"I'm serious, Dwaine. Besides paying for the doll, I'll have to cover the cost of your services."

He swiveled his chair, bumping heads with her in the process.

"Ouch!"

"I'm so sorry." He wrapped his arms around her, and she fell into his lap.

Sheila let out a gasp, but he covered her mouth with his before she could protest. His lips were soft, warm, and inviting. She responded by threading her fingers through the back of his hair.

Dwaine wished the kiss could have gone on forever, but the spell was broken when another customer entered the store.

Sheila jerked her head back and jumped up. Her face was the shade of a ripe Red Delicious apple.

"I—I'd better get to work. I've got a lot more cleaning to do in the back room." She stumbled away from Dwaine.

"We'll stop work at noon so we can take our drive to the country with a picnic lunch," he called after her.

"I've changed my mind and decided not to go."

The door to the storage room clicked shut before Dwaine could say anything more. He turned to the elderly woman who had entered the shop and forced a smile. "May I help you, ma'am?"

Chapter 9

Sheila paced back and forth, from the living room window of Grandma's old house to the couch, still covered by a sheet. She'd left The Older the Better almost two hours ago and hadn't heard a word from Dwaine. He'd said he would call her tonight if he heard from the doll collector.

Of course, she reasoned, *it might take days for him to get a reply about the doll. But I'll be leaving soon, and then what?*

The phone rang in the kitchen, and Sheila rushed out of the room to get it. "Dwaine?" she asked breathlessly into the receiver.

"No, it's Grandma."

"Oh, hi." Sheila stared out the back window into the neighbor's yard. A young couple with a baby were getting into their car. Her heart took a nosedive. Would she ever fall in love, get married, and have children?

"Sheila, did you hear what I said?"

She jerked her gaze away from the window. "What was that, Grandma?"

"I asked if you would like to have supper at my place tonight with Dwaine."

"Thanks for the invite, but I'm not in the mood to eat with the group at the retirement center."

"I wasn't planning to eat downstairs," Grandma said.

"You weren't?"

"No. I hoped to try out a recipe I found in a magazine, and I wanted to cook it for someone besides myself."

Sheila laughed. "You're needing a guinea pig, huh?"

"Actually, I'd prefer to have two guinea pigs."

Sheila groaned. "Grandma, you're not trying to play matchmaker, are you?"

Grandma cleared her throat and gave a polite little cough. "Of course not, dear. What would give you that idea?"

Sheila thought about telling Grandma how she and Dwaine had made a date for this afternoon and how she'd changed her mind about going. If she invited Dwaine to join her for supper at Grandma's, it would be like sending him mixed signals.

"Sheila, please don't say no. You'll be leaving next week, and I'd like to spend as much time with you as possible before you go." Grandma's tone was kind of pathetic, and Sheila figured she would feel guilty for days if she turned down the invitation.

Sheila shifted the phone from one ear to the other. "Okay, I'll come, but let's make it just the two of us. I'm sure Dwaine is busy."

"No, he's not. I already invited him."

Sheila flopped into the closest chair at the table. "You asked him first?"

There was a pause. "I was afraid you might refuse."

"Dwaine and I aren't right for each other. So you may as well give up your matchmaker plans."

Grandma chuckled. "Who are you trying to convince, sweet girl? Me or yourself?"

"I live in California, and Dwaine lives here in Wyoming. A long-distance relationship would never work."

"One of you could move."

"My job is there, and his is here."

"Have you prayed about this?"

Sheila hated to admit it, but she hadn't. It wasn't like her not to pray about a situation she knew only the Lord could resolve.

Grandma clucked her tongue. "Your silence tells me you probably haven't taken this matter to God. Am I right?"

"Yes, Grandma, you're right."

"I think you're making excuses and should give the situation serious thought, as well as a lot of prayer. Jobs are to be had in every town, you know."

Sheila drew in a deep breath and released it with a moan. "I'll admit, I am attracted to Dwaine, but I don't know why, because we're as different as east is from west."

"How so?"

"For one thing, I'm a neat freak; I'm always organizing."

"I can't argue with that. The last time you dropped by, you organized my kitchen cupboards so well I couldn't find anything for two days."

"According to Dwaine, his shop was a mess when he bought it, but to tell you the truth, I'm not sure he is much better about organization than the previous owner," Sheila said, ignoring her grandmother's teasing comment. "That receipt for your old doll is probably someplace in his shop, and we can't unearth it because of all the clutter."

"I would think with your ability to organize, you'd have

found the doll or a receipt if it was still there."

"I've checked everywhere I could think of, and so has Dwaine."

"I'm sorry you came all this way to get one of my attic treasures, and now you'll be going home empty-handed."

"I guess the doll's not really that important, and I do have Grandpa's Bible." As the words slipped off her tongue, Sheila knew she hadn't really meant them. Would she be okay going home without the Bye-Lo baby? Could she return to California and never think of Dwaine Woods again? Would his kisses be locked away in her heart forever?

"Sure wish you'd consider taking something else from the attic," Grandma said. "I could come over to the old house tomorrow and help check things out."

Sheila shook her head, although she didn't know why; Grandma couldn't see the action. "Actually, Dwaine might have another lead on the doll."

"Really? Why didn't you say so before?"

"He found a Bye-Lo baby advertised in a doll collector's magazine, and it looks like your old doll. There's even some writing on the cloth body, but it could be another false lead."

"Writing? Why would there be writing on the doll?"

Sheila's face heated with embarrassment. She'd been only eight years old when she wrote her name on the doll's stomach, but she'd never told Grandma what she'd done.

"I—uh—am sorry to say that I wrote my name on Bye-Lo's tummy when I was a little girl."

"Whatever for?"

"Because I wanted her to be mine someday, and I hoped maybe. . ." Sheila's voice trailed off.

"Oh, I see."

"It was a stupid, childish thing to do, and I'm sorry, Grandma."

"Apology accepted." Grandma chuckled. "Who knows, your name might be the very thing that helps you know for sure if it's my doll or not."

"That's why I'm hoping the person who placed the ad responds to Dwaine's phone call soon."

"While you're waiting to hear, won't you join me and Dwaine for supper this evening?"

Sheila nearly choked. "He said yes?"

"Sure did. Now how 'bout you, dear? Will you come, too?"

Sheila felt like she was backed into a corner, but she didn't want to disappoint Grandma. "What time should I be there?"

"Six o'clock. Dwaine will pick you up at a quarter to."

"You arranged that as well?" Sheila's voice rose a notch.

"What else are grandmas for?" Grandma giggled like a young girl. "See you tonight, and wear something pretty."

Sheila lifted her gaze toward the ceiling. "Sure, Grandma."

⋆≈⋗⋗

At a quarter to six, Dwaine arrived at Lydia Dunmore's stately old house to pick up Sheila. His ankle felt somewhat better, so he'd left his crutches at home. He lifted his hand to knock on the door, but it swung open before his knuckles connected with the wood.

"I saw you through the peephole," Sheila said before he could voice the question.

"Ah, so you were waiting for me." He chuckled, and she blushed.

75

"I'll grab my sweater and then we can go." Sheila disappeared into the living room and returned with a fuzzy blue sweater. Instead of blue jeans and a sweatshirt, like she'd had on today, she was dressed in a pale blue dress that touched her ankles.

"I felt bad when you didn't want to drive to the country this afternoon," Dwaine said as they headed down the steps side by side.

She halted when they came to the sidewalk and turned to face him. "I didn't think it was a good idea for us to go on another date."

He opened his mouth to comment, but she cut him off.

"For that matter, I don't think tonight is such a good idea, either, but I'm doing it for Grandma."

A wave of disappointment shot through Dwaine, and he cringed. "Am I that hard to take?"

She shook her head. "Except for our completely opposite ways of doing things, I find you attractive and fun to be with."

"I enjoy your company, too; so what's the problem?"

Sheila held up one finger. "I live in California, and you live here. Not an ideal situation for dating, wouldn't you say?"

He shrugged his shoulders. "I'm sure we can work something out."

She lifted her chin and stared at him. "Are you willing to relocate?"

"I moved from Montana to Wyoming because I like it here. I also like my antique store, and I think in time I'll make a fairly decent living because of it."

"And I have a great job in Fresno," she countered.

Dwaine opened the car door for Sheila, glad he didn't have

to share the confines of his compact car with anyone else. He needed this chance to speak with Sheila alone before they headed to her grandmother's retirement center.

When he climbed into the driver's seat and clicked his door shut, Dwaine leaned toward her. "Sheila, I thought we had something going between us, and after that kiss the other night—"

She pulled away. "Can we please change the subject?"

"What do you want to talk about?"

"How about my grandmother's doll? Did you hear from the person who placed the ad in that doll magazine?"

He shook his head. "Nope. They haven't returned my call or sent any e-mails."

Her eyes clouded with obvious disappointment. "Oh."

Dwaine wanted to pull her into his arms and offer reassurance, but he figured a hug wouldn't be appreciated, and he could tell she didn't want to talk about their relationship. "If I don't hear something by tomorrow, I'll call again," he promised.

"Thanks. I appreciate that."

❧❀❧

This lemon chicken is delicious," Sheila said as she smiled across the table at Grandma.

Dwaine smacked his lips. "I second that, and to prove it, I'll have another piece." He stabbed a chicken leg with his fork and plopped it onto his plate.

"Sheila says you may have found my old doll," Grandma said.

He swallowed the meat he'd put in his mouth before answering. "It's a collector who buys and sells antique dolls."

"I understand there's some writing on the doll's body."

He nodded. "That's how it was stated in the description, only it didn't say what the writing said."

"I can't believe that Sheila doing something as naughty as writing her name on a doll could prove to be helpful years later." Grandma chuckled behind her napkin. "Sheila always was possessive of the doll. I never knew how much until she confessed she'd written her name on its stomach."

Dwaine laughed and shoveled another bite of meat into his mouth.

Sheila gritted her teeth. *The way these two are carrying on, you'd think I wasn't even in the room.*

"Sheila, dear, you haven't said more than a few words since we sat down." Grandma wagged her finger.

"I've—uh—been eating."

"She did say she likes your chicken," Dwaine said.

"If you don't mind, I prefer to speak for myself." Sheila's voice sounded harsh, and Grandma and Dwaine looked at her like she'd taken leave of her senses.

"Are you upset about something?" Grandma asked.

Of course Sheila was upset. She'd taken a week's vacation to look for a doll Grandma had apparently sold and no one could find. Then she'd asked her boss for another two weeks so she could continue to search for the doll while helping Dwaine at his shop because he'd sprained his ankle on her account. To make matters worse, every lead they'd had so far had turned up nothing. Unless the magazine ad brought forth helpful information, it was likely Sheila would return to California without her attic treasure. Her final frustration came from falling for a guy who lived hundreds of miles from her.

"Sheila?"

"I'm fine, Grandma. Just tired, I guess."

"I'd like to date your granddaughter," Dwaine blurted, "but she's not interested."

Sheila didn't wait for Grandma's response. She leaped to her feet and raced out of the apartment.

❦

Dwaine limped down the hall after Sheila, his heart pounding and his mind whirling with unanswered questions. She'd acted strangely all evening, but what had happened to set her off like this?

Dwaine caught up to Sheila as she stepped into the elevator. "Wait!"

The door started to close, but he stuck his hand out and held it open.

"Where do you think you're running off to?" he panted.

Sheila averted her gaze and stared at the floor. "Home. I'm going home."

"But you said you weren't leaving until next week."

She looked up, and her eyelids fluttered. "I'm going back to Grandma's old house, where I won't have to spend the evening being talked *about* rather than *to*."

Dwaine stepped into the elevator and pushed the button so the door would close more quickly. He didn't want to chance her bolting again.

"Ever since we sat down to supper, you and Grandma talked about me like I wasn't even in the room." Sheila's chin quivered. "I'm already upset over not finding the Bye-Lo doll, and I don't like being treated as if I'm a child."

"I'm sorry. I didn't realize that's what I was doing."

Sheila blinked, and a few tears rolled down her cheeks. "That's not all."

"What else is bothering you?"

"I feel like all you care about is going on dates and having fun. Finding my grandmother's doll doesn't seem to be a priority anymore—if it ever was."

He shook his head. "That's not true, Sheila. I told you about the magazine ad, didn't I?"

"Yes, but what have you done to contact the person who placed it?"

"I told you before; I called and left a message on their answering machine." He sighed. "Can't really do much more until I hear back, now can I?"

She shrugged and hung her head. "I've never run out on Grandma like that before. I don't know what came over me, and I need to go back and apologize."

"I guess it's my fault. I'm the reason you got so upset."

"No, it's my fault. I shouldn't have let myself—"

"I've enjoyed spending time with you these past few weeks, and I hope we can keep in touch after you return home," he interrupted.

The elevator door swished open, and Sheila hurried toward her grandmother's room. Dwaine did his best to keep up, but the pain in his ankle slowed him down.

"I'll give you my e-mail address so you can let me know what you hear on the Bye-Lo baby," she said over her shoulder.

"Right, but I was thinking more along the lines of our keeping in touch so we can build a relationship," he mumbled.

She stopped walking and turned to face him. "Again, I

don't see how we can have a relationship when we live in two different states."

He gave her a sheepish grin. "Ah, that. Well, I figure if the Lord brought us together, He will make a way."

Chapter 10

S heila couldn't believe her vacation was over and she was back in Fresno. Her flight had gone well, and she'd called a cab to drive her home. She should be happy and content, but instead, her heart was filled with a sense of loss that went deeper than just losing a doll. Was it possible she could love Dwaine after knowing him only a few weeks?

The first thing Sheila did when she stepped inside her house was check her e-mail. Sure enough, there was one from Dwaine, entitled "Response from doll collector."

As she read the message, Sheila's heart plummeted. The writing on the doll confirmed that it wasn't Grandma's. As if that wasn't bad enough news, Dwaine didn't even say he would continue to look.

"He did say he misses me," she murmured. "Guess I should be happy about that."

She glanced around the living room and loneliness crept into her soul. "I'll be okay once I'm back at work tomorrow morning. Too much vacation isn't good—especially when you return home with nothing but an ache in your heart."

Sheila wasn't sure if the pain she felt was from not finding

Grandma's doll or from missing Dwaine. Probably a little of both, she decided.

"This feeling of gloom will pass. All I need to do is keep busy." She headed for the kitchen. "I'll start by cleaning the refrigerator, and then I'll go to the store and buy something good to eat. Work and food—that's what I need right now."

⚜

The next few weeks went by in a blur as Sheila immersed herself in work and tried to forget she had ever met a man named Dwaine Woods. She'd had several more e-mails from him, but he never mentioned the doll. Sheila figured he'd either had no more leads or had no interest in trying to find the Bye-Lo for her.

"It's just as well," Sheila muttered as she turned off her work computer on Tuesday afternoon and prepared to go home.

"Were you talking to me?" Dr. Carlson asked as he passed her desk.

Sheila felt heat creep up the back of her neck and spread quickly to her cheeks. She hadn't realized anyone else was in the room. She thought the doctor had gone home for the day.

"I didn't know you were still here."

He chuckled and pulled his fingers through the thinning gray hair at the back of his head. "If you weren't talking to me, who then?"

She stared at the blank computer screen. "Myself."

"I see. And did you have a suitable answer to your question?"

She shook her head. "I'm afraid there is no answer."

He snapped his fingers. "Sounds like a matter of the heart."

"It is," she admitted.

"Want to talk about it?"

It was tempting, for Dr. Carlson was not only an excellent chiropractor, but also a good listener, full of sound advice and godly counsel.

"It's nothing. I'll be fine," she murmured.

"All right then. I won't press the matter, but I will be praying for you."

"Thanks. I appreciate that."

"See you tomorrow morning." Dr. Carlson grabbed his briefcase from under the front counter and headed out the door.

Sheila picked up her purse and followed.

Dwaine had closed his shop for the day, deciding to clean out the drawers of an old rolltop desk he'd discovered in a shed out behind his shop.

He gulped down the last of his coffee and pulled open the first drawer. Inside were a bunch of rubber bands, some paper clips, and a small notebook. He thumbed through the pages to be sure there was nothing important, but halted when he came to the last page.

DOLL HOSPITAL—SEATTLE was scrawled in bold letters.

"That's odd. I wonder if Bill Summers took some old dolls there to be repaired."

Dwaine thought about the box of dolls he'd acquired several weeks before. He'd been planning to take them to Seattle during Easter vacation.

"I need to get those out, because I'll be leaving for Seattle next week," Dwaine muttered as he ripped the piece of paper with the bold writing from the notebook. "Don't have a clue what this is all about, but I sure am glad for the reminder that

I need to take the dolls in for repair."

He shook his head. "I think Sheila was right about me being forgetful."

Dwaine closed the drawer and stood. He hadn't heard from Sheila in a couple of days and decided to check his e-mail.

A few minutes later, he was online. There was a message from his sister Eileen, saying they were looking forward to seeing him. There were a few e-mails from other antique shops, but nothing from Sheila. Was she too busy to write, or had she forgotten about him already?

As soon as he clicked the icon to get off-line, he closed his eyes in prayer. "Father, I miss Sheila, and I really need Your help. If You want us to be together, please show me what to do."

He opened his eyes and glanced around the antique shop. Sheila had done so much to make the place look better when she was here. "I think I'd better give her a call when I get back from Seattle."

❧

Sheila had decided a few days ago that she probably wasn't going to hear from Dwaine again. It had been over a week since she'd received an e-mail from him.

"Maybe he's given up on me because all I ever ask about is Grandma's doll and I've never said how much I miss him." She shut the computer down and pushed away from her desk. "It's probably for the best. He needs to find someone who lives there in Casper, and I need to. . ." What did she need? Sheila headed for the kitchen. "I need to fix supper and get my mind off Dwaine and the doll he's never going to find."

She chuckled in spite of her melancholy mood. She was

calling dinner "supper" now. She'd been converted to Casper, Wyoming's, way of saying things. Or was it Dwaine's ways she'd been converted to? Had he gotten under her skin more than she realized—carved a place in her heart she could never forget?

Sheila spotted the black Bible with worn edges—the one Dwaine had found on Grandma's old piano. Grandma had told Sheila it belonged to Grandpa and said she'd like for Sheila to have it. At the time, Sheila had thought Grandma was trying to make up for the missing doll, but now, as she stared at the cover, she was filled with a strong desire to read God's Word. She'd forgotten to do devotions that morning and knew her day would have gone better if she had.

She sagged into a chair and breathed a prayer. "Lord, please speak to me through Your Word, and give me a sense of peace about the things that have been troubling me since I returned home."

She opened the Bible to the book of 1 Timothy. Her gaze came to rest on chapter 6, verses 7 and 8. "For we brought nothing into the world, and we can take nothing out of it. But if we have food and clothing, we will be content with that."

Tears welled up in her eyes. "Father, forgive me for putting so much emphasis on worldly things. You've obviously decided I don't need Grandma's doll, and I'm realizing how wrong I've been for concentrating on a worldly possession. I should be more concerned about my relationship with You, as well as friends and family. Help me to care more, love more, and do more to further Your kingdom. Amen."

The doorbell rang, and she jumped. "It's probably the paperboy, wanting to be paid for this month's subscription."

She padded down the hall to the front door and peered

through the peephole. No one was there. At least, she couldn't see anyone.

Cautiously, Sheila opened the door. Nobody was on the porch, but a small cardboard box sat on the doormat. A yellow rose lay across the top of it.

She bent down and picked them both up.

"Sure hope you like roses."

Sheila bolted upright at the sound of a deep male voice. A voice she recognized and had longed to hear. "Dwaine?"

He peeked around the corner of the house and grinned at her.

"Wh—what are you doing here?" she rasped.

"Came to see you."

"What about the rose and package? What are they for?"

He stepped onto the porch. "The rose is to say, 'I've missed you,' and what's in the box is a gift from my heart."

She looked at the package, at Dwaine, and back at the package again. "What's in there?"

"Open it and find out."

Sheila handed him the rose and lifted the lid. She gasped, and her eyes clouded with tears as a Bye-Lo baby came into view. The skin on her arms turned to gooseflesh. Could it possibly be Grandma's old doll?

With trembling fingers and a galloping heart, Sheila raised the cotton nightgown. It was there—her name scrawled in black ink on the cloth stomach.

She clutched the Bye-Lo baby to her chest. "Oh, Dwaine, where did you find her?"

"In Seattle. It's an interesting story. Can I step inside out of this heat?" Dwaine wiped the perspiration from his forehead.

"Yes, of course. Come in and I'll pour you some iced tea."

When they were both seated at the kitchen table with a glass of cold tea, Sheila said, "Don't keep me in suspense. Please tell me how all this came about."

Dwaine set his glass down and grinned. "It was an answer to prayer."

"Going to Seattle, finding the doll, or coming here?"

"All three." He leaned closer and she shivered, even though she wasn't cold.

His lips were inches from hers, and she could feel his warm breath against her face. Mustering all her willpower, Sheila leaned away. "H—how much do I owe you for the doll?"

"What?" Dwaine looked dazed.

"Bye-Lo. How much did she cost?"

"Nothing."

"Nothing?"

He shook his head. "Let me explain."

"Please do."

"Last week I was cleaning out an old desk I had found in the shed behind my shop, and I came across a notebook. One of the pages had the words 'Doll Hospital—Seattle,' written on it."

"That's all?"

"Yep. I had no idea what it meant, but it reminded me that I had a box of old dolls I wanted to take there." Dwaine paused to take another sip of tea. "After spending Easter with my sister and her family in Seattle, I went to the doll hospital the following day."

"That's where you found my grandmother's doll?"

He nodded. "As soon as I told the lady where I was from

and that I was the new owner of The Older the Better Antique Shop, she lit right up. Said a Bye-Lo doll had been sent from the previous owner several months ago and that she'd never heard back from him."

"I'm surprised she didn't call the store."

"She said she'd tried but was told the number had been disconnected. Turns out she'd been given a wrong number." Dwaine set his glass back on the table. "Since she knew the number she'd called wasn't in service, she assumed the business had closed."

"So she kept the doll?"

"Right. She put in new eyes, since that's what it had been sent there for, and placed the doll in her display cabinet. Said she didn't want to sell the Bye-Lo in case the man who sent it ever tried to contact her."

Sheila stared at the doll lying on the table. Its pale pink bisque face looked as sweet as it had when she was a child. "You didn't have to buy it then?"

"Nope. Just paid the woman the bill to fix the eyes."

"But what about the amount my grandmother was paid by the previous owner of your shop?"

Dwaine shrugged. "Don't know how much that was since I can't find a receipt."

"I'm sure Grandma knows what she sold it for."

He shook his head. "I called and asked, but she said she forgot."

"At least let me pay for the cost of the doll's repairs and your plane ticket to bring it to me." Sheila smiled. "You could have saved yourself the trouble and mailed it, you know."

He squinted and shook his head. "And miss the chance to see you?"

She squirmed in her chair as his expression grew more intense.

"I've missed you, Sheila. Missed your laughing eyes, beautiful smile, and even your organizational skills." He leaned closer. "I believe I've fallen in love with you."

Her mouth went dry. "You—you have?"

He nodded and lifted her chin with his thumb. "I know we haven't known each other very long, but when God brings a good thing into my life, I'd be a fool to ignore it."

"I agree."

His eyes twinkled. "You think I'm a good thing?"

"Oh, yes," she murmured. "God's been showing me some important verses from His Word, and as happy as I am to have the precious Bye-Lo baby, I'm even more excited to see you."

As Dwaine's lips sought hers, Sheila felt like she was floating on a cloud. When the kiss ended, they both spoke at once.

"Does Fresno need another antique shop?"

"Does Casper need another chiropractor's receptionist?"

They laughed.

"I could use a secretary. As you already know, my shop was a mess before you came along." Dwaine took hold of her hand and gave it a gentle squeeze. "And I've been a mess since you left town."

"Me, too." Sheila smiled through her tears. "I've been doing a lot of thinking lately, and I've decided there's really nothing keeping me here in Fresno. I know, too, that building a relationship with someone as wonderful as you is far more important than my job or the old doll I used to play with as a child."

"You mean it?" He sounded hopeful, and his eyes searched

her face. "What about your parents' house? Would you sell this place if you moved to Casper?"

She shook her head. "Just a minor detail. The house can be put up for rent."

His lips touched her forehead in a kiss as gentle as the flicker of butterfly wings. "I know it's probably too soon for a marriage proposal, but if you move to Casper, we can work on that."

She fingered the cloth body on the Bye-Lo baby. "And to think none of this would have happened if I hadn't come to Wyoming in search of Grandma's doll."

WANDA E. BRUNSTETTER

Wanda E. Brunstetter lives in Central Washington with her husband, Richard, who is a pastor. They have been married forty-one years and have two grown children and six grand-children. Wanda is a professional ventriloquist and puppeteer, and she and her husband enjoy doing programs for children of all ages. Wanda's greatest joy as a Christian author is to hear from readers that something she has written has touched their hearts or helped them in some special way.

Wanda has written nine novels with Barbour Publishing's Heartsong Presents line as well as three novellas, and her collection of four previously published Amish novels, *Lancaster Brides*, was a best seller. Wanda believes the Amish people's simple lifestyle and commitment to God can be a reminder of something we all need.

Visit Wanda's web page at www.wandabrunstetter.com.

Fishing for Love

by Tammy Shuttlesworth

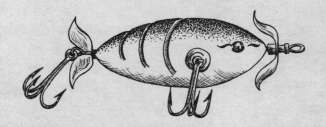

Dedication

To the fishermen in my life: my husband,
Dad, Grandpa, and my Lord and Savior.

Many thanks to www.antiquelures.com for permission
to use whatever information I needed from their Web site.

I will instruct you and teach you in the way you should go;
I will counsel you and watch over you.
PSALM 32:8

Chapter 1

I can't believe how long it's been since I've seen you either, Grandma."

Kimber hugged the woman she'd spent so many after-school hours with during her early childhood, then stepped back. Grandma's familiar smile graced her lips, but gauging by the shadows under her eyes, the recent move to a retirement home hadn't been easy. Kimber imagined that leaving behind the old Victorian family home of fifty years was going to have the same impact on the family matriarch's soul as losing Grandpa two years ago.

Grandma Dunmore peered over her bifocals. "Kimber, you look more like your mother every day. You have the same bouncy red-brown curls and a clear complexion highlighting those expressive brown eyes I've always loved. I'm glad you got your dad's brown eyes, you know, instead of the family's hazel ones." Grandma turned to the young lady standing beside Kimber.

"And this is Casey. I'd know you anywhere; you haven't changed a bit." Grandma enfolded the young woman in a welcoming hug. "I can't believe what a small world we live in. I can remember how crushed our little five-year-old Kimber was when your family moved away. Kimber was so sure she'd never see you again."

"I bet Grandma also recalls how happy I was when I called to tell her that you'd moved practically next door to me eight years later in Louisiana," Kimber inserted.

"That I do," Grandma assured them both. "Casey, I'm glad you accompanied Kimber on this trip. You be sure to make yourself at home while you're here, and if there's anything you need, you just let me know like in the old days, all right?"

Casey nodded. "Thanks, Mrs. Dunmore. It's good to see you again, too. My mom and dad send their love, by the way."

"I hear they're solving the problems of Uncle Sam overseas now, is that right?"

"I don't know about fixing our government, but they are in Hawaii," Casey affirmed.

"I've made chocolate chip cookies and there's plenty of ice-cold milk in the fridge," Grandma said. "I figured you'd need food before you take on the attic. My new kitchenette is this way, so follow me. By the way, Kimber, have you thought about what you're going to pick yet?"

"No, Grandma. I'm going to wait 'til I get there and see what brings back the most memories for me. I knew Sheila would want the Bye-Lo baby doll because no one could get that doll away from her when we were little. I haven't spoken to Lauren and Jessica, so I don't know what they'll choose. I only hope I don't take something they have their hearts set on."

Grandma put her arm around Kimber's shoulder as they walked toward the small kitchen table. "I'm sure whatever it is you select will be exactly what the Lord has in mind for you. He wouldn't have it any other way, you know."

"I know, Grandma. I need to have more faith and wait to see what His plans are. Can I help you serve those cookies? I hope they taste as good as they did when I was little."

"You and Sheila sure could put those cookies away, couldn't you?" Grandma laughed. "I haven't changed the recipe, so I'm sure they're just as good as you recall. You and Casey sit down and relax. It does my heart good to have my granddaughter and her best friend back where I can give them snacks like I used to."

As they shared the late afternoon treat, Kimber wanted to be a young girl again. She longed to race home from school to find Grandpa sitting on the back porch of the old Victorian house, swinging in the porch swing and waiting for her. She wanted to see him sitting across from her at the big family-sized table as she learned to write and read.

Kimber smiled as she recalled how she believed that Grandpa knew the answers to everything about life and how she thought he'd always be there to advise her. *Not so,* she thought. Her smile faded. Time moved on. Grandpa was gone. She and Grandma might be more than forty years apart in age, but they had one thing in common; they were both alone.

❧❦❧

Kimber listened as Casey's footsteps followed behind her, plodding up the old wooden stairs, the fourth step from the top squeaking as it had in the days when they had come to the attic to play.

"I know I came along to help," Casey said, "but I can't take staying up here with these boxes and things. I feel like an intruder or something. I think I'll go check out the rest of the house if you don't mind."

"Not at all," Kimber replied. "You know where I'll be. Just don't forget to come check on me when you're finished downstairs."

In a way, Kimber was glad to be alone with her memories while she searched for the perfect treasure to take home with her. A few songs from an out-of-tune upright piano drifted up to Kimber, but mostly she worked uninterrupted and focused her mind on the task in front of her.

"No time like the present," Kimber mumbled, opening a small trunk and looking through some old family photos. Relatives from the distant past she didn't recognize or couldn't remember were identified in Grandma's scrawled handwriting on the back of the pictures, along with the date and event.

"I wonder if Grandma knows these photos are up here. I'll bet she'd like to have them." Kimber closed the lid and moved it aside, making a note to mention them to Grandma when she visited with her the next day. She then turned to a larger trunk.

"There has to be something here that means a great deal to me, especially after all the time I spent in this house as a child." Kimber began to look through the top layer.

"Here's a bunch of old long-playing records from Grandma's collection," Kimber said, thumbing through some album jackets. "I remember her playing those old Lawrence Welk songs all the time. That crazy canary of hers, which never sang any other time, chirped like crazy to those tunes." Kimber chuckled. "Grandma and Grandpa would waltz around the room as if they were on a grand ballroom floor.

The rest of the trunk contained nothing but another layer of albums, some with names such as *Fibber McGee and Molly*.

Kimber turned her attention to another box, finding only old papers and long-forgotten journals of weather observations in her grandma's handwriting dating back to the 1950s and '60s.

Frustrated, Kimber sat back on her heels. She envisioned Casey walking around below and finding nothing but lumps of furniture covered with sheets as they awaited final disposal. A small twinge filled her soul. *I should join Casey, but I can't make myself go down there.*

Kimber had stopped short of looking around the house upon her arrival, worried about her reaction. Maybe before they returned to Louisiana she could make herself go through the home, but right now she didn't think she could stand to see the Dunmore family home practically abandoned.

I'm not up to joining Casey...yet. I'm here to find that something special. Kimber rose and spoke to her reflection in a cheval mirror leaning against a wall. "It's bad enough knowing I won't be able to come here again and enjoy spending the day with family and friends. This house will belong to another family. They'll make their own happy memories in it, but I'll bet they won't give any thought to those who lived here before them."

Kimber wished well whomever purchased the house, though it sent a pang through her heart that she probably wouldn't return to it ever again. She'd only be able to drive by and look at the outside and remember what had been all those years before.

"Are you going to be much longer?" Casey's Southern drawl called out from the doorway.

Kimber turned and faced her friend. "I don't know. There are so many things from my childhood still here, but I just can't seem to find anything that grabs at my heart," Kimber answered.

"Besides that, I've been thinking of Grandma giving up her home. Now that I've seen her in person, it's hard for me to accept that she's getting older and isn't able to take care of herself as she used to."

Casey moved to stand beside Kimber. "It must really hurt." She reached out and squeezed Kimber's hand. "I'm here for you, Kimber, but you only have four days."

"I know. I'm beginning to wonder if that's enough time." Kimber pushed her bangs away from her brows. "Whew! I can see where someone has cleaned and sorted a little recently up here, but I don't remember this place being so dusty when we played up here as kids."

Casey poked her head around a stack of boxes. "If I recall correctly, it was clean because we used to beg your grandmother to let us come here and pretend to keep house. I can almost smell that lemon polish we always used."

"If I remember correctly, *you* had nothing to do with the cleaning," Kimber pointed out. "You just wanted to play with the baby dolls up here while *I* cleaned. You'd dress them, sing to them, and put them to bed in some of those dresser drawers." Kimber closed her eyes a moment. "I guess when Grandma lost Grandpa, cleaning must not have been important anymore," she offered quietly.

Casey made her way to a chair and sat down. "I can't believe you don't have any idea of what you're going to keep. I'd think it would be easy to find something."

"It isn't turning out to be like that for me. I understand Grandma's thinking. I'm flattered she wants each of us cousins to pick out our own thing, but it would have been a lot easier if she'd just chosen something for me before she moved to the retirement home. I've never been good at making decisions. You know that."

"Maybe what you pick from here will lead you to find your one true love." Casey gave a melodramatic sigh.

"I don't think there's someone out there for me anymore," Kimber said skeptically.

"You're only twenty-two. Besides, there's someone for everyone. Isn't that what our young-adult minister always tells us?" Casey patted her stomach. "What do you say we go get something to eat? We've been here for hours. I'm starved."

Kimber glanced at her watch. "We've only been here three hours, and we ate all those cookies and milk at Grandma's, so you can't give me that 'I'm starving' bit. With as much as you eat, I don't see how you manage to stay so slim anyway."

"I'm not the only one," Casey rebutted. "That tall, svelte figure of yours doesn't carry any extra padding."

"I work at staying in shape," Kimber countered. "I don't plan on turning to mush just because I sit most lunch hours and weeknights in college classes. You're welcome to join me any time you want. All you have to do is get up every other morning and go for—"

Casey put one hand in the air to stop her midsentence. "A three-mile run. Whatever. Can we go eat now? It will give you more time to think about what you're going to pick. Besides, I want to hit the stores so I can buy a cowgirl shirt. I used to have a whole bunch of them when we lived here. I'm hoping it'll impress our friends back home."

"You can get the same kind of clothes at one of the Western-type stores back home in Louisiana, Casey. And probably at a much better price, too. It's not exactly going to match the rest of your Southern-belle type wardrobe, you know."

"I figure I can borrow a pair of your jeans to wear with it," Casey replied. "At least I'll know I bought it here. It'll have that real Western flavor then, plus serve to remind me of some of my childhood."

"Don't get mad, but if you keep eating the way you are, you won't fit into my jeans much longer," Kimber joked.

"It's the clear, country air up here in Wyoming," Casey rebutted. "It makes me hungrier."

"I suppose a poor excuse is better than none," Kimber scolded. "The mall is only twenty minutes away. Give me a few minutes to brush away the dust and cobwebs and I'll join you. You might even persuade me to help you pick out that perfect cowgirl shirt."

Casey gave a doubting harrumph but raced to the stairs. With Casey gone, Kimber swung her flashlight into a dark, unexplored corner beside a dresser. Two medium-sized wooden boxes sat beneath a pile of newspapers and a couple of books. She removed the items on top and pulled the boxes out. After struggling with the rusty front hasp on the top box for a minute or so, it finally gave way.

"Oh, no!" Kimber shouted as a pair of beady glass eyes stared up at her from both sides of a wooden green head.

Chapter 2

I can't believe you two are leaving already. I do wish you could stay longer, like another week or so." Grandma's voice contained a small catch in it, but she hummed as she put plates piled with grilled cheese sandwiches in front of Kimber and Casey. She added sliced sweet pickles beside each sandwich and poured some iced tea into tall drinking glasses decorated with blue waves Kimber recalled from her childhood.

At least the drinking glasses are with Grandma in her retirement apartment, even if most of her old familiar furniture can't be, Kimber reflected. The contemplation only made her wish that life hadn't taken the turns it had, made her sad that she didn't live closer to Grandma and that she hadn't kept in closer touch with Grandma once Kimber and her parents moved down South.

"Kimber, would you mind saying grace?"

"Not at all, Grandma," Kimber replied, glad for the diversion. She asked God's blessing on the food and on their relatives who weren't present, then closed by asking for a safe trip for her and Casey's return to Louisiana.

"Amen," rang a trio of voices.

Grandma spoke first while the girls began nibbling at their sandwiches. "I've been thinking. Do you think you both could come back next summer and visit with me? I know funds are tight since you're college students, but I'd be glad to contribute toward airline tickets. I might even purchase them entirely if the sale of the house goes well. I'd planned on giving—"

"Why don't we wait and see what things look like next year in early spring before we make plans for the summer?" Kimber interrupted. "I don't know if Casey or I will have to take summer classes or not. If we do, I'm not sure how much vacation time we'll get."

Kimber caught sight of Grandma's frown. "What about Christmas next year?" she asked, trying to ease the pain apparent on Grandma' face. "I know school breaks for a couple of weeks then."

"Christmas would be wonderful!" Grandma reacted with excitement, then sobered. "We don't know where any of us will be next year, do we? Man can make all the plans he wants, but the good Lord will sort the order of his footsteps, or something like that. Isn't that what the Good Book says?"

"It's pretty close, Grandma," Kimber concurred, wishing anew that she and Casey didn't have to leave so soon. Tears edged Grandma's eyes, proving how the aged woman felt inside. Kimber realized Grandma went through these same emotions each time she saw a grandchild or other family member arrive to make a selection from the Dunmore home.

How much pain does a person have to bear before life quits hurting? Kimber wondered. *First, Grandma lost Grandpa, and now, on top of that, she has to say farewell to a home she's lived in for over fifty years.* Kimber offered a silent prayer for the Lord to cover Grandma with an extra blessing of peace and strength as she dealt with the upcoming sale of her home.

"Has Kimber told you yet what she's taking from the attic?" Casey asked, breaking the silence as they ate.

Grandma turned to face Kimber. "I figured you'd tell me in your own good time, hopefully before you left for the airport. You've avoided talking about it for three days."

"Well, go on, Kimber," Casey urged. "I can't wait to see what your grandma thinks. I don't think she could guess what it is, and she won't ever believe it."

"Go ahead, child," Grandma encouraged. "While you've been searching these last few days, I've been sitting here trying to remember what's still in the attic. I'm afraid my memory isn't as good as it should be. What did you finally decide on?"

Kimber didn't respond immediately. What she'd elected to take wasn't what the majority of today's young ladies would choose. Casey didn't approve and had voiced that fact continually since they left the Dunmore home a half hour ago.

What if Grandma doesn't approve either? Kimber wondered. *We're due at the airport in two hours.*

Grandma lowered her hands to her lap and looked expectantly at her granddaughter. Kimber swallowed the lump in her throat and hoped her voice gave no sign of the uncertainty she felt knocking around in her stomach.

"I found a couple of Grandpa's old fishing tackle boxes. Since they were buried under some cardboard boxes and newspapers, I didn't think anyone else wanted them."

"Tackle boxes?" Grandma queried. "Yes, I remember now. Grandpa hadn't fished in a very long time. I recollect the day he finally put those boxes in the attic." A tear trickled down her cheek, which she ignored. "Let me see now. If I recall correctly, those boxes are full of nothing but a bunch of tangled up fishing line, some old damaged lures, and fly-fishing flies. Are you sure that's what you want?"

"Yes," Kimber admitted. "These four days sped by, but once I saw the tackle, I knew they were meant for me. I did find some quilts and bundled them up and set them aside as I couldn't stand to see them all forlorn and forgotten."

"Which ones would those be?" Grandma asked.

"I remember using them for sleepovers when I was a child," Kimber answered.

"I personally think quilts are a better choice for a proper young lady instead of some stinky old fish bait," Casey put in.

"Casey, please." Kimber threw a warning look toward her friend. "Grandma, there's a blue quilt with different colored interlocking circles. The other one is dark maroon and it has small butterscotch flowers on it and pale yellow tufts of yarn pulled throughout. They're in a plastic bag. I hope that's okay with you." Kimber fell silent.

Grandma smiled. "Casey might think the quilts are a better choice, but if those tackle boxes are what you want, then I'm not about to question your decision, Kimber. You go right ahead and take them with my blessing, dear. I'm sure those quilts will find their way to someone who will put them to good use."

The rest of the meal passed rapidly, much as the four days split between visiting Grandma's new apartment and rummaging in the Dunmore attic had done. Kimber had finally forced herself to go through the rooms in the half-empty Victorian, but she hadn't stayed long in them. She still couldn't imagine not being able to return again, except as an outsider—an idea she didn't think she'd ever accept. Kimber abruptly halted her line of thinking. Nothing was going to ruin her good mood or her last few minutes with Grandma.

Chapter 3

"Those things give me the creepy crawlies. I don't see how you can look at them. I certainly can't. I'm glad they're locked up in the trunk of this car, as far away as possible from me." Casey's inflection expanded her last word into three syllables for emphasis. "You're my friend, Kimber, and I do a lot of things for you because of that, but I *will not* help carry those boxes into the house."

"I'll carry them myself," Kimber assured Casey. "They aren't that heavy."

"Tell me you're joking about this," Casey went on. "Tell me you honestly *are not* keeping those—that—them as your 'treasure.'"

Kimber held back a chuckle, keeping her gaze on the rest of the traffic leaving the airport and heading toward downtown Shreveport. "Casey," she said, trying to sound as stern as possible, "we are on Interstate 20 headed east to Haughton, Louisiana, from the Shreveport Airport, right?"

"Yes," Casey replied.

"We just spent eight hours in Dallas, Texas, due to a weather delay on our way back from Casper, Wyoming, right?"

"Yes," Casey replied again, her voice not quite the Southern-belle voice she usually spoke with.

In the darkness of the car, Kimber pictured every emotion from horror to dread flickering across her friend's face. The idea that Kimber had selected some "stinky ole fish bait," as Casey called the items from the attic, didn't make sense to Casey. Right now, Kimber wasn't too sure it made much sense to her, either. But for some reason, once she'd seen the old fishing tackle and the wooden boxes holding it all, she knew she couldn't leave them behind in Wyoming.

Casey gave a deep sigh. "I don't see why you didn't pick something like the family Bible or some of your grandma's jewelry. Or, hey, here's a better idea! What about dishes or silverware you used as a child? You know, nice, common, everyday, down-to-earth stuff. Why did you have to pick some ugly, ole fishing whatchamacallit stuff?"

"I'll admit that some of what's in those boxes isn't in the best condition, but some are antique lures, not just stuff, Case. You might not understand this, but I'm keeping them because as soon I opened that first tackle box, memories came back to me that I'd forgotten all about. I recalled trips to Canada and other places. I think of more fishing trips and conversations with Grandpa every time I pull out a different piece of tackle to look at it or clean it up."

Kimber shifted her small car into the next higher gear and swapped lanes to pass a line of slow traffic in the right lane. "I don't think I've ever told you this, but I was five years old when Grandpa and Dad taught me how to fish. That was the summer you moved away."

"So?" Casey challenged. "What's that have to do with you

choosing that stuff for your treasure?"

"It's part of my memories where the tackle is concerned. I was brokenhearted, school was out, and I didn't have anything to do," Kimber continued. "One day, none of the boys could go with them, so they took me on their fishing trip. Fishing filled my lonely days that summer and for the next few summers until we moved to Louisiana. Now that I think about it, Dad and I haven't fished at all since we got here."

"So you're blaming your choice on me?" Casey quizzed.

"No, I'm just pointing out when and why I learned to fish," Kimber answered. "Casey, I was five. You were gone. I was crushed. Fishing gave me something to do. It made me forget how much I missed you. I'd forgotten all about that until I found those tackle boxes. Now that we're going to college together, it seems right that the tackle should be mine, doesn't it?"

"I have a feeling there is some deep mystery to this I'm not ever going to figure out," Casey replied.

Kimber downshifted and prepared to exit the interstate toward her home. "Keeping the fishing gear just feels right. I don't know how else to explain it."

"You put the quilts off to one side in case you decided not to keep the tackle, didn't you?" Casey queried. "You didn't tell your grandma that, but I could hear it in your voice. However, the fishing things are the *only* items you brought back."

"All right, I confess. The quilts were a backup choice. I wasn't sure about the tackle to begin with, but the more I think about it, the more it means to me, Casey."

"Kimber, I've been disagreeing because a treasure should be cherished and special and loved, which I definitely *don't* think fishing stuff qualifies as. You did say there are some old things in there, right? They could be worth money, like, quite a lot of money."

"There might be a few, but mostly it's a jumbled bunch of fishing line, old wooden and plastic lures, and some other things. I'd say they're mostly memories, but I did think about calling around to some antique shops to see if they can give me an idea of the value of the oldest pieces."

"It can't hurt to find out. You said the other day you were worried about how you were going to keep paying for your college since the grant you applied for didn't come through. I don't know much about the value of fishing lures, but isn't there usually a market for antiques? If you sold a few, the money could help pay off your student loans. If there's enough, you might even be able to finish college without any money worries."

"Being able to pay off a loan isn't why Grandma asked me to select something from her attic," Kimber insisted. "She wanted me to have an item that meant a lot to me. I want to be sure what I chose helps me realize how fortunate I was to grow up in the family I did."

"If you want to know, we have a mutual friend from church who enjoys fishing and runs his own bait shop. I'm sure he can give you an estimate."

"Jake Evans? He doesn't know I'm alive."

"Jake says you're the one who always goes some other direction when he wants your attention after church. He can't get close enough to find out more about you. Why is that?"

"I don't know." Kimber gripped the steering wheel, then checked the rearview mirror as if nothing bothered her.

"I think you do. Jake says he thinks you're not impressed with him."

"He's a fisherman," Kimber replied, hoping this conversation would end soon.

"As was Jesus." Casey's answer left no doubt that there were still unfinished comments. "Plus he does own his own business."

"Yes, but do you think Jesus walked around smelling like crickets and earthworms?"

"I have it on good authority that Jake wears an aftershave called Lucky You," Casey rebutted. "He looks more like Keith Urban—that tall, blond, blue-eyed country music singer you listen to once in a while—than Mel Gibson, but he's so handsome in a suit and tie. Besides, you're the outdoorsy type, so outdoorsy smells shouldn't bother you."

"They don't." Years of fishing had taught Kimber to respect the open air, not to fear it.

"So why do you avoid Jake, or why do you avoid answering my question about why you avoid him?"

"Look, we're home. Can you help me unload the suitcases since it looks like Mom and Dad have already left for work?" Kimber released a deep breath as she hurried to open the car trunk.

"Everything but those stinky old tackle boxes. I'm not touching them," Casey replied. "Now that I think about it, it's interesting you want your grandpa's fishing boxes but you won't go near Jake who owns a bait shop. Hmmm."

<hr/>

"I see," Kimber spoke into the phone receiver. "Thanks for your help." She replaced the phone on the base, straightened the tangled cord, and flopped onto the well-loved floral sofa. "That's another dealer who says he can't help me find the value of those lures. I've called every antique dealer within fifty miles, and so far, only one wants to help. What do you think I should I do?"

Casey looked up from doing algebra homework. "Go ahead and visit the one who's interested and see what he says. It will give you an idea of what you have."

"If I'd taken Grandma's quilts, I wouldn't be spending my free time dialing phone numbers only to be disappointed over and over," Kimber said as she fiddled with the fringe on the edge of a pillow.

"Oh!" Casey exclaimed. "I called Jake. He's eager to see your lures. He lives near Lake Bistineau, so that's only twenty-five minutes away, and his bait shop is called Hook and Lure. It can't hurt to see what he says about your antique stuff, can it?"

"I guess not." Kimber hoped she could escape before Casey grilled her again about why she tried to stay away from Jake. The reason may sound silly now, but at the time, Kimber had been humiliated. "I have to finish some reading for an English paper that's due in two days. Can I get you anything before I go to my room?"

"Thanks, but I'm fine."

Kimber trudged up the stairs, trying to decide what she'd gain by having someone who owned a bait shop look at her collection.

What could it hurt? All he can do is tell me he doesn't know anything about the lures I have, which is what the antique dealers have done so far.

After reading three different reviews on her English story to help prepare for her paper, she closed her books and sat at her student desk, bowing her head and whispering her nightly prayer.

"Lord, You know I want to do what's right, but it seems like I'm getting nowhere as far as Grandpa's tackle goes. I don't want to sell it; You know that's not my intention. But, Lord, if Grandpa's fishing tackle is the right treasure for me to keep, and if it be Your will, please send me someone who will tell me what I now own."

Chapter 4

J ake says if we stay on the main road, we can't miss his store," Casey said from the passenger seat. "It shouldn't be much farther if I remember how he said to get there."

"I told you to write the directions down." Kimber wondered if this trip would be as bad as some fishing expeditions she'd been on. "I've never driven this way before, so I'm not sure where we're at."

"I brought my cell phone in case we need to call Jake for directions," Casey assured.

"I could have come here by myself."

"You still haven't told me why you avoid Jake. Why should I believe you'd make this trip to his shop alone?" Casey prodded.

"Because we've been friends a long time," Kimber replied, ignoring the question at the heart of the matter. "Friends trust friends to do as they say they'll do."

"Okay, friend. Tell me why you won't go near Jake." Casey's challenge seemed to hang in the air between them.

"He taught our adult Sunday school class once and spoke about Jesus being a fisher of men. His sermon was quite. . . imaginative."

"I've heard talks on that topic before," Casey said. "What made Jake's so special that you remember it and now avoid him?"

"For one, he took our class outside and wanted us to cast a lead weight into a bucket from twenty yards away. Some of the guys caught on quickly, and a few even nailed the bucket on the first try. Most of the girls were horrible, myself included. Would you believe I got the line tangled up in a tree branch? They had to cut it out in order for the rest to use it. I was so embarrassed, but Jake turned the whole experience into a message."

"By saying what?"

"He told us that learning to cast is like starting out as a new Christian. You won't always do or say the right thing— just don't forget to learn from your mistakes or you'll repeat them over and over. He said it's the same with casting. You have to work at it if you want to improve."

"So with effort, you grow, either as a Christian or a fisher-man. That is a different approach," Casey admitted. "What was so horrible that now you won't speak to him?"

"Because I was bragging before we went outside about how I'd be a great caster because I'd fished since I was little. When I got the line fouled in the tree, I wanted to disappear right then and there."

"Jake didn't seem bothered," Casey commented.

"No, he might not have appeared so, but later he offered to give me lessons. That added to my agony," Kimber confessed.

"So you avoid him now because he wanted to help you then?"

Kimber nodded.

"You'd better get ready, because there's his store."

Jake watched as two young women walked across the parking lot. The taller of the two, Kimber Wilson, stumbled slightly in one of the split sections of asphalt. He wished now he'd had the lot repaired last week. If the business were doing as well as it normally did, he would have.

Glancing back from the crumbled parking section to the young ladies, Jake noted that Casey Tullgrove, who'd phoned him about the fishing tackle, accompanied Kimber. Casey, a cheery, happy-go-lucky person he knew from church class, was a transplanted Northerner.

Jake knew Kimber was from somewhere out West originally, but Jake had little chance to get to know her better since she usually ducked the other way any time he headed in her direction. It was a situation he often vowed he'd change but never did. Now he might have a chance to do so. Jake smiled.

Kimber's faded blue jeans and sunshine-yellow T-shirt almost matched the ones Jake wore for his business. Her shirt was adorned with a huge purple Mardi Gras slogan across the front, where Jake's had a large bass jumping out of a body of water. A glow on her cheeks said she was no stranger to the outdoors, which Jake, being a fisherman, respected. A bright April sun shone on her bouncy shoulder-length brown hair, creating tints of red and orange and reminding Jake of the brilliant colors on the best sunfish Louisiana offered in its waters.

"I see my directions worked," he said, holding the front door open as they arrived. "It's nice to see you, Casey. You, too, Kimber."

Jake extended his right hand to shake hands first with Casey, then Kimber. As his hand closed around Kimber's, his heart shifted in a way he wasn't familiar with. Her brown eyes reminded him of a lake trout he'd once caught and returned back to nature. *Better stick to business,* Jake warned himself.

"Kimber, Casey says you have some rather old fishing items you want me to look at."

"Yes. I got them from Grandpa. I mean Grandma. In Wyoming. In her attic. I'm sorry. I don't usually have this problem speaking." Kimber lowered her glance to the floor.

Jake willed her to look back at him. He wanted to mind-paint her every feature so he'd always have the memory of how she looked today. "Some of them could be quite old if they were in an attic, then," he managed.

"I'm glad you could see us on such short notice," Casey interrupted.

"Always glad to help," Jake replied, turning his gaze toward Casey. "I have to ask why you called me, though. I certainly don't call myself an expert on lures. I run a bait shop."

"That's not what our young-adult minister insists," Casey answered. "He's convinced you're the best there is in these parts as far as fishing is concerned."

"I'm sure he meant when it comes to selling bait or catching fish. Nothing more," Jake replied.

"Nope. He said you were the one who could help Kimber with her antique fishing stuff."

"Why don't we have a seat?" Jake motioned them forward while he went to a refrigerated cooler containing chilled water and sodas. "How about something to cool us off since it's so hot out there?"

Kimber and Casey accepted chilled bottled water and took seats in lawn chairs positioned around a huge wooden table, made from a spool that had once held telephone cable. Kimber gazed around the tidy store, impressed with the array of corks and assorted fishing gear for sale. On the walls hung various pictures of water in river, lake, and ocean form. A striking photo of Niagara Falls filled a four-by-six-foot frame on the wall behind the cash register.

"My grandpa offered to take me to Niagara Falls once, but I wouldn't go," Kimber pointed out. "We were coming back from a fishing trip to Canada that he and Grandma took me on, but we'd been gone ten days. All I wanted was to get home to see my parents and brother. Now that I'm older, I wish I'd gone with them."

"I've been there once," Jake said. "With my mom and dad. I always said I'd go back someday, but I've never found the time to go."

"You can look at Kimber's fishing stuff, right?" Casey questioned, abruptly changing the subject.

"Sure can, but I won't promise what I can do. I just dabble with old lures, mainly because of the ones I inherited from my dad." Jake looked at Kimber. "Ready to show me what you brought along today?"

"I only brought a couple of them," Kimber replied, reaching into her purse and removing a neatly folded plastic grocery bag with a local chain name emblazoned in red across the front. From inside the bag, she withdrew two pieces painstakingly wrapped in tissue paper.

"It's all right if you don't know what they are." Kimber

found it hard to speak with Jake's full attention on her. "I'm not going to sell them. I just want an idea of what they might be worth. Casey is convinced they're unusual and are going to bring in lots of money."

Kimber watched as Jake donned a pair of thin rubber gloves, removed the tissue and laid it aside, then positioned the lures on top of a piece of bubble wrap he'd put on the countertop. Her throat tightened as he picked up the first one. It was weird seeing Jake hold it and not Grandpa, but after a few seconds, Kimber didn't mind. The lure looked as much at home in Jake's hands as she remembered it once being in Grandpa's.

Jake lifted the minnow, avoiding the hook on its underbelly, and gently turned it around to check it out before returning it to the counter. He picked up the second one, wooden and faded green in color, and immediately turned it over to examine the belly section.

"I haven't seen this before other than in magazines. I need to do some more checking, but if it's what I think it is, young lady, this little critter is worth a fortune. I'll be glad to do the research, but only if you'll help me. What do you say, Kimber? Care to find out if it's as rare as I think it is?"

Kimber glanced at Jake. She grabbed the edge of her chair to steady herself against an unusual feeling rocking through her. "Sure," she said. "How soon do you want to start?"

"Money to pay off those student loans." Casey went unheard in the background.

Chapter 5

I thought we'd start on the Internet," Jake said. "I did some looking on my computer when I got home last night. You won't believe how many Web sites out there deal with antique fishing tackle or lures."

Kimber paused. There wasn't any way to handle this other than to say what had to be said. "Jake, I have to be honest. I don't know anything about computers." Kimber settled back onto her chair and waited for his reaction.

"Nothing?" Jake sighed. "You don't know anything?"

"Nothing at all. I don't even know how to turn one on." Kimber felt as if she'd just tossed her fishing line in a tree all over again.

"But you're a college student," Jake said.

"I hear the doubt in your voice. Let me explain. I was home-schooled, not to mention going to a good number of country-type grade schools with low budgets before computers became necessities. My parents don't believe in cable television, cell phones, or a lot of other newfangled technology, either. What I'm saying is that any research involving electronic gadgetry is yours. Do you still want my help?"

"I'm here for the long haul, Kimber, no matter what I have to do. I don't want it to sound as if I'm only doing it because of the money, because that isn't my reason. I've seen most of the lures you have, and a good number of them may be valuable. I wish I could remember the name of the frog one, because it would make looking it up online much easier."

"Me, too. I remember Grandpa used to talk about it all the time when I was little. I meant to ask Grandma about it when I last phoned her. Besides the Internet, what do you think about visiting antique dealers to see what they think of the lures?" Kimber queried.

"Getting another opinion can't hurt," Jake responded. "I thought I was the only expert you wanted."

"Someone once told me an 'ex spurt' is a drip under pressure. Ever heard that one?"

Jake groaned and slapped his hand against his forehead.

"All right, you've already heard it. Casey chose you. She called you because our young-adult pastor said you could help."

"Kimber, can I ask something else?"

"Sure." Kimber knew what Jake was going to ask, and she knew he deserved an answer. She didn't know how he'd respond, though. She swallowed hard, feeling like a fish out of water.

"Why do you avoid me at church?"

⚜

"Do you remember when you spoke to a class about being a new Christian and compared it to fishing?"

"Yes, I wanted the class to try to cast a weight into a bucket."

"I tried—or trying was the theory behind my attempt that day."

Jake nodded, feeling his eyebrows rise in surprise as the memory returned. "You're the one who. . ." He stopped. It wouldn't do to make more of this than Kimber had, especially since he knew he wanted to see more of her.

"Got the line snarled in the maple tree next door? Yes, that was me. You cut it out of that poor tree so you could continue the lesson with the remainder of the class."

"So you stay away from me at church because. . ." *Is this the right way to downplay this?*

"The incident still haunts me."

"Several others failed to hit the bucket at all that day. At least you hit something." Jake kicked himself under the table. *Not the brightest thing I could have said.*

"Yes, but shortly before that, I'd bragged about what a great fisherwoman I was because I'd been fishing since I was five."

"We all make mistakes, Kimber. You might have hit the bucket with a second cast, but you didn't try, did you?" He hoped that comment was better than his last. "I didn't ask you to try, either, did I?"

"I wouldn't have anyway. I was too ashamed."

"If I recall, I tried to show the class that all Christians make mistakes. Kimber, I'm sitting here doing so right now."

"How's that?"

"I'm letting you continue to feel awful about something that happened three or four years ago. What if we get back to researching and forget about the sermon for now? I'll take care of the computer stuff and I'll even give you computer lessons while we work. You might find you pick it up quickly."

Kimber scoffed.

"Don't be so negative. You might be as good with computers

as you are with catching fish. Since the last is still an unknown to me, someday you'll have to prove your skills."

There, Jake thought, *I've planted a different reason than research to see her again.*

"Okay. I admit computer lessons would be good since I can definitely use it for college papers." She grinned at him. "Could you teach me to e-mail, too? Grandma mentioned she's learning how to use e-mail at her retirement home. It would be nice to surprise her one day with an e-mail from me."

"E-mail isn't too hard. You know what else? We've forgotten the antique dealers. Would you mind if I went with you to visit them?"

"I thought it might be asking too much with your business. I can go myself."

"I'm sure you can. With all this rain, there's not much going on at the store right now. It won't hurt if I close for an hour or so."

"I appreciate the offer. Casey thinks I should have picked a couple of Grandma's quilts, and once in a while, I even think so. But I'm glad I chose the fishing tackle, jumbled lines and all."

"I know I'm happy you did." Jake smiled his biggest smile yet.

✤

Kimber's Wednesday noon English class passed quickly. She enjoyed her professor, although she was one of the few in her class who seemed to have that opinion according to what she heard others say during breaks. Professor Minnow was a self-professed lover of eighteenth-century English romance. As such, she used her classroom for in-depth discussions about her ideas on love and romance—nonstop.

Kimber didn't know if the professor was married or not, but if she was, Kimber imagined the professor's husband no taller than the barely five-foot-tall professor herself. He probably had an old-fashioned handlebar mustache and wore a bow tie when he dressed up to go to the opera. The image made Kimber smile. That was not at all the type of man she'd choose, given the chance. She found herself thinking of someone like Jake Evans, a man who dressed in blue jeans and T-shirts and whose blue eyes—eyes that reminded her of the palest blue herons Louisiana offered—sparkled when she told a bad joke.

"That is all for today," Professor Minnow intoned with perfect articulation. "Do not forget that your four-page critical analysis on *The Old Man and the Sea* is due at the beginning of our next class. Details are in your syllabus, which you received on the first day of class. I will see you then."

Kimber gathered her notes, tapped them against the desktop to straighten them, and placed them into her binder that was decorated with a huge Eeyore on the front. She dropped her pen and highlighter into her purse and slung it on her shoulder before leaving. She was due at Jake's in an hour. It was enough time to stop by her house, make sandwiches for them to have for a late afternoon snack, change clothes, and drive to his bait shop.

Kimber didn't want to explore her reasons to get to his store in a hurry. If forced, she would answer research. Jake had graciously offered to bring his laptop from home for him to surf the Web while she learned how on the store desktop. The words *laptop* and *desktop* were beyond her grasp, but Kimber knew Jake would set her straight within minutes of starting.

Kimber thought it was a glorious day, made even more so by

the remains of a morning shower still sparkling on the leaves of the cypress and sweet gum trees she passed as she drove to the lake. Humming her favorite hymns made the drive go by quickly, and she pulled into the parking lot in no time at all.

"Have any luck?" Kimber slid into the seat beside Jake, swung her legs off to the side, and straightened the skirt of her plaid sundress before leaning toward the biggest monitor to read the print listed on it.

"Not much," Jake admitted. "I've been waiting for you. If you're ready, let's get started."

"I'd rather watch today," Kimber said, observing as Jake maneuvered a somewhat small oval object to the right of the desktop computer monitor.

"No watching allowed. Not in my classroom. Now this is called a mouse," Jake explained. "It moves this blinking line on the screen known as a cursor. The laptop normally uses the dark area below the keyboard, called a touch pad, to move its cursor. I've already opened the Internet program on the desktop that allows us to search the Web." He pointed to a long rectangular white area beneath some words and objects near the top of the screen.

"This is where you type the Web address of the search engine and then press the ENTER key. That brings up a search engine page, and when it does, type in 'antique fishing tackle' and press ENTER again. The search function will find as many pages on the Web as it can that contain those words. I'll do it the first time, but then it's all yours."

Kimber moved aside as Jake used the desktop and entered some sequential letters interspersed with periods and backslashes. He pressed the ENTER key again and waited for a few seconds. She watched while a page appeared containing several blocks of text with the words *antique fishing tackle* boldfaced throughout them.

"Great," Jake said. "We'll use the cursor to select the link by starting with the first one and working down the page. To do it, when the cursor is over the text at the bottom of the descriptive paragraph, push down twice on the mouse's left button quickly—that's called double-clicking—and the program will automatically load that new page for us to view."

Kimber watched as another set of pictures and print filled the screen. How the Internet functioned was beyond her comprehension, but she was delighted to see a few pictures that somewhat resembled what she'd seen in Grandpa's tackle boxes. She studied the monitor intently as she went through link after link. She discarded those without pictures and returned to what Jake called the home page to begin her search over and over again.

"All right," Jake said. "I know somewhere out there, there must be pictures of specific tackle, like that frog one, for example."

Kimber noted Jake's irritation and realized she could resolve the situation. "You mean the Heddon Frog?"

"That's it! How did you find the name?"

"Last night I remembered Grandpa used to call it a 'head-on frog' because head-on is how it hit the water."

"Go on. You have to type the words in."

Kimber pecked the words *Heddon Frog* into the search block. She tentatively pressed the ENTER key then waited for the return page.

"Now I select the link, right?" she asked when the page appeared on the computer screen.

"Yep. See, you already understand how to do this much."

"Start with the first one and work down," Kimber said, feeling proud of what she'd already managed to accomplish.

While they sat back and waited for the next page to load, Kimber was suddenly filled with anxiety. What if her lures weren't worth anything? On the other hand, what if she had a rare lure? She'd already said she wasn't going to sell, but in the back of her mind, the numbers were adding up. Student loans. No more grants. Two more years of college.

"Before I forget, thanks for taking time to teach me about computers," Kimber acknowledged. "Although I'm not sure how well I'm doing."

"You're smart, Kimber. You're doing great for someone with so little knowledge about computers. Aha, I wondered why it took so long to load the first page. There's a picture of your frog. I think you'd better read the caption."

"One of the rarest wooden lures in existence," Kimber said, her voice weak, but not as weak as her knees.

Chapter 6

J ake whistled. He'd seen some great fishing lures in his day, but the one on the computer screen was definitely top-of-the-line.

"Do you think the one I have is worth that much?" Kimber asked.

"I'm no expert, remember," Jake joked, trying to lighten the mood.

He wasn't sure if Kimber's was a replica or a real-world version of the $20,000 lure. To him, either was an accomplishment. He wasn't sure what she'd do once she found out, but he couldn't wait to find out.

"I know, but what do you think?" she pushed.

"I don't know. I'd hate to say one way and have it be the other."

"Surprise me."

"You won't give up, will you?" She was as stubborn as a northern pike after forty-five minutes of hard fighting, he'd give her that much.

"Nope." She laughed, a sound that did more to lighten the mood than Jake's earlier joke.

"I'd say it might be real, but it might not. Did anyone in your family ever carve wood?"

"No one I can think of," Kimber answered. "Why?"

"It might be a hand-carved replica. If so, it isn't worth but three or four thousand instead of twenty thousand."

"Oh. That's all."

He didn't like the way she frowned. "I thought you weren't going to sell."

"I'm not. It's—I have to insure them, so I need to know their value."

"Right." She didn't sound sincere, but Jake didn't push. "Did your grandfather buy lures to have them or to use?"

"I think he fished with most of them. If he didn't, wouldn't they be in their original boxes?"

"Good point. The ones my dad left me were in boxes when I got them."

"What do I do now? With the frog, I mean?"

"I think we need to find someone who can verify whether it's real or a replica." Jake scratched his head. "Probably easiest to find someone who can tell us, which means more searching."

"On the Internet? Sounds too complicated for me." Kimber scooted her chair back. "I'll gladly let you have this one."

Jake moved his chair in front of the computer and began, speaking while he typed. "Have you thought about what you'll do if it's real?"

"Not really. I've been saying all along I won't sell, and I don't want to, but twenty thousand dollars is a lot of money."

"It's probably not the only lure you have that's worth money." Jake reminded Kimber there were other possibilities in the tackle boxes.

"That means plenty of chances for us to get together for research, then, doesn't it?" Kimber asked.

Jake liked the hopefulness in her tone. He'd gotten her from where she didn't want to be near him to looking forward to seeing him again.

<hr>

Kimber pushed open the door to Bygone Memories and peered around in search of the owner. A mixture of plastic flowers, chipped pottery, broken toasters, furniture, and other odds and ends filled every nook and cranny. Thick layers of dust covered items that seemed not to have been touched in years. Uneasiness filled her spirit until she reminded herself this was the only antique dealer who'd expressed any interest in helping her.

"How can I help you?" A voice boomed out from behind a huge wooden desk near the back of the room. Papers rustled as they were shoved aside, and into view came a large man who apparently owned the irritatingly loud voice.

"I'm Kimber Wilson. I called yesterday and you said I should come by today to show you my antique tackle. I only brought a few of them. I do want to tell you up front that—"

"Name's McDermott," interjected the owner. "I wondered when you were going to get here." He carried a separate stack of papers as he made his way to her and dropped them near a cash register. "It's almost lunchtime, you know."

"Yes, sir. I know. I explained on the phone I'm a college student and I could only come after my lunchtime class was over." Kimber fought a wave of apprehension that pushed through her. She wished now she'd waited and let Jake come with her as they'd originally planned.

"Might as well show me what you brought," McDermott demanded. "I got a cousin that says he'll help me appraise it, but he's in Dallas for the next month or so on some personal business, so it won't be fast."

"This is it for today." Kimber pulled two wooden lures from their nest within the tissue paper and set them softly on the counter.

"I ain't so sure about that minnow-looking thing or that frog," Mr. McDermott said. "They're going to take some looking into."

"Do you charge for researching?" Kimber suddenly worried this adventure might cost money she didn't have.

"Nah, it's part of the deal. My money comes from other sources. So what else do you have? Are there more like these or are they different?"

"I also have some hand-tied flies," Kimber replied. "There are more wooden ones and they're what I'm most interested in having appraised. As I tried to tell you earlier, I'm not—"

"You got my assurances you've come to the right place," McDermott interrupted. "You just have to wait 'til my cousin comes back." He reached for the lures. "You leave these with me 'til then, and I can do some research on my own. That way we can save ourselves some time."

Kimber picked the lures up before the shopkeeper could and hurriedly replaced them in the tissue paper and stuffed them into her purse. "I'll take them with me, if you don't mind."

"Not at all," McDermott said, sliding a yellow sheet of paper with some hand-drawn lines sloppily centered on it her way. "Complete this and make sure you put your name and phone number on it. That way I can get in touch with you when my cousin comes back."

Kimber did so and hurried to her car. She sat behind the wheel, waiting for the air conditioner to cool it off. It gave her a chance to sort out her feelings. She didn't trust this McDermott character. Antique dealer or not, he made her feel as if he were involved in some type of crooked business, something she wanted nothing to do with.

That evening while chewing down a microwave meat and potatoes dinner before rushing to class, Kimber recalled her visit to the antique dealer. Despair and frustration filled her soul anew. Others might choose to inherit dolls, rings, or dishes, and there was nothing at all wrong with those items, but Kimber wasn't like other people. The more she struggled to find out the value of the fishing tackle, the more responsible for it she felt. How was it possible that in less than three weeks she'd become so attached to Grandpa's old fishing tackle?

❧❦❧

When we find pictures online of what we're looking for, then what would I do?" Kimber quizzed Jake while they took a break from more research.

"First you e-mail the page owner, explain what you have, and ask what he thinks the value might be."

"There's only one problem with that option, Jake."

"What's that?"

"I don't have an e-mail address," Kimber confided, laying aside her candy bar. "I'm pretty sad, aren't I? Even Grandma mentioned the last time I spoke with her that she met a gentleman at the retirement center who's quite proficient with computers. He showed her how to set up a free e-mail account and she's learning how to use it. I guess I'm not a very with-it granddaughter, am I?"

"You can use my business e-mail for the bait shop. It's easy to remember." He handed her one of his business cards and pointed to the address. "It's Hook and Lure at fishmail dot-com. As for the other, I think you're a caring granddaughter whose parents have solid Christian values." Jake leaned over and patted Kimber's hand. "Don't worry. When we find a Web business with a photo of some lure you have, I'll help with e-mail and correspondence 'til you get the hang of it."

"Isn't that dangerous? I've heard horror stories about Internet hoaxes and virus things on the news. It scares me to think I might do something I shouldn't."

"No. Nothing says you have to respond to any or all of the replies you get. By all means, do *not* open any attachments anyone sends to you. The exception is if they tell you in advance they're going to send you something, then it's usually okay."

"I don't know, Jake. I'm not sure about all this computer talk."

"Kimber, wipe that worried look off your face. It'll probably confuse you more if I tell you I have a server scanning all my incoming mail for viruses. I'll explain more about attachments when we get to that point, okay?"

Kimber blew out a sigh of relief. "Thanks, Jake. I guess now is as good a time as any to confess I went by the college lab on my own after class. I tried some Web surfing you showed me. I didn't find anything, but at least I didn't fumble around. I would have last week if you hadn't shown me so much. I'm also glad you wrote down the search engine Web address letter by letter, though. I wouldn't have remembered it on my own."

"I'm happy my lessons helped. I'm glad you took the first

step and tried it on your own. With some practice, you'll get comfortable with e-mail, too," Jake encouraged. "I wish you'd waited for me to go along to the antique dealer, but I know you wanted to go right after class. How was the visit?"

"Horrible. He was upset when I arrived later than he expected even though I'd made it clear on the phone that I couldn't come until after class was out. He says he has a cousin who can appraise the lures for me, but before I left, he tried to convince me to leave them with him."

"You didn't, did you?"

"No way. He made it sound as if I'd be doing him a favor, that he wanted them so he could do more research. I got this weird feeling about him, you know, as if he's not to be trusted or something."

"If you go there again, I'm definitely going with you," Jake declared. "Got that?"

"Yes, sir," Kimber replied, trying to shake off the ominous feeling that just thinking of the dealer had returned to her. "I don't think I'll go back, though. He gives me the creeps when I think about him. I'm sure all antique dealers aren't like him. It was just something about him in particular."

"I guess that means you have to let me help you find out what your lures are worth now."

"I guess so," Kimber answered, feeling unexplainably relieved. She didn't know what it was about Jake, but she wouldn't mind spending more time with him.

Chapter 7

"Feel brave enough to check for e-mail responses yet?" Jake asked Kimber as she reentered the bait shop two weeks later after her English class. He'd been waiting all day to see her and was glad she'd finally arrived. He hoped her grin meant she was as glad to see him as he was to see her.

"You tell me, Mr. Computer Teacher. Am I ready?"

"Why not? You've mastered Turning on and Starting the Computer Lesson One, Surfing the Internet Lesson Two, and Writing E-mails Lesson Three. I think you're ready for Checking E-mail Responses Lesson Four."

"Very funny, Jake. Too bad you don't teach college computer classes."

"Why's that?"

"You'd have all the young ladies waiting to get in your class to listen to your wit."

Jake held his hand across his heart. "The lady doth wound me."

"Is that eighteenth-century English or twenty-first-century Computer?"

"I think we'd better check the e-mail before I lose the battle."
Jake made a wide sweeping motion toward the chair for Kimber
to sit down.

"What's first?" Kimber turned to Jake. "Don't you dare say
first I have to turn on the computer."

"All right. How about first you reach down to the main
power switch?"

"Jake Evans. I mean it."

"Okay. I can take a hint. No fun and games. You show me
what you remember. I'll sit and watch."

Jake settled back, observing as Kimber booted the computer,
brought the Internet program online, and then the e-mail program. She stumbled a few times, but she didn't refer to her cheat
sheets once. Jake thought about saying something to encourage
her but didn't. She didn't seem like she was in the best of moods.
He decided to stay quiet and let her take the lead.

"I need help," Kimber said. "I have four replies. I brought
up the first one, but I forget how to close it out and get the
next one. I know it's simple, but I can't remember."

"Here you go." Jake showed her what to do. "You don't have
to reply to all the e-mails if you don't want to," he reiterated. "Or
you can, but I think it's good to be vague about your collection
right now. Just state that in your opinion, it's in good shape. Tell
them you're only looking for an idea of what it's worth."

"He wants me to send pictures of the lures. How will I manage that?" Kimber snapped her fingers. "My youth group has a
digital camera they let people borrow. It's supposed to be easy to
use, according to our minister. I have to provide batteries and
something to store the photos on. Some kind of memory card or
something."

"I have digital media and I'll help with instructions," Jake said. "You can use my computer to check the photos before we send them out. It'll be a breeze."

Kimber looked hopeful. "I'll make it work somehow. As for e-mail, there's no time like the present." She pecked away at the keyboard. "What do you think of this for a reply?"

"Dear Antique Rod and Reel," Jake read aloud. "I possess some antique lures and I'm trying to find out their approximate value. I'm not an expert, but I believe most are in fair condition as they have little rust on them. Can you help? Please advise. Thanks, KJ."

Jake nodded. "I think it's a great start. You might mention you'll be able to forward digital pictures within a few weeks. That way he won't send another e-mail to ask about them. Besides that, I can't think of anything else, can you?"

"No. I press this button, and that's it?"

"The one marked SEND," Jake confirmed.

Kimber complied. "I can't believe all I do is press a button to send a letter hundreds of miles away in a couple of seconds."

"It's more involved than that, but as far as you're concerned, that's about all there is to it," Jake answered, proud of how much Kimber had learned where computers were concerned. She seemed more comfortable about them and more relaxed around him, which was good. There were several lures yet to research, so there were lots of opportunities to get together. But Jake was ready for more than computer time. He wanted to get Kimber away from a computer and do something different.

"I think I'll surprise Grandma with an e-mail," Kimber said, interrupting Jake's thoughts. "I wrote down her e-mail address last time I talked to her and put it in my wallet just in case I got brave enough to attempt e-mailing her."

❧❦❧

"I want to read Grandma's e-mail first." Kimber brought up the e-mail and read through the script. "She was surprised to hear from me, especially since the e-mail showed it came from your business address." Kimber turned to Jake. "If I hadn't put 'Grandma, it's Kimber!' in the subject line, she wouldn't have known. I should have explained to her on the phone I was using your e-mail before I sent it off, shouldn't I?"

"You're learning, Kimber. I'll bet she was glad to hear from you and didn't think a thing about it."

"At least now I have a less expensive way to keep in touch with her more often. Thanks for letting me use your e-mail for that purpose, Jake."

"Don't mention it. I'm glad to help any way I can. Now how about those responses to the lures?"

"The first one says: 'KJ: I'll be glad to look at and evaluate your collection in person. My business headquarters are located in Dallas, Texas. Our organization has a convention scheduled in Tyler, Texas, soon, which is much closer to you and may be more convenient for travel purposes. If you wish to make arrangements to meet during that time frame, let me know.' He says this is the link for more information about the convention." She pointed to the blue underlined text in the e-mail.

"Sounds like it's worth looking into," Jake said, rubbing his palms together. "You think?"

Kimber nodded. "Yes, but I'm not going to get excited yet. I have a few others to go through." She read through the other replies, but none showed as much promise as the first. "This isn't going to be easy, is it?"

"Nothing good ever is," Jake answered. "Nothing good ever is."

"Jake, you're repeating yourself," Kimber warned.

"I know. For good reason."

❧

"I'm taking individual pictures of every lure I have," Kimber said. "It's time-consuming, but I'll have an inventory, plus it'll give me practice with the digital camera. We can't do anything else since it's raining again."

"I thought you'd never take a break. I feel like I've been watching you work all morning." Jake gazed at the sportsman-type watch on his left arm, its digital display flashing noon. "I guess I have."

Kimber laid the camera aside and moved to stand near him at the table. "I'm worried about your bait shop. What if a customer stops in and wants something?"

"There won't be customers if there's rain," Jake reminded her. "We've had this conversation before in the last four weeks. Every time it's rained." He was concerned about the financial state of his shop, but Kimber didn't need to know. The store had come through worse times in the past and survived. Jake offered a silent prayer that God would see him through this time as well.

"I can still worry, can't I?" Jake watched Kimber pick up a minnow lure and remove a smudge on it before returning it to the tabletop for the next picture.

"Please don't. I know few people around here who fish when it's raining. I know a lot who fish before it rains, and some who fish right after it rains, but hardly any who fish in driving, cats-and-dogs downpours like we're having today."

"I'll try not to then. I think I finally have the hang of this camera. I'm glad I'm not taking pictures of the hand-tied flies, though, since there's a couple hundred of them."

"I'd be here to help even if you did, you know."

"It's the casting lures only today. You can help me make a written inventory of whichever flies you know the names of later on."

"I can't wait to help with that. It's been awhile since I've worked with flies, so it will be challenging. Anything else?" Jake had finally seized on an idea for an outing with Kimber that didn't involve research, but first the rain had to stop.

"I don't think so. I've been trying to recall what Grandpa told me about the original lures. I know he said some were made of string, wood, and rubber, before newer plastic-type ones were developed."

"There were metal ones, too," Jake offered. "The oldest lures have glass-type eyes, though some manufacturers used tacks."

"I have some lures with glass eyes. Does it make them more valuable?"

"It might. It's something we'll check on."

"Whatever they're made of, they're memories I'll always treasure."

"I'm glad you think so," Jake said.

Casey stopped by the kitchen as she headed out to a Saturday afternoon class. "I overheard that last bit of conversation. Glass eyes. Tack eyes. Doesn't matter to me." She shuddered and covered the last lure Kimber had photographed with a dish towel. "It gives me the creeps, and it's only lying on the counter. You once said fishing kept your mind off of me moving away, but why did you decide you liked to fish, Kimber? How could you even try to catch a defenseless little fish, let alone tug on him then put your hands in his mouth to take that wretched hook out? Don't you think the hook hurt him?"

"I'm sure I didn't mess with hooks when I was little, Casey. I don't know about the pain the fish feels, but as far as fishing goes, I remember Grandpa telling me once if I handed a man food, I fed him for that meal. If I taught that same man how to fish, I fed him for the rest of his life." She fell silent for a moment, her eyes misting over. "On the other hand, Dad says God put fish in the water and they snap at our lures because they know we enjoy a fight and they don't want to disappoint us."

"I prefer your grandpa's explanation," Casey said.

"Me, too." Jake realized Kimber's background in fishing gave her more in common with him than any woman he'd ever dated. He was drawn to her every time he saw her, and it wasn't only because of the love of fishing they shared.

"Me three. Grandpa did have a great way of looking at things," Kimber said. "It's time for lunch, Casey. Care to join us? We're having fish sticks."

Casey groaned. "None for me. I'm glad I'm on my way to class. I'll pick up a burger or something. Are you going to stay here and eat those things, Jake? Eww."

Jake grinned. "Only one thing could be better, and that's if it were fresh-caught."

❦

After their lunch, Kimber's return to digital photography went well. When she tired and wanted to give up, either Jake spurred her on, or she closed her eyes and called up her favorite memory.

She sat on a large, glacier-carved rock near a thick stand of trees watching as Grandpa cast his fishing line across a blue-black ribbon of water. A lure flashed through an afternoon sky then dove into the water and sunk out of sight, taking with it the hope it would be reeled back in with a fish attached.

Before the afternoon ended, digitized photos worthy of the best amateur photographer contained pictures of all the casting lures in Kimber's recently acquired collection.

The rain finally ended and Jake left to check on his store. She felt lost without him and sat down at the table to think over the last few months' events. She'd progressed from avoiding Jake at church to wanting to be with him every spare minute. In the beginning, she was embarrassed to be near him because he'd seen her at what she thought was her worst—casting a weight into a tree. He hadn't made fun of her at all, and now Kimber knew she'd been silly to make a big deal out of nothing. Her own pride had kept her from getting to know Jake a few years earlier.

Kimber remembered something Grandma had said in Wyoming. "I'm sure whatever you select will be exactly what the Lord has in mind for you. He wouldn't have it any other way."

"I know, Grandma," she'd replied. "I need to have more faith and wait to see what His plans are."

Kimber gazed at the countertop. If she'd picked the quilts, what man would be in her life right now? Jake Evans? She didn't think so. May sunshine filtered through the window blind, casting a warm glow across a variety of rubber lures and wooden plugs lying every which way that Kimber hadn't put away yet. A similar type of glow filled her heart as she glanced over her collection. Faith had brought her to this point and put Jake Evans into her life. She smiled.

Not only that, but the idea that something from her childhood existed now in much the same state as it had then reminded her of all the times in Grandpa and Grandma's kitchen after school when he'd advised her. The old tackle might be wooden lures, unused for many years, but they reminded Kimber of her childhood. Seeing them again rekindled within her how much she valued the family she grew up with.

Thoughts of family brought her brother, William, to mind. He'd been in the marines for three years, and he wanted to make it a twenty-year career. With the current state of affairs in the Middle East, Kimber worried about his safety, but William had assured her that he was assigned with the best-trained and best-outfitted unit the marines had.

"Besides, Kimmy," he'd said, using his favorite nickname for her when she pressed him with her concern about current events, "if the Lord calls me to fight in His army sooner than I plan, who am I to question Him?"

Kimber was glad that through everything, William kept his faith. He liked the military so much he wanted to continue in it. In his bimonthly phone calls, William often brought up a girl named Jenny McElveen. Kimber wondered if she would have a sister-in-law before long. If so, she was thrilled William had found his soul mate. She hoped as he'd found his, she might find hers, too.

"Lord, thank You for dying for me and saving me from sin. Please protect my mom and dad while they work mid-shifts as

I hardly get to see them since I'm in school most nights. Please protect William as he defends our country. Be with him as he and Jenny decide whether they are right for each other. And, Lord, thank You for sending Jake Evans my way to help me research Grandpa's fishing lures. I'm glad he's in my life and I'm getting to know him. Please slow down or stop the rain so his business can rebound. Amen."

Chapter 8

"Why are you calling so early? Did you hear something back on the frog?" Kimber asked.

Jake paced the front of his bait shop, tied to it by the reception on his cordless phone, one of the first models made. "In a way. The guy e-mailed and said he'd have to see it in person to give his professional opinion. He's going to be at the convention coming up in Tyler, Texas. He suggested we bring it to him then if we want him to look at it."

"Do you think it's a good idea?"

"It's your lure. Whatever you want to do is fine with me."

"You're not much help, Jake." Her voice had a not-quite-awake, not-quite-asleep quality.

"I already told you I'd ride along."

"I'm not sure I'm ready to find out if it's real or not. What if it is? What if it isn't?" Now she sounded almost fully awake.

"We won't know if we don't go."

"You're a poet and don't know it."

"Then I take it we're going to the convention in Tyler, Texas?" Jake ignored her dig at him and looked forward instead to spending the day with her.

"Yes. Will you e-mail him and let him know, or are you going to make me drive there and type it myself?"

"I will because it will save you driving in another storm. Can you believe we have more forecast for later today? It's ridiculous. No one here remembers getting rain like this in twenty years or more."

"I've only lived here seven years, so you can't prove it by me," Kimber interjected. "How have you been since you helped me with my photography project the other day?"

Jake enjoyed her conversation, because he knew if he hung up, there'd be more than a phone connection broken. "Business has dropped some," he admitted, careful not to reveal the full extent of his financial mess.

"Does it usually do so this time of year, or is it the rain?"

"Mostly the rain, but that's okay. It gives me a chance to take you fishing."

"You can't seriously want to fish. The lakes must be nothing but red mud from all the red clay around here and the rain we've had. When did you want to go?"

She was definitely awake now. Jake walked the length of the bait store, running his hand through the minnow tank and bothering the tiny baitfish much as his heart was disturbed any time he talked to or thought of Kimber.

"In about an hour. I told you once I know people who fish before it rains. I'm one of them. I believe an incoming weather front makes the fish more active. If you want to go, I'll pick you up at eight."

"I warn you I haven't fished in years. You saw what I did with that cast at church. I've also been known to toss my plug in the wrong direction, let loose of the rod completely as I cast, or toss my line across another's at the most inopportune moment. I also have another college English paper due I haven't started on, but you sound rather insistent. Are you sure you don't have news about my Heddon Frog lure?"

"Nothing more than what I've already told you," Jake answered.

"All right. I'll go. I doubt we'll catch anything since the water will be muddy."

Knowing Jake would be there within the hour, Kimber dashed to shower. She then gave her appearance a quick once-over in the full-length mirror, patted on sunblock and some light face powder, and finally pulled her hair up in a ponytail centered on the back of her head. Next, she threw on a lime-green T-shirt with a MudBug Madness—Shreveport/Bossier City's salute to the crawfish—slogan on the front and a pair of blue jeans with tiny holes at the knees. A pair of shabby sneakers stained green from helping with lawn work finished her outfit.

"I wish I didn't have to dress so shabbily to fish," she said to her reflection in her bedroom mirror. "I'd rather Jake saw me looking more presentable."

≪≫

"This isn't an insult, but you do remember how to bait a hook, right?"

Jake stood beside Kimber in the shade where only a few buzzing insects broke the early morning quiet. He disliked making it sound as if Kimber didn't know anything, but he knew women who insisted they knew what to do when fishing yet, when it came down to it, expected him to do everything. He thought it best to review what Kimber understood before they headed toward the lakeside.

Kimber put her hands on her hips. "Bait a hook? I've put live earthworms on hooks by myself since the first summer I learned to fish, and I was only five years old!" Kimber retorted. "Besides, I can't believe you'd bring someone along who didn't know his or her way around a fishing rod or a lake."

Jake stood so his shoulders blocked the sun's glare in her eyes. He enjoyed how a light breeze tossed her dark brown hair into waves of its own choosing. Better get back to fishing, or he'd stand and stare at her all day.

"Five?" Jake managed to reply. "Most girls who visit my bait shop are at least eleven or twelve. The majority turn up their noses at the live crickets, minnows, and earthworms and head for the plastic worm section. I guess you're one of those progressive women I hear about on the news. Trying to break the glass ceiling and demanding equal money for equal work?"

"Progressive?" Kimber echoed. "Not me. I might go to college, but I'm just a girl whose grandpa happened to take her fishing one long-ago summer." She told Jake the background of how she began to fish and why, ending with Casey's move near her seven years ago and their reestablished friendship.

Jake stared toward the lake for a long moment. "You said you could bait a hook. Do you also recall how to string new line and add a new hook? Do you remember the knot to use so the hook won't come off the first time you set the hook in a fish's mouth? Can you choose the correct size lead weight and select the proper tackle for the weather and water conditions?"

Kimber smirked at him. "I figure most of it will come back once I get started. If you ask all the girls you take fishing these types of basic questions, Jake, I'll bet they don't hang around too long, do they?"

"I'm not worried about 'all the girls,' Kimber. Just you. Here, I brought Mom's old rod and reel. It hasn't been used for a few years, but if you show me you know what you're doing as far as setting it up properly, you're the right person to use it."

"I'm flattered, Jake, but I can't use your mom's rod."

"If you're half the fisherwoman I think you are, it's in the right hands. Go ahead. Don't just stand there. Get busy and get it rigged so we can start fishing. Here's what you need." He handed her two empty sections of rod and reel. "You can get anything else you need from my tackle box."

Kimber set to work and Jake listened to her hum. He waited until she finished to speak.

"I guess humming Christmas songs in summer is one way to keep cool, although today is almost chilly since that cold front is bringing more rain our way."

"I don't hum it to stay cool, and besides, show me where it says you can only sing that song at Christmas," Kimber countered. " 'Joy to the World' is my favorite song because it helps me concentrate. Something about the words reminds me God came to guide the world. With Him on my side, I can handle pretty much anything. I don't always remember that when I should."

"I never thought of the song in that way," Jake commented. "I prefer a tune called 'I Can Only Imagine.' Ever heard it?"

"Sure. I hear it on the radio when I'm doing homework or driving to class," Kimber answered, still working at putting the new line on her rod. "I'll admit it's a great song, but it doesn't relax me the way 'Joy to the World' does. I think it's because my grandma used to sing what I called 'the joy song' when I was little." She held up the assembled rod and reel. "Want to see if it passes your inspection?"

Jake took the rod, his fingers lingering against hers for an instant. It took great effort to pull the rod away and turn it over. He held it up and checked to ensure the small silver circular guides that the fishing line threaded through were lined up properly. He completed his checklist of items and was confident the rod was ready to use. A smile showed his approval.

"You do know what you're doing. Most women put the rod together wrong and the guides don't match. From there, it's all downhill. You tied the hook tightly and you've chosen a decent-sized weight to go with the plastic red-and-white bobber you selected. I take it we're fishing for what we Southerners call bream, otherwise known as bluegill to some Northerners. Ready to hit the water?"

"Figuratively speaking, of course," Kimber said. "Lead the way, Mr. Evans."

❧❧❧

She didn't know why she'd addressed Jake so properly, but she didn't miss the change in his demeanor. His entire face darkened, despite their facing the sun.

"Did I say something wrong?" she probed. Of all things, she didn't want to hurt his feelings on their first real outing. She didn't count all the times they spent together doing research as outings or dates, though they certainly counted as together time.

"No. I was thinking about. . ." Jake stumbled over a tree root but didn't drop any equipment as he struggled to stay upright. "I'd better watch where I'm walking."

"I'm usually the one who does that," Kimber admitted. "Are you okay?"

"You bet," Jake said, reshuffling the rods in his arms. "Do you want to pick our starting spot, or do you want me to?"

"You go ahead. You're more familiar with the area."

"Let's head for that bank. I've caught several nice bream in the last year or so and a few crappies, too." Jake pointed toward an incline a hundred feet or so away where several tree trunks stuck out of the water's edge. "There's underwater cover for both types of fish, so maybe we'll be all right today. I doubt it with the muddy water, but fishing's always worth trying."

Kimber walked behind Jake where the path narrowed and was as careful as she could be since the last thing she needed was a repeat of the tangled-line-in-the-tree-at-church incident. She watched Jake maneuver around some tree roots. This was one early morning phone call she didn't mind being awakened by. After spending time with Jake, she understood that beneath his handsome, rugged exterior was a tender, gentle person. In fact, Jake was everything she wanted in a mate: Christian, sincere, humorous, and compassionate. He also loved fishing. What more could she ask for?

Chapter 9

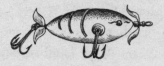

I can't believe you went fishing with Jake!" Casey flopped onto the sofa, crossed her arms, and pouted. "I thought you were only seeing him because of the research for your fishing things."

"We fished, but the water was so muddy from so much rain that we didn't catch anything. We ended up talking about different types of lures and bait you use depending on weather conditions and the color of the water. Hardly the sort of conversation you're interested in, is it?"

"That's not my point," Casey rebutted. "I thought you were only going to see him for the fishing stuff you brought back from your grandma's. That's all."

"I see," Kimber said, slowly recognizing the signs of jealousy. "If the weather holds, we're going out fishing again this weekend. If you're worried about what Jake and I are up to, why don't you come with us?"

"I've never fished before," Casey said. "I wouldn't know what to do."

"Jake has a list at the store where people can sign up for fishing lessons. There were several names on it, so he must be a capable teacher. I'll bet he can help you learn. He's calling tonight to tell me what time we're leaving this Saturday. I'll tell him you're coming with us so he can pack enough in our picnic lunch for one more. I'm sure he won't mind having you join us."

"I'll bet your fishing knowledge impresses him, doesn't it?" Casey sat up and leaned forward.

"Why's that?" Kimber asked, pulling out her books and preparing to work on her final English paper.

"I never told you this, but Jake and I dated a few times before my parents moved to Hawaii. He *never* packed us a picnic lunch, nor did he ever take me fishing."

"Do you want me to call off our fishing trip, Casey?"

"Don't cancel because of me. I'm glad Jake found someone to fish with. Who knows? Maybe something serious will come of your relationship with him. What I wonder about is his motive where your antique tackle is concerned."

"His motive? If you thought Jake would take advantage of me somehow, then why did you ever introduce us in the first place?"

"Because in the beginning, I thought Jake would help you find out what they were worth. I didn't think he'd need the money you'd provide if he bought your lures and then resold them for a profit."

"Jake wouldn't do that." Kimber recalled a comment by Jake. What had he said? *"I don't want to sound as if I'll help because of the money, but most of your lures are going to be valuable."* That was pretty close. Had she misinterpreted his interest?

"Personally, I think you're jealous, Casey, but maybe you'd better come with us and make sure Jake doesn't try anything questionable."

"I told you I shouldn't have come," Casey whined, swatting her hand in the air around her head. "There are bugs. If they aren't biting, they're buzzing me like I'm target practice for aircraft from the air base that fly over here all the time. I don't have any business trying to fish. It doesn't matter what I do; I can't get the hang of it."

Jake and Kimber looked at each other, then Jake turned to Casey. "I'll work with you again on what to do. It's not a problem. I like helping people learn. There's great satisfaction in doing something right, you know."

"I'd rather do well on my college algebra final," Casey snapped. "Teaching me to fish is hopeless. I think I'll go unpack lunch and get it ready. You and Kimber can keep fishing until you're hungry, then join me at the picnic table."

"Casey," Kimber said, "why don't you sit here beside me? We can talk and watch Jake 'til he's done."

Casey dropped her rod and squinted into the sun. "I'm not into getting all sweaty. I'd rather be in air-conditioning, but since there isn't any here, I'll take shade trees instead. I brought my algebra book because I knew this would happen. I'll be fine. Don't worry."

Kimber and Jake watched as Casey pushed her way through some brush and headed to where Jake's pickup sat near a covered eating area.

"Do you think I should volunteer to help her get the food and drinks out of my truck?" Jake asked. "The cooler they're in is fairly heavy."

"She probably doesn't want either of us around her right now," Kimber said. "Casey's ego is bruised because I can fish and she can't. Setting up lunch is something she can do on her own. You understand, don't you?"

Jake nodded. "Casey doesn't have to get all worked up because she doesn't know how to fish. Some men and women were never taught at all. They don't understand how relaxing and enjoyable it is. I'm glad if one person I work with appreciates the sport."

"There is a lot to learn about it, though," Kimber said. "You started talking to Casey about the difference between a slamming and a spinning reel. Then you mentioned trolling with a corrosion-resistant three-bearing reel with a worm-gear level wind with titanium-coated line guide. I was almost overwhelmed, so I can imagine how she felt. I say give her room and she'll be fine once she composes herself."

"Whatever you say." Jake cast his line out and reeled it back toward the bank a few feet before sitting down.

Casey's scream interrupted the ensuing quiet.

❧

"I was just—and then I—was going—to get—but then I turned—and then this—thing. . ." Casey gulped huge deep breaths between her sobs. She wiped at her face and pushed away tears streaming down her face. "Not only can't—I fish. I can't even—set up—a picnic lunch—I'm hopeless."

"Did you happen to get a good look at this 'thing'?" Jake quizzed. "Can you tell me what it looked like?"

"Does she have to do so at this very moment, Jake?" Kimber asked, standing beside Casey. "She's scared to death. Can't you see how she's shaking?"

"Yes, but I'd like to know in case there are more of them in the back of my truck. Good to know if what I'm looking for bites. For all our safety's sake on the way home, of course."

Kimber considered Jake's request. "What do you think, Casey? Do you think you might try to describe it?" She patted her friend on the back in reassurance.

Casey nodded, but her words came out still smothered by sobs. "Ugly. Black. White stripe. Legs. Blue tail."

Jake leaned against the bumper of his truck. "I think Casey saw what we call a skink in the South. It won't let go very quickly if it bites, but it's more of a nuisance than anything. It's like a chameleon. You know, those lizards that change from brown to green depending on what they're up against, except a skink doesn't change colors."

"How comforting." Casey sounded slightly more composed. "All I know is it looked huge. I must have disturbed it when I pulled the cooler back toward the tailgate. I thought if I reached in and took stuff out a little at a time, I wouldn't have to carry it all at once. Just as I went to pick the cooler lid up, that *thing*—skink—whatever—popped his head up above the lid on the opposite side away from me. I tell you, it was glaring at me!"

"I imagine seeing it was probably pretty scary. Did it bite you?" Jake asked.

"Are you kidding? I didn't give it a chance to! I dropped the lid and screamed for help."

"Let me look around. I'll check out the truck bed and see what I can find. I'd guess that particular skink is long gone, though," Jake volunteered.

"Please hurry," Kimber said. "Then I think we'd better pick up our stuff and head home."

"If that lizard is in the cooler, I don't want anything to do with those sandwiches," Casey insisted.

❧❧

"I told you I should have stayed home," Casey said. "I ruined the whole day."

"Don't apologize," Kimber replied. "I probably would have screamed, too, if I'd seen that thing pop its head up like you described."

"No, you wouldn't, because you belong in the outdoors. Jake knows it. That's why he likes you and takes you fishing. I don't belong there and I knew it, but I let you talk me into going with you."

"I wanted you there because you were sure Jake would talk me into selling my lures to him first, then resell them for a profit. He didn't do that, did he?"

"I ruined things before he could," Casey answered.

"I still can't believe you think Jake would take advantage of me in that way," Kimber rebutted. "I'll admit I haven't known him long, but it doesn't fit with what I do know about him."

"Did you read your copy yet of the newspaper article about his store that Jake left here this morning before our fishing trip?"

❧❧

"I need to see you today, Jake. Not tomorrow. I'll be there in thirty minutes."

Kimber replaced the receiver on the phone and glared at her reflection in the hallway mirror. A hint of too much sun covered her nose and cheeks. She didn't bother to brush her hair and remove the wind-induced tangles from the lake trip earlier. Her appearance didn't matter, since she wasn't going to see Jake to go out with him; she was going for the opposite reason. Now. Before her heart got reeled in any further. She wasn't sure if Casey's allegations were right, but she needed to find out.

"I'll ride along if you want," Casey offered.

"No. We have more severe storms forecasted, so I won't stay long. This is something for me to do alone," Kimber said.

"Let's pray before you go," Casey requested.

"Thanks for the reminder," Kimber replied.

"Of what?"

"To let God work out the details."

Chapter 10

I need you to explain this," Kimber said, waving the newspaper section around in the air seconds after she entered his store.

"I can tell you're upset, but I'm not sure what I'm supposed to clarify. The article relates how the bait shop is doing because of all the rain we've had these last few months. That's it."

"That's not *it* at all," Kimber replied. She turned so Jake wouldn't see her clasped hands. Looking out the window and facing the lake wasn't any better. It took her back to the good times she and Jake had had fishing together. Times she was probably tossing away because of the accusation she was about to make. Lightning strikes on the opposite side of the lake added to her misery.

"I don't know what you're looking for." A clap of thunder accented Jake's statement. "The piece says the store has some financial trouble. I'm not the only business to have problems because of the continual rainfall. Since I have a bait shop, and most people, present company excluded, don't fish because of high, muddy water, I'm losing more stock than I'm selling."

"Now that's more like it," Kimber replied over her shoulder

as calmly as she could. "Which is why you plan to buy some of my lures at a ridiculously low price and turn around to sell them at their real market value. You'll make money *and* save your store at the same time."

In the window reflection, she saw Jake step toward her then apparently change his mind and remain where he was. "Where would you get a crazy idea like that? I've done nothing but encourage you *not* to sell those lures."

"Be more specific, Jake. You didn't want me to sell them to the antique dealer."

"Because he's dishonest. You pretty much called him that when you told me about the your first visit with him. Those lures belonged to your grandpa, and I think, no, *I know* they should stay with you, no one else."

In the background, a weather radio near the cash register sounded an alarm. He walked over and silenced it with one push of a button.

"No one else," she parroted when the noise subsided. "I'm not that easily convinced."

"Where did this idea that I wanted to make money off of you come from? You've never mentioned anything like this before, so it isn't something that. . ." Jake stopped unexpectedly. "Casey put you up to making this claim, didn't she? Do you honestly believe her?"

Kimber swallowed the lump in her throat.

"Kimber, please turn around and look at me while I'm talking. I'd rather not say this to your back."

She turned slowly to face him. "Go ahead."

"I don't know what I can say that will persuade you differently. Someone once said that 'good things come to those who wait.' It might not sound original, but I'll wait forever for you to change your mind. I've spent my life waiting, Kimber."

"How so?"

"When I was four, I wanted to be older so Dad would teach me more about fishing. When I was fifteen, I waited for Mom to finish chemo treatments after her cancer surgery, successfully I might add. When I was nineteen, I waited for them to return from a trip to Arkansas where they went to pick up a rare lure to add to Dad's collection. Neither came back alive."

"The paper said the accident happened five years ago. I'm so sorry," Kimber whispered.

"I have a lure worth eighteen thousand dollars, but it might as well be a branch broken from a tree. I have Dad's store, but I'd rather have them here alive more than anything else, except you."

"I don't know what to say," Kimber admitted. "Originally, it was Casey who brought up the idea of you making a profit from my lures. I half believed her because, well, because it was easier than letting my heart get all the way involved with you. It sounds silly now that I say it out loud."

Jake moved and put his hands on her shoulders. "Do you honestly think I'd hurt you? Kimber, in a few months you've taught me more about living than I've learned in the last twenty-five years of my life. What does the word *love* mean to you?"

"Trusting, caring, always being there, being able to laugh with each other. You'd better not be headed where I think you are, Jake. I don't think it's possible to fall in love in a few months."

"Maybe you don't think you can, but if I'm not all the way there, I'm—"

Lightning hit one side of the building, a clap of thunder immediately following. Together the noise drowned out the rest of Jake's declaration.

Kimber turned a worried glance toward the parking lot. "The lake is overflowing! It's over the rocks at the edge!"

"This way." Jake grabbed her hand, pulling her toward the rear of the store. "My truck is out back. I was going to load up some things from the store to take home later today. We can make it out of here before the high water gets here, but we're going to have to hurry."

"You're going to let everything get covered by water or swept away? Won't you lose it all?"

"I don't have a lot of choice about the items on the shelves. You're all I care about staying safe." Jake tugged at Kimber's hand and pulled her close to his side. "Let's go."

"Can't we try moving a couple of things? How much room is left in the back of your truck?"

"A lot. I hadn't put much in it yet." Jake turned to gaze at the lakefront. "We might have time to grab a few things, but it will be *very* few."

Kimber rushed to the front of the store, grabbed some small cricket containers off a shelf, and swung the lid of the main cricket cage open. She started scooping the crickets into the personal-size cages as fast as she could. "Don't just stand there. Move something. Help me, Jake!"

Jake shook his head and strode toward the earthworms. The large wooden box he kept them in was heavy and awkward, but he managed to get it off the cradle it sat on and onto a nearby dolly.

"Let me help," Kimber said when it was full. She tugged on the front of the box while Jake pushed on the back. The dolly began to move across the wooden floor, squeaking as it did.

"Wait a sec." Kimber piled six cages filled to the brim with crickets on top of the earthworm box. "Okay, now let's give it another go."

Before long, earthworms and crickets were stashed safely in the bed of the truck. Jake kept a continued watch on the water while Kimber tossed corks, fishing hooks, and spools of line into an empty box.

"What about the minnows?" she asked, glancing toward the huge tub where small baitfish swam in endless circles.

"I can release them into the lake. I don't have anything to put them in."

"Yes, we do." Kimber grabbed the infamous cooler that had once hid the skink from Casey. "Won't some of them fit in here?"

"They won't last long without aeration," Jake answered as he moved water first, then nets full of minnows into the fifty-gallon insulated plastic cooler.

"It's worth a try." Kimber tried her best to keep the cooler balanced on the now-empty dolly while Jake poured minnows into it.

"That's about all my little truck will hold. Right about now I wish I'd had the money to buy a big four-by-four instead of a small Nissan truck." Jake wiped his forehead and reached for the bottled water Kimber held out.

"Is this on the house, or will I have to pay for it later?" he asked, grinning in an effort to ease the tension.

"That was close," Jake gasped, wiping his face with the sleeve of his shirt. He looked over his shoulder and out the rear window of the truck as floodwaters reached the store's front door. "I can't believe you went back in there and helped me move that stock."

"I'm not sure I believe it myself." Kimber looked back at the water also. "I want to apologize. If I hadn't been so persistent about arguing with you, you wouldn't have turned off the weather alarm. You'd have heard the flash flood warning and saved more of your supplies."

"I have insurance," Jake said. "I already said you were all I cared about saving."

"I'm not sure I'm ready for a relationship, Jake. I don't know what to expect where love is involved. While I was in Wyoming picking my attic treasure, I watched Grandma. You know where love got her now that Grandpa's gone? She's alone and hurt, that's where."

"Kimber, I've learned you can't go through life afraid of being loved. If I hadn't gone back to being a churchgoing man when I lost Mom and Dad, I wouldn't be here today."

"Why not?" Kimber asked.

"If I hadn't, I wouldn't have preached the sermon about fishing to your class that day, which means you wouldn't have tangled your line in a tree, which means I wouldn't have had to untangle it, which means you wouldn't have been embarrassed, which means you wouldn't have avoided me, which means Casey wouldn't have had to hook us up."

"Hook us up. Very funny, Jake Evans. You realize I'm not some trophy fish you can catch with a fancy lure."

"Yes, ma'am," Jake agreed. "You're a lot more than that to

me, Kimber Wilson. I promise I'll keep our fishing lines untangled for the rest of our lives. I hope my word is good enough for you to trust."

"Anyone who helps move minnows by putting them in a cooler when they should leave a flood zone instead is crazy, but a lot like myself. I do still wonder about one thing, though."

"What's that?"

"Does the flood mean you'll close? You have insurance, but will you want to reopen the bait shop in the same location?"

"Why not? It's all I have left of Dad and Mom, besides the house, which isn't much more than a lakefront cabin."

"A lakefront cabin? Those are worth a small fortune in today's market, Jake. You could sell it and start a new business somewhere else, couldn't you?"

"I could have done so when my parents first passed away. I didn't want to then and I sure don't want to now. The shop and the home are all I have left of them. My life's treasures are made up of times that happened in one of those two places. I won't sell either, no matter what."

"How do you stand living and working so close to the water? Don't you tire of worrying about floods?"

"When I was little, I worried all the time. Dad finally convinced me the lake wouldn't flood every year. I've learned there are going to be trials in our lives and it's up to us to work at overcoming them if we're going to be happy. Besides, God promises to walk beside us and guide us through them, remember?"

"He's the real reason we made it through the flood and saved some of your bait stock," Kimber said.

"I believe so. Staying at the shop could have been a wrong decision. If it had been someone else there with me, I doubt I'd have stayed and tried to save anything."

"So why did you with me?"

"Because your willingness to help was a test of how much fishing and my world means to you and that you're the right person for me."

"I'm glad God put those lures where I'd find them so I could find you."

"Me, too. Which means what I was saying before lightning hit was the wrong thing to say."

"I couldn't hear you the first time for all the noise."

"I was about to say I was fairly close to being in love with you, but that's not exactly true now."

"Not true." Kimber bit her lip, holding back her tears. Just when she was ready to tell Jake she loved him, he decided he was wrong about his feelings for her. Was he not the soul mate she'd waited for? Were her efforts in the bait shop all for nothing?

"Did you hear me?" Jake asked.

"No," Kimber confessed.

"Before disaster struck, I was about to say I was *fairly close* to loving you. That's what isn't true. I'm *all* the way in love with you, Kimber Wilson."

"All the way," Kimber repeated slowly, with emphasis, liking the way the words sounded on her lips.

"Do you need more time to think about what I said?" Jake probed.

Kimber studied him. There was no evidence of the man she knew hours ago. His blond, somewhat curly hair lay plastered to his head because of the rain. His heron-blue eyes shone with the character of one who'd raced a flood and won.

"No more time is necessary," Kimber said. "Just a few favors."

"You name them."

"Will you help me tell Casey I shouldn't have listened to her but trusted my heart where you were concerned? I should do it on my own, but it won't be easy. That's why I'd like you to be there."

"I'd be honored to help you with that. And?"

"We're supposed to meet the dealer in Tyler at the convention next weekend so he can appraise the Heddon Frog. You're still riding along to give your opinion on what he tells me, right? It's only a couple of hours over there. We can leave at seven in the morning and be home before sunset. I'll pack the picnic lunch this time."

"I wouldn't miss the trip for anything else in the world. I've always dreamed about seeing the lures other people have collected. Is there anything else?"

Kimber smiled. "Be there when I call Grandma in Wyoming and tell her what's come from choosing those tackle boxes as my attic treasure. I think she'll be tickled I found such a unique use for them."

"I'll always be here to assist you in any way you need, but there's one condition." Jake returned Kimber's smile and squeezed her hand.

"What's that?"

"We tell her we're flying in to visit her a few days after our wedding."

"That will be when?" Kimber asked, a tremble evident in her voice.

"Your choice, my dear," Jake said, pulling his bride-to-be to his chest and enfolding her into his arms.

"I think Grandma will be more pleased about the wedding than the fishing tackle," Kimber said, leaning into Jake's hug before pushing slightly away. "Wait a minute, Jake. When we marry, we combine our tackle collections, right?"

"Generally that's the way things go. Why?"

"We'll have duplicates and some triplicates of some of the antique lures."

Jake thought for a moment. "When we go to Tyler, we can start looking into what they're worth. What if we sell some of the extras and use the money to finance the rest of your education?"

"We can't use the money just to help me out. What if we also rebuild our bait shop?" Kimber said.

"Our bait shop." Jake grinned. "I like it. I imagine once you see our lakefront home you'll think it needs remodeling. I hope you know I look forward to fishing with our children."

"Boys or girls?" The idea of holding their children in her arms spun as crazily through her heart as a Heddon Frog cut through lake water.

"As long as they're healthy, gender doesn't matter. I happen to know this great fisherwoman who I'm certain will help me teach them."

Kimber gazed at the man who'd taught her the meaning of love and the real value of tomorrow's promise. "God has truly blessed me with the catch of my life."

Jake's eyes overflowed with love as he pulled Kimber into his arms and replied, "I was about to say that very same thing to you."

TAMMY SHUTTLESWORTH

Tammy Shuttlesworth is an Ohio native who lives in Louisiana. She misses the changing seasons of the rolling hills of home, but being in the South gives her an excuse for one vacation trip back to Ohio every year or so. A U.S. Air Force (USAF) veteran who was blessed with twenty years of peacetime service, she now teaches JROTC at Haughton High School. The highlights of her ten years with the LA-801st are seeing both daughters as "Buccaneers in Blue" and sponsoring numerous award-winning Color Guards at inter-service competitions.

Tammy's husband, also retired from the USAF, supports whatever she attempts, from writing to bowling to cross-stitching. Their seventeen-year-old will soon head off to college while their oldest daughter's family includes their first grandson, Kaleb. With him, coloring books and "worm-finding walks" are once again part of weekend activities. Her favorite relaxation tools are opening the Bible to a surprise verse, walking her long-haired miniature dachshund, or watching Home and Garden TV to get ideas for her growing flower garden.

This Prairie

by Janet Spaeth

Dedication

To Helen and John Galegher.
Your smiles warm even the coldest winter.
Thank you for sharing this prairie with me.

"For this child I prayed."
1 Samuel 1:27 KJV

Chapter 1

The late afternoon thunderstorm had ended, but the streets were flooded in places with its aftermath. Lauren Fielding knew that by the time she got home, her new red BMW wouldn't look any more spectacular than the rusty old Nova she'd driven through college, but she didn't care. At night, all cars looked the same, right? Just as long as it got her home—back to her own splendid home and her own splendid husband.

She parked her puddle-splattered car next to his Lamborghini. Both cars had been Christmas presents to themselves. For a moment she sat in her car, enjoying it, enjoying everything. She'd worked hard, and some of the sweetest rewards of her success were moments like these. Quiet moments. Easy moments. Loving moments.

Speaking of loving, she thought as she tucked her keys into her pocket, *I should go inside.* She had some tremendous news for her husband.

❧❦❧

"It's a big, splashy deal," she said as she sat next to him on the couch, waving her hands as she painted the scene in the air.

"Radio, television, even billboards. Magazine, newspaper, Internet. You name it, we're doing it."

He nodded, his eyes—as brown as warm morning coffee—fixed on hers. A small fire was burning in the fireplace, warding off the damp chill of the thunderstorm, but she couldn't settle down and enjoy it.

She leaped to her feet, too antsy to sit still, and paced around, still drawing invisible road maps. "I'm going to have to hire a whole new complement just to deal with them. Lauren Fielding Advertising, honey pie, just hit the big time. This is enough to boost me into *Advertising Age*'s top ten."

He folded the newspaper and laid it beside him.

Lauren picked it up and slapped it across her hand. "One day, very soon, you'll see an ad in here for Comfort Home Hotels, and it'll be my ad. My ad, Bob, my ad!"

He smiled.

"In some weird way, I'll be famous. I mean, I will. Okay, actually I'll be making someone else famous, Comfort Home Hotels, but every time I see that name, I'll see mine right behind it." She dropped to the chair beside him. "I never dreamed of this when I started the agency. Never."

She jumped up, spun around, and gushed, "And did I tell you how much they've given me for the campaign? Well, I can't. Contracts and all that. Hush-hush, secret-secret, but let me give you an estimate: *a lot!* We thought last year was big, big enough for the cars, but oh, this is even better!"

He moved the footstool out of her way.

She stopped spinning giddily and faced him, a bit wobbly after all those revolutions, and put her hands squarely—or as squarely as she could—on her hips. "Excuse me, but have you noticed something here? Like I'm the only one talking?"

He cleared his throat. "You do it well."

She sank next to him and laid her hand on his. "Are you okay? Is something wrong?"

Bob smiled into her eyes, and her heart did that funny squiggly thing it did when they were close. "Not wrong. No, I don't think so."

Her heart plummeted. This didn't sound like him. "You don't think so? What do you mean?"

She saw the pile of mail on the table beside him and sorted through it quickly. She pulled out an envelope with the statement from an upscale clothing store and grinned. "Okay, that's enough to make anyone gray, but it's their shoe department. Blame it on their shoe department."

She filtered through the other envelopes. "Ad, ad, ad, bill, ad, bill, bill. . . . Oh, look! An invitation to the Murrays' May Flowers Brunch." The May Flowers Brunch was the bash of the year in their neighborhood. The Murray family owned a series of very exclusive, very expensive pastry shops, and their party was a calorie-ridden paradise. "Is this what's got you down?"

He shook his head and pointed to the last envelope in the stack, a thin, violet-strewn letter addressed in a deep indigo ink. "It's from your grandmother."

Her hands shook as she took the paper from him. "It can't be bad news," she said, trying for a confidence she didn't feel. "Not with her. She's fine. She'll always be fine."

Her eyes scanned the letter. " *'Dearest Lauren, I've been so enjoying the cards you've sent me. The Valentine's Day one is especially sweet with that picture of the kitten sitting in the box of chocolates. It reminds me of Raggsy, the barn cat you loved so much. But I wonder if Raggsy would have posed that willingly! Perhaps for you, he would have.'"*

She looked up from her reading to explain to Bob, "Raggsy was the messiest cat I've ever seen. Grandma always had a soft spot in her heart for homeless animals, and Raggsy had been living in an abandoned farm when one of her friends found him and gave him to her. Poor cat. He always looked like he'd been living in a haystack, and maybe he had been. His fur was terribly matted and dirty, but I loved him so much. He'd let me brush him—probably because I always gave him kitty snacks afterward, though."

She returned to her reading aloud. *"I've been so remiss in not telling you how much your cards and notes have meant to me.'"* She looked up with tears in her eyes. "I haven't been at all good, Bob. I've done cards and notes because I've been too busy for letters. Too busy for my own grandmother! What kind of a schmuck am I?"

He patted her arm. "She understands, I'm sure."

Lauren sniffed. "I hope so. *'This big old house holds so many memories for me, but the problem is that it's big and quite old. I can't keep up with it any longer, so I've made the decision to sell it. I'm moving into a retirement home.'* A retirement home! Oh, no! I can't imagine her without that wonderful house. It was like a castle to me."

"Honey, it's probably too much for her to maintain now. She's alone, and let's face it: It's got to be hard for her to get around the way she used to. That's a big house."

She swiped her nose across her sleeve and then laughed ruefully. "You can take the girl out of the country, but she's still going to wipe her nose on her sleeve!" She blinked several times and looked back at the letter.

I know that I have many years of memories from this house, and although I can take the memories with me, I can't take all of my things with me. I thought and prayed about what to do, and I've decided that the fairest thing to do is to let you girls—Sheila, Kimber, Jessica, and you—come out here and pick what you want. You can each select one thing from my attic.

The tears came unstoppably. "I'm going. I have to go."

"Of course you do, Lauren. When do you need to leave? Do you want me to go, too?"

There was something incredible about Bob's strong chest, Lauren thought as she leaned against the wool of his sweater, now soggy with her tears. Money was good, but it didn't do anything to relieve the sudden need she felt to go to Wyoming and see her grandmother.

"We can leave tomorrow if you want," he said, his breath warm against her hair. "It'll only take me a minute or two to get the other attorneys to cover for me. I'll call Roger tonight and get him up to speed about what's going on for the next week. Nothing he can't handle."

She looked at the violet-covered letter and frowned. "Bob, we should go as soon as possible. This letter was mailed back in March! I can't believe it took this long to get here. She must think I'm terrible for not answering!"

His fingers wrapped around hers as he continued, "I'd kind of like a trip out of the city for a while. It'd be good for us to get away, take a break. Hey, I have an idea. Let's fly to Nebraska, rent a car, and drive on to Wyoming. I can show you where I grew up."

The idea was appealing. They had each been so busy that they hadn't had much Bob-and-Lauren time. She'd been totally occupied wrapping up the deal with Comfort Home Hotels that most of her evenings and weekends lately had been spent at the office. The irony had not been lost on her—she'd been working on a campaign for Comfort Home Hotels while she had rarely experienced the comfort of her own home.

He continued, "You know, I think this would be a great time to go. The trees will be fully leafed out, and maybe we can even see a flower or two growing out of the ground instead of tucked in vases in a street vendor's cart. . . ." The calming cadence continued, and she felt herself relax against him.

"I love you," she said, her words muffled into his warm embrace, and from the way his hug tightened almost imperceptibly, she knew her words had gone straight through the polo sweater, past the matching shirt, and into his heart. "I just love you."

Big money contracts were nice, very nice indeed, but they paled beside sitting on the couch, curled in the arms of the man she loved. That, she decided, was beyond price.

❧

The plane jolted and bounced its way across the landing strip, and Lauren prayed. They weren't the words her childhood Sunday school teacher—Mrs. McMurtry of the eternally pursed mouth—would have approved of, but they were heartfelt: *Lord, keep me safe.* With each bumpy landing that ended happily, as they all had, Lauren vowed to look for a church home, but somehow the determination simply got away from her. Time, time—there was never enough.

"You okay?" Bob's voice was soft against her ear. She knew he was aware of how much she dreaded flying.

She rubbed his arm. "I'm okay, but I think I'm so much in debt to God for all these prayers for safe landings that I'd better get to church quickly."

To her surprise, he nodded. "Sounds good to me."

"Really?"

"I'm always ready to give credit where credit is due, and if you've asked Him for something, you probably owe something."

She studied his face as the voice of the flight attendant reminded them to stay seated even though the pilot had turned off the safety belt sign. "Are you serious?"

He grinned and reached down to retrieve the magazine that had slithered under the seat ahead of him. "Sure. We can talk about it later. This might not be the time or the place."

A passenger leaned across her to open the overhead bin, and she had to twist to avoid getting his round paunch in her face. "Excuse me, little lady," the owner of the stomach said to her in a Texas drawl so thick it seemed to ooze out of him. "My Collette keeps telling me, 'A little less of the barbecue and a bit more of the treadmill,' but I seem to do a bit more of the barbecue and a little less of the treadmill."

She laughed at his dry humor, and the conversation with Bob was momentarily lost.

But her mind wandered back to it as she gathered up her carry-on bags. She pondered it as she stood in the crush of people in the aisle of the plane, not so patiently waiting to deplane.

She thought about this even as she and Bob made small talk waiting for their luggage to appear on the carousel at the baggage claim. Bob—religious? They'd been married seven years, long enough that she felt she knew her husband as well as she knew her own self. This was a surprise. But on the other hand, he was an honorable and fair man, so perhaps she shouldn't be so amazed that he'd turn to God.

The woman at the rental car agency had everything ready for them, and within minutes Lauren was stuffing her bags in the trunk of the black Chevy Blazer they'd be driving. Bob had been right. Spring was already here in Nebraska. The grass was sprouting a brilliant new green, and the flowers in the planters outside the airport, while clearly from a nursery, were a welcome change from Chicago's storm-locked spring.

"I don't know if I can remember how to get to the old home place," Bob mused as he pulled out of the airport. "Nothing looks at all the same."

"Well, it's been, what, twenty years since you've been out here?" She unfolded the road map and tried to make sense of it. "We're in Lincoln, so we need to get on, well, wait a sec."

She peered at it. "Hang on. This can't be right. Are we really way over here?"

"Pretty much. We're not as close to the border as Omaha is, but we're still on the eastern side of the state."

"Got it. What am I looking for? Which interstate?"

The big blue line on the map—that was the interstate. This wasn't at all hard, she told herself. "Eighty. But, Bob, look at this. Look at it go west, over to that little cutout part." She held the map out in front of her and jabbed at the lower left-hand corner of the state. "Bob, we have to go all the way across the state. Listen to me. All—the—way. It's going to take us forever to drive to Wyoming."

He glanced quickly at the unfolded map and smiled. "Nah.

We'll be there by tomorrow night. We can spend tonight in Broken Bow."

She tried to find the town on the map but couldn't. She knew he'd grown up in the area of Broken Bow, and when he'd suggested that they stop by for a nostalgic look at where he'd been raised, she had said yes and not given it another thought—her mind had been too wrapped up in the advertising coup and her grandmother's letter. Now she was embarrassed to tell him she hadn't even picked up an atlas or anything to find out where her dear husband had grown up.

"We could go straight through if you'd rather," he said, the cheerfulness in his voice only a bit strained. "It's nine hours and twenty-two minutes to Casper from Lincoln." He made a point of looking at the clock and making some mental calculations. "We could be there by one seventeen in the morning if we don't stop for dinner or restroom breaks."

"Nine hours and twenty-two minutes?" she echoed. "How would you—oh, got it. The Internet."

He'd spent a lot of time planning this, she realized, whereas she had done zippo, nothing, nada. And to make it even worse, this trip was for her. He'd done all this—for her.

If he could do that for her, the least she could do for him was keep her mouth shut for at least a little while. It wasn't impossible, but it came right to the edge of what she could do.

Nebraska is pretty, she told herself as they journeyed westward, but it was somewhat, well, repetitive. *Nicely repetitive,* she reminded herself. This was her husband's birthplace. She began to look at it with a dawning respect.

She slouched against the window as much as her seat belt would allow her, taking inventory of the man she'd married—

181

could it really have been seven years ago? Except for the tiny lines beginning to etch their way from his eyes, a map of laughter. . . When had those lines appeared? Had she been so wrapped up in her career that she hadn't noticed them?

Or even the first strands of silver woven into his hair?

He frowned teasingly at her. "Do I pass?"

"I was staring, huh?" She felt a slight flush rise to her cheeks.

"A bit." He winked at her, and her heart melted. Her gorgeous husband. She smiled at him, and he turned his attention back to the road.

The road stretched on ahead, glimmering in the late morning sun. Was Nebraska actually that much different from Illinois?

It was clean. She had to give it that. And it sparkled in the spring morning under a cloudless blue sky.

But it needed billboards—billboards selling Comfort Home Hotels—and lots of them. She imagined how they'd look against the pristine background of fields new with corn. Blues, nice bright blues, water blues. Greens, the same shades as the stalks that rolled on and on in mathematically precise rows. Yellows, the echoes of corn that caught the sunlight and packaged it into neatly wrapped ears.

Against it all, a silver ribbon of highway that invited travelers to pause, to take a refreshing dip in a pool, to rest in air-conditioned comfort, to unwind with room service. It was all a part of the overall theme that had sold the account. Each Comfort Home Hotel was designed to fit into the environment, so one in Santa Fe would have a hacienda feel, or a Miami hotel would utilize the lovely colors associated with the city's architecture. She would be interested to know what the company would decide to do with the Lincoln hotel—she had checked and there was one scheduled to go up in two years.

This was the kind of account that agencies craved. Comfort Home Hotels had a clear identity; it was up to her to decide how to build on it. This was exactly the kind of work she enjoyed the most. She loved digging into the back creative recesses of her mind, letting her imagination run while the business-oriented part of her brain made sense of it all.

"Working, hon?" Bob's voice broke into her thoughts.

She nodded. He knew her so well after all these years. What made him especially perfect for her was the way he respected her. He never tried to change her into something she wasn't.

"Are you worried about your grandmother?" he asked, and she was once again struck by how kind he was.

"To tell the truth, yes, I am," she confessed. "I can't imagine the house without her in it."

"That may be the most difficult part," he acknowledged, "seeing the house without her there. But you know, Lauren, maybe I'm reading too much into what she said in the letter, but she sounded as if she was settled within herself about going to the retirement home."

"You're right. Grandma's always had a philosophy about a God-led life. To be honest, it kind of went over my head, but it seemed to work for her." She looked out the window at the landscape, which didn't seem to change much, except for the switching of fields with cows and fields with corn.

In the quiet of the car, she had to face one immutable fact. Her life was about to change. It was as clear—and yet as unprovable—as knowing that a storm was in the offing by the smell in the air. Something major was just over the horizon.

Chapter 2

Bob glanced at his wife, her cheek against the window. She was sound asleep, her neck bent at an impossible angle thanks to the seat belt.

He had been so blessed, having Lauren at his side these seven years. He could still remember the first time he saw her. She was standing outside Fresca, a tiny new restaurant, holding an umbrella that kept collapsing against a fierce wind. He also was standing in front of the building, waiting to meet the couple who were going to introduce him to a blind date for the evening, when an early summer thunderstorm struck. He had an umbrella with him, but it was no match for the winds.

He tucked his head down and darted inside. The woman standing near him apparently had the same idea at the same time, and they managed to wedge themselves together in Fresca's tiny doorway.

One look and he'd been smitten. He laughed silently at the memory of how he'd gotten the soul of a poet—him, the corporate attorney with the mind of legal steel—when he saw in her eyes the pansies that had grown around his old home in Nebraska. They were blue, tinged with purple. It was a deeply intense color he'd held in his memories, a hue that certainly a romantic bard would be able to name.

He'd had to say something, and the first words out of his mouth were, "I'm stuck."

She laughed, and soon they were free of the door and sitting inside the restaurant. When he told her he was on a blind date, she said she was, too—and somehow it hadn't surprised either one of them that they were waiting for the same couple and they were each other's blind date.

If ever two people were perfect for each other, they were.

God had introduced them before their mutual friends had the chance to.

God.

He stole another look at his wife. This was one thing he hadn't shared with her—his growing hunger for God. It was too new, too unformed yet. But soon he would.

Something else was changing in him. The Lamborghini wasn't enough. The penthouse wasn't enough. Dinners out at five-star restaurants weren't enough.

He wanted roots. Real roots that didn't dig down into concrete but went into deep, rich soil. A high-rise apartment was wonderful, but he wanted—he needed—so much more. He wanted to be able to grow tomatoes. How long had it been since he'd eaten a sun-warmed tomato, fresh from the vine? He wanted to smell a newly mown lawn. Admittedly, he knew the appeal would run out eventually, but right now his arms ached for this connection with the land.

He wanted to watch fireflies blink to each other in the dusk. To go for an evening bike ride. To walk in the bright morning sun and think.

And now this visit to Nebraska, this walk down memory lane, was intensifying his ache. He was home.

He felt a little catch in his heart. In his dreams, he saw a third person with them, a baby. But the news of the Comfort Home Hotels contract meant that once again, a family would be put on hold. How many times had he heard Lauren say that she didn't hear the ticking of her biological clock because she had a digital one? And how many times had he agreed with her?

This wasn't a good time to bring up beginning a family. His spirit sagged as the thought came, unbidden, that it had never been a good time.

It was still all right, he told himself. He loved her, and someday it would be the perfect time. He just had to be patient.

He also had to, at some time, respond to the shade of doubt that made him wonder if he'd be a good father. Did he want a baby—or did he want to take the responsibility of raising and nurturing a human being who would, at some time, be sixteen?

He recalled some of the wild tricks he'd done as a teenager and shuddered. Maybe fatherhood could wait.

Lauren stared at the gas station, trying to look fascinated.

"Yup," Bob said, leaning back against the car. "This is where I grew up. Well, not here. Not in this gas station. But this is where my house was."

"It's a very nice corner," she commented. "Look at the lilacs." The back of the gas station's lot was edged with lilacs, all profusely blooming and perfuming the air with their delightful aroma.

He frowned. "I don't think they were there then. I don't remember them, at least. But to be honest, when I lived here, I was in my anthill stage. I could watch ants for hours on end."

She stood on her tiptoes and kissed him right below his ear. He was such a dear, so full of surprises. "How could somebody so nerdy become such a world-class lawyer? Anthills, indeed."

"Hey, anthills are fascinating. There are times when I'm rushing around downtown Chicago that I think back to those ants scurrying around. All they lacked were little briefcases."

An ant chose that moment to run across Lauren's toe, and she pointed at it. "I don't think I've ever seen an ant just walk. They're always rushing around."

"Feel a kinship?"

If he'd slugged her right in the stomach, he couldn't have hurt her worse. She touched his arm. "Bob?"

He smiled a bit weakly. "I'm sorry. That wasn't fair."

"But it didn't come out of nowhere, honey." She felt as if the wind had been knocked out of her. Why would he say something like that? Was he rethinking his love for her?

Had she neglected him in the process of building her advertising agency? She tried to think back to anything she might have done—or not done, any time she might have overlooked him. It was an exercise in futility, she realized. If she wasn't aware of it then, what were the chances she'd recognize it now?

The thought that she'd hurt him was almost too much to bear.

He draped his arm around her and hugged her tightly to his side. "I'm sorry; I really am. That was rude and uncalled-for."

She leaned against his reassuring shoulder. "Well, I hope so. I mean, I hope it was uncalled-for. Although, you know, Bob, ants are pretty efficient creatures. They could use a little downtime, though."

"I agree. And so could we. Hey, I see the Dairy Barn down the street. I'll treat you to an extra-large hot fudge sundae with triple whipped cream."

They strolled down the street, hand in hand, as he reminisced. "I think there was a clothing store there. It was three stories high, and the elevator in it had a copper panel with pearlized buttons with the floor numbers on them. It took every ounce of my strength to do it, but I always thought it was the coolest thing to push those buttons."

Elevators to go up three floors. She thought of downtown Chicago, where sunlight was filtered through skyscrapers that towered overhead. Three floors. This was another world to her.

She looked around her. Prairiedale was—well, she didn't know how she felt about Prairiedale. It wasn't exactly stuck in the past, but it wasn't as zippy as Chicago. That was it. It was slower.

A fellow in overalls balanced himself against a streetlight while talking to a man with a dog. Obviously they'd been there for a while; the dog was asleep at his owner's feet.

Two women stood in front of the beauty salon, their hair perfectly done in precise white curls. The shorter one of the two glanced at her watch, and Lauren heard her say to her companion, "Earl is late picking me up again, Min."

"He was late dropping you off, too. You like to have lost

your place with Esther for your perm." Min straightened her back, making her look even taller and more gaunt. "You should get that man a watch."

"I did. He's saving it for Sundays."

"So he'll be on time for church?"

"So he'll know how late he is for church, you mean."

The two women giggled, and Min gave the other woman a poke in the arm. "You are bad, Caroline Snead. Bad, bad, bad."

Lauren tried not to grin, but it came out anyway, and she was rewarded when both women beamed back at her. "Hello," they both said at once.

She could tell their curiosity was difficult to restrain, and impulsively she said, "We're visiting here. My husband grew up in Prairiedale."

He stepped forward and introduced himself. "I'm Bob Fielding, and this is my wife, Lauren. I lived here until I was ten, down where that gas station is."

The women looked at each other and their faces plumped into smiles. The taller one took his hand and pumped it up and down vigorously. "Bob Fielding! You must be Mary and Tim's son, the one who became a lawyer in Chicago! I haven't seen you since you were a little tyke. I'm Min Sanders. My husband, God rest his soul, used to run the gas station off Maple Avenue. You used to come in for pop."

"Oh, I remember that!" Bob grinned.

"And I'm Caroline Snead. Used to be the county librarian. You were quite the reader, as I recall. My husband is Earl Snead. We farmed out by your aunt and uncle, but we retired awhile back."

"Awhile back!" Min snorted. "About a decade or twelve ago."

Caroline ignored the remark, and Lauren realized the exchanges between the two women were part of their friendship. "We've been hearing about you all these years. Greta and Sam used to keep us up-to-date on all of the Fieldings."

Bob turned to Lauren and explained, "Greta and Sam were my great-aunt and great-uncle." He dropped his voice to a stage whisper. "Kind of a human news team, if you know what I mean."

Min and Caroline leaned together in amusement. "Oh, Bob, you haven't changed at all!" Min gushed.

"Now, Caroline, that's not true. He's taller. He was only six when they moved away!" Min reminded her.

That remark prompted a new cascade of laughter, and soon the four of them were seated in the Dairy Barn with huge mounds of ice cream in front of them.

"This is just like I remember it," Bob said, glancing around him in awe, "especially how red it was—red tabletops, red counter, red linoleum."

"Oh, a few things are different." Caroline rolled her eyes at Lauren, and Lauren knew that she was already accepted by the two women. "The prices have gone up."

"And I just don't think this ice cream is as rich as it used to be." Min took a spoonful of the vanilla ice cream heaped in her bowl and sampled it. "No, definitely not."

"Min Sanders, your taste buds have shriveled up and died," Caroline scolded her friend. "This is good Nebraska Valley ice cream—always was, always will be."

Min sniffed. "They could call it caviar—doesn't make it so."

Caroline leaned over the table. "You have to excuse Min. She's having a bad hair day and is a bit cranky."

"I am *not* having a bad hair day. At least not since I saw Esther."

Lauren sagged happily into the corner of the booth and listened to the exchange. She glanced over at Bob. He had a goofy smile on his face, and he looked different somehow. Younger.

His forehead wasn't furrowed. That was it. He was relaxed. How long had it been since she'd seen him so at peace?

With the voices of the Min and Caroline Show playing in the background, her mind played over her life with Bob. They'd been fortunate to have careers that, with a lot of work, had brought them success. But that success needed a high level of maintenance, and they'd continued to work hard. It was a treadmill they hadn't ever gotten off of, mainly because they liked it.

But perhaps the pressure had been invisible. She could see how his face was softening as the stress drained away. Maybe they needed a vacation—some time away from their jobs. That would be good. Maybe they could go to Maui. They could work on their tans and wear leis and eat at a luau on the beach. Or maybe they'd head off to the place in Mexico her receptionist had told her about. San Something, where they would scuba or snorkel in water so clear and pure that it was like heaven, and where the fish swam right by their outstretched hands.

Bob's voice brought her back from her musings. "We'd love to go."

"Go where?" She struggled to an upright position and blinked. As everyone looked at her, smiling, she realized she'd fallen asleep right there in the booth. "Sorry, I must have drifted off."

"That's okay." Min patted her hand. "We were talking about

going out to visit Greta and Sam's place."

"They've passed on," Caroline explained in a hushed voice. "About eight years ago, right, Min? Greta got pneumonia and never did get better, and even though Sam wasn't sick—he had the constitution of a workhorse, I'll tell you—he followed her into heaven within two months."

Followed her into heaven. It took a moment for the meaning to sink in. *Followed her into heaven.*

Somehow that wasn't quite the same as "He died." Not as harsh—but was it as real?

Her philosophical meanderings came to a stop as they all stood up and reached for the bill simultaneously. After much bartering and trading, Bob ended with the bill, and the women insisted on driving them to the farm.

"Is it safe?" she whispered to him as they left the small diner. "They could be a couple of ax murderers for all we know."

He squeezed her hand in reassurance and grinned in the direction of the two women, with the contrast of their heights making them seem for all the world like an elderly female Mutt and Jeff.

They had to walk quickly as they trailed after the women, who moved at quite a clip toward Min's car, which, to Lauren's surprise, was a bright yellow Mazda coupe.

Within minutes they were tearing down a gravel road as a cloud of dust billowed around them. "Roads were graded this weekend," Min shouted as they rocketed forward. Lauren's teeth seemed ready to jar right out of her head as the car bounced along at a death-defying speed. "Makes it a much nicer ride, doesn't it?"

Caroline leaned over the seat and confided, "Tom Abbott

drove the grader. The man drives like a demented taxi driver."

The Mazda became airborne again, and Min hollered, "Wheeeee!"

Lauren had ridden in her fair share of Chicago taxis, and none of them had been as terrifying as this ride. She could only imagine what kind of driver this Tom Abbott must be—she wasn't really sure what a grader was, but she figured it was responsible for the graveled surface of the road.

The car swung to the right so suddenly that she nearly landed across her husband's chest.

And then, just as sharply, the car turned the other direction, and she was launched into the window.

Enough was enough. She just might not survive this ride. She'd been worried about Min and Caroline's criminal past when she should have been concerned about their driving records. Just as she opened her mouth to say something, Min slammed on the brakes and announced, "We're here."

The thick dust from the abrupt stop obscured their destination at first, but when at last it settled, she could see the farm. It wasn't charmingly picturesque, like those in New England. In fact, it looked fairly run-down to her. The house once had been white, but years of not being painted had softened it to a splotchy ivory.

The yard needed to be mowed, and the garden was so overrun with weeds that it was hard to tell what had been grown there.

But from her husband's expression, she could tell he was looking at paradise.

"Aunt Greta grew the best tomatoes," he said, almost to himself, as he strolled over to the garden and pulled some weeds aside. "She said they were extra special because the dog slept on them. Apparently Fur Bug—that was the dog's name—liked the smell of the tomato plants and would lie on top of them. Oddly, it didn't kill the plants. Instead, their tomatoes were wonderful."

Lauren couldn't see even a remnant of a tomato plant. The entire garden plot looked weed-covered. None of it looked familiar except the thistle plants with their fine, sharp spines.

She followed him to the barn, which still smelled slightly of milk and an earthier animal scent, then on to the house, all the time listening to his stream of memories. "In the summer after church, we'd pile into Uncle Sam's pickup truck and head out here for fried chicken and tomatoes. Talk about heaven on earth."

Caroline clucked as she noticed the sway of the front door. "Nobody's lived here for a year now. The prairie takes back any house that isn't lived in. If somebody doesn't buy this house soon, it'll go back to the land."

Lauren looked at the tattered farmhouse and the unkempt yard and the decaying barn. To her eyes, the prairie had a head start on the process.

No wonder it hadn't sold. It was a mess. Nobody could live here without pouring a fortune into rehabilitating it.

"That'd be a pity," Bob said sadly. "A real pity. You'd think somebody would want it, wouldn't you?"

Her heart was screaming an answer, but her brain was busily overruling it.

Chapter 3

It's a crazy idea," Bob said as they neared the Wyoming border. "Just crazy."

He chewed the inside of his lip. It *was* crazy. They couldn't just pick up and move to Nebraska. Their lives were back in Chicago, where the sidewalks teemed with life and dinner out meant prime rib at the Ritz Carlton, not chili dogs at the Dairy Barn.

"Well, for one thing, we have our jobs." Lauren spoke quietly.

The Comfort Home Hotels account. He knew how important it was to her. The challenge, the excitement, even the status. He didn't want to do anything to take away even a moment of that success.

"True," he said.

"Our parents live in Chicago."

"That's something else to consider."

They both stared ahead, then she said, "I don't know if I'm ready to leave Chicago. Maybe I am. This is a lot to think about."

"Lauren, it was just a nutty idea. It's hard, I guess, to let go of the things of the past."

"Grandma used to quote me something from the Bible about letting go—'*When I was a child, I* spake *as a child,*' is how it began I think. Odd that I remember that, but I think it's because she said "spake," which I thought was the funniest thing in the world."

"I wonder how she's doing."

Lauren looked at him, and her tear-filled eyes were now the color of rain-drenched pansies. "I think the retirement home is a good place. I looked it up on the Internet."

He took a deep breath. "And I had an attorney I worked with in Laramie check into it. The Mountain Springs Retirement Center is well respected. We can be sure she's getting excellent care there."

She nodded. "It's not the place—I trust her judgment on that. She wouldn't have chosen a place that wasn't good. I'm, oh, I don't know. I'm not worried, exactly. Concerned? That's become such an impersonal word. *Any cares or concerns about your new loan, Mrs. Fielding?* Bob, I just love her, and I want her to be safe and healthy and happy."

He reached across and touched her hand briefly. He'd only met her grandmother twice: at their wedding and then two years ago at the funeral of Lauren's grandfather. Lydia Dunmore was sweet and kind, and clearly proud of Lauren. He knew, too, how much Lauren treasured her grandmother.

Lauren was silent for a moment, and he wished he could read her mind. But these seven years of marriage had taught him to give her room to formulate her thoughts.

"Min and Caroline sure were cute," she said at last. "I wasn't quite ready for Mr. Toad's Wild Ride, though."

He laughed, and it felt good to leave the heart-heavy things they'd been discussing. "Mr. Toad's Wild Ride is absolutely the way to describe it," he agreed. "I never would have pegged Min as the yellow sports car kind of woman, and I certainly wouldn't have thought she saw herself as an amateur NASCAR driver."

They chuckled over some of the funnier moments together, and at last Bob said, "It was good to visit Prairiedale. It sure didn't look the same as it used to." The small town had changed. . .or maybe he had. He shelved the idea in the back of his mind. This wasn't the time to mull it over.

Lauren's head was resting against the back of the seat, and her eyes were closed, but he knew she wasn't sleeping.

He turned the radio off. The music station had gone to static, and he wasn't in the mood for news. If they'd been in the Lamborghini, he would have gotten out a CD to listen to. Lately he'd been buying those nature CDs—classical music with the sounds of loons or ocean waves or wolf howls. Lauren didn't like them. She'd told him that if she wanted to listen to a loon, she'd go to Minnesota. She didn't want to hear a loon chorus as backup singers for Vivaldi.

He smiled. For all their differences, they were a good match. God, he admitted, had brought them together, and God would keep them together—as long as they were partners in His work.

The question, he knew, was how Lauren would take it. But right now, the focus had to be on her and her grandmother. And God would see them through that, too.

Lauren fought the headache that was crowding into her thoughts. She didn't want to see Grandma in a retirement home. Grandma was supposed to be at home in the sprawling

Victorian, awaiting Lauren's arrival with freshly baked chocolate chip cookies.

The Mountain Springs Retirement Center wasn't hard to find. The large, elegant brick building sat squarely in the center of the block, like a broody hen.

Like a broody hen? She rolled her eyes at her own phrasing. She'd spent one afternoon in a small Nebraska town and now she was Miss Country Lane, USA.

Her eyes turned to the building. *Grandma lives in there,* she said to herself, trying to make the fact palatable. It didn't work. She couldn't go in yet. She couldn't even move to get out of the car. All sorts of terrible thoughts flew into her mind. If Grandma were sick. . .

She shook herself mentally. One of her cousins—Sheila or Kimber or Jessica—would have let her know if anything were wrong.

"It's probably going to be easier to see her if we actually go into the building," Bob reminded her gently.

"I'm ready." She wasn't, of course, but she was as ready as she'd ever be.

He held her hand as they walked to the front door. Inside, a receptionist greeted them cheerfully. "Lydia Dunmore? Oh, I think I just saw her heading into the computer room."

Computer room? Lauren mouthed at Bob.

They were directed to a room with three computers along a thin table.

"Bill, I can't get my sig line to work," said a voice behind a large monitor.

"Sig line? My grandmother is making a sig line?" Lauren asked in surprise.

"Honey! What a wonderful surprise!" Grandma pushed back her chair and heaved herself up. "Excuse my ungainliness. Age isn't quite as graceful as I'd like."

Lauren wrapped her grandmother in a hug. "You're still beautiful, Grandma. And look at you, using a computer and talking about sig lines!"

"A sig line is an automated signature line for e-mail," Grandma said proudly. "We just learned about it in computer class. Bill—that's him over there—teaches us."

A thin elderly man bowed politely. "We have a lot of fun in class. Lydia is a fast learner."

Grandma's blue eyes lit up. "I'm really enjoying it, Bill. You're a wonderful teacher. Right now I'm having some trouble. I'm trying to set up my sig line, but I want it in bright blue and I can't get the color to change."

Lauren's fingers almost itched with the urge to reach across and change the line herself. She certainly could do it easily. She caught Bob looking at her and grinning. After seven years of marriage, he knew what she was going through. Restraining herself was almost impossible.

Grandma looked over and nodded knowingly. "Drives you batty, doesn't it?"

"You still remember, don't you?" Lauren squeezed her grandmother's hand. "You called me Roarin' Lauren because I wanted everything done right away. I had absolutely no patience. I still don't."

"And you, bless your heart, turned what could have been a failing into an attribute. I hear that your energy, your go-get-'em attitude, is working in your favor."

"Grandma, I just got a big account, the account of a lifetime.

Have you ever heard of Comfort Home Hotels?"

Grandma shook her head. "Sorry, I can't say that I have."

"Well, you will. You'll see the name everywhere, and whenever you do, I want you to think of me. . .and remember that I love you."

"You've been very blessed. God has been good to you."

"Yes, He has." Lauren was surprised at how easily she agreed with her grandmother. God was certainly Someone she hadn't thought about lately. She'd just been too busy to even pick up the phone book and find a church near her. Well, at least she did quickly acknowledge His handiwork when she admired a rosy sunset or a perfect daisy or a puppy frolicking in the park.

"And look at your handsome husband. Bob, it's so good of you to come out here. This is quite an unexpected pleasure!"

Bob clasped her in a bear hug. "It's a joy for us, too."

"Let me give this sig line thing one more try, then we can go to my apartment and I'll get you the key to the house."

Grandma turned back to the computer and, with Bill hovering helpfully in the background, typed a few more characters. "Wahoo!"

Lauren looked at her husband and saw her amusement mirrored there. Seeing her grandmother taking such pleasure from learning how to use a computer relieved her worries immensely.

"Next thing you know, she'll be learning how to play the electric guitar and joining a rock-and-roll band," Bob whispered to Lauren while her grandmother shut down the computer.

Lauren rewarded him with a poke in the ribs.

Somehow she couldn't see her grandmother playing guitar

in a group, unless it was a praise team in a church. But on the other hand, the computer stuff here had taken Lauren totally by surprise.

Grandma probably never would have learned to use the computer if she'd stayed in her house, she realized. Maybe this wasn't a completely devastating move.

She studied her grandmother surreptitiously as they followed her to her apartment. Grandma seemed as chipper as ever. Life in the Mountain Springs Retirement Center was apparently agreeing with her.

Her grandmother's apartment was charming and spotlessly neat, which didn't surprise Lauren at all. Neither did the photographs and plaques that covered the walls. Family was everything to Lydia Dunmore, and the abundance of framed photographs was evidence of that. Even the snapshot of Lauren and Bob she'd tossed into her Christmas card was there, lovingly framed.

Most of the plaques had butterflies on them—a favorite of her grandmother—and a Bible verse. Lauren recognized them from the house, and apparently Grandma had brought them all with her. Every wall had several of them.

She had to examine one closely. It was a bit different from the others in that there weren't any butterflies or dragonflies or even birds on it. It was a simple piece of wood, almost rustic, and the letters were a bit uneven.

" 'For this child I prayed.' First Samuel 1:27," she read aloud. "I remember this. It hung over my bed when I stayed at your house."

"Your bed and every child's bed." Her grandmother joined her. "Don't you know the story of it?"

"No, I guess I don't. Tell me."

"Your grandfather and I had been married for a year, and then two, and then three, four, five. After all that time, it was still just us and the dog and the parakeet and two cats and whatever strays happened to drop by the house. I wanted a baby so badly that I became an early version of the Humane Society."

"You always had a soft spot for animals."

"But a softer one for babies. Your grandpa and I really wanted to fill that big house with children's voices. I wanted to hear them learn to play the piano. I love the sound of a child earnestly picking out a melody on the keys. But nothing happened."

Grandma's eyes got misty as she remembered. "We waited, and after a while we quit—well, I don't want to say we quit hoping, because we never, ever did that. But we quit thinking it might happen. And then God surprised us. He surprised us five times."

Bob chuckled softly. "I love it."

"The evening that Lauren's mother was born, my husband went outside and got a piece of wood and carved those words in it himself. We hung it over your mama's cradle, and every child since then has slept under those blessed words."

Her grandmother's bright blue eyes shone as she looked from Lauren to Bob. "I don't want to be nosy, and I won't ask because I know how much it hurt when people asked us when we were going to get around to having a baby. But I will say this: If you two have a baby, and you want this old piece of wood, I'd be honored to give it to you."

Lauren stiffened. This was a road she did not want to go

down. Not now, and maybe not ever. But this was her grandmother, and she softened her voice. "We're not quite ready
yet, but when we do, we'd be privileged to have it in our baby's
room."

Our baby's room.

Why did she suddenly have tears in her eyes?

Chapter 4

I
t wouldn't be so bad if everything weren't draped with sheets. It looks like a scary movie set."

"I don't think we need to whisper." Bob threw open the drapes, and late afternoon sunshine poured in. Immediately the house became friendlier. "It's really stuffy in here. Let me try a window." He tugged on one, but it wouldn't budge. "It's either swollen shut or nailed in place."

"Oh, swell. I can only imagine what the attic will be like."

"Do you know what you want from up there? I bet there are some splendid antiques tucked away." Bob wiped droplets of sweat from his forehead. "I should have brought a fan."

"I do know what I want, and I think I know right where it is. This won't take long."

Each step took Lauren further and further back into her childhood. Days of playing dolls with her cousins. Nights of staying up late and giggling past midnight. The weddings, baptisms, and funerals that had brought them together.

The attic was even more stifling than she was prepared for, and both she and Bob gasped at the airless heat.

"It's over here." She went to a trunk decorated with travel

stickers. Before opening it, she ran her hand over the black surface and the colorful decals. "This was my special suitcase. I kept everything in here."

Memories flew around her head like Grandma's butterflies when she unlatched the suitcase and examined the contents. A pencil with a miniature plastic milk carton on the end. A tiny brass teapot Aunt Marlene had given her. A mirror with bright silver backing. A large cardboard L that Uncle Stanley had gotten from a theater before she was born.

Then, at last, the object of her quest.

Wrapped lovingly in yellowed tissue paper, the tiny white dress was still soft and delicate. She held it up for Bob to see, and in the filtered sunlight, dust motes danced like pale glitter.

"It was my great-grandmother's," she said in a reverent whisper. "Grandma let me play with it. Once I tried to dress Raggsy in it."

"How'd that go?" Bob asked, mopping his face. "Cats aren't big on modeling clothing."

"Raggsy was no different. Talk about an uncooperative cat. He clawed me so badly I still have the scar." She pointed to a faint white line along her wrist. "Anyway, Grandma didn't get mad, but she gave me a long talk about family and heritage. I never tried to dress Raggsy in the dress again." She ran her fingers over the white-on-white embroidery that crossed the bodice of the dress. "I have been so blessed by her."

Lauren sat on the floor, surrounded by her past, and cried.

❧

"I need a restroom break."

Bob looked at his wife. "Can't you wait until Prairiedale?

205

It's just twenty-five miles away."

She looked at him, her pansy-colored eyes alight with laughter. "Let's see. Three cups of coffee and a glass of orange juice for breakfast, and two glasses of iced tea when we said good-bye to Grandma, and a root beer back in Scottsbluff—um, no. I can't wait."

"Okay. There's one up here."

"I know. I saw the sign back there."

He waited inside the rest stop for her and leafed through the maps and brochures. One about Arbor Lodge in Nebraska City evoked a barrage of memories. He couldn't have been more than eight when he'd gone there with his parents and Aunt Greta and Uncle Sam. He could still remember the huge columns of Arbor Lodge.

This trip was drenched with memories.

"Okeydoke." Lauren was smiling broadly as she came out of the ladies' room. "I'm ready for lunch at the Dairy Barn."

How she could put away all that food and not be the *size* of the Dairy Barn was beyond him. She was quite an incredible woman.

"You're sure happy," he commented as she sang along with the radio on the way to Prairiedale.

"I'm just excited to be seeing Min and Caroline again," she said.

He didn't believe her, not entirely, but maybe it was just a delayed reaction to seeing her grandmother. The entire visit had gone well, and the small white christening gown was on the backseat of the car, wrapped in new tissue paper and safely boxed.

The little yellow Mazda was parked outside the Dairy

Barn. "Look at that," he said. "Min and Caroline must be in the Dairy Barn. That's terrific. Then we won't have to try to find them to say hello."

"Yes, isn't that fortunate?" Lauren turned her head away quickly, but didn't he detect a wide smile on her face?

He pulled into a spot right in front of the Dairy Barn—now this was true small-town America, he told himself, finding a spot so conveniently located. His eyes took in all the details of Prairiedale's Main Street—Anderson's Drug Store, Glamour Beauty Salon, Gillette's Clothing. It might be another twenty years before he returned, and he wanted to imprint it all in his mind.

He opened the door of the Dairy Barn and let Lauren precede him. After the bright sunlight outside, his eyes took a moment to adjust to the lowered light inside.

"Over here, over here!" Min called from a corner. "We've got this booth saved for us."

He reined in a grin. The Dairy Barn was empty except for the four of them. They could have each had their own booth.

"Did you have a good trip?" Caroline asked solicitously. "And how was your grandmother?"

The conversation stayed light and floated around his head. He couldn't stop looking around, trying to memorize each piece of cracked red vinyl, every detail of the tabletop jukebox players that were probably worth a fortune to collectors. This was the stuff of his childhood, just as surely as the christening dress in the car was part of Lauren's.

He felt as if in leaving, he was tearing away part of his past. . .and it hurt.

Lauren's cell phone buzzed. They were so squished into the

booth that he could feel it vibrate. She pulled the tiny phone out, glanced at the glowing display, and turned it off without answering it.

"Well, time to go." Lauren stood up so abruptly that he wondered if he'd missed something.

"Can I drive for a while?" she asked when they returned to the car. "I'm getting a bit sluggish just sitting there, and you've been driving all day."

"Sure." Actually, the thought of not driving for a while was refreshing. "But if you get tired, let me know."

He sank into the rental car seat and let his muscles relax. It had been a long day, and he—

❦

"Wait, wait!" Bob shouted. "You were supposed to turn there."

Lauren couldn't suppress the laughter. "You can't tell me where to turn. I'm going this way."

"But the interstate's back that way!" he protested.

"Who says I want to go on the interstate?"

He groaned. "Lauren, dear, sweetie, honey, I love you with all my heart, but you just cannot go this way. Lincoln is in the other direction."

"I don't want to go to Lincoln. Not right now anyway."

He'll like it, she told herself. *I've done the right thing. Please, God, let him be happy.* Her prayer was heartfelt. She'd been working in secret, using every bit of tiny technology available to her, from her cell phone to her PDA. He hadn't even noticed.

"Lauren, you really have to—"

"Bob Fielding, if you can't zip it for five minutes, I'm going to have Min drive you back to Lincoln." She had to bite her lip to keep from laughing.

That made him sit up. "Oh, no thank you! But why you won't—wait, what are we doing out here? This is Aunt Greta and Uncle Sam's place."

She pulled over to the side of the road. "Hon, we can buy it. It's for sale. What do you think?"

She studied him as he looked out the window at the old farmhouse, sitting in a pool of early afternoon sunlight. He didn't speak. He didn't turn back to look at her. He just sat, staring.

"Bob? There's more. Something happened today that I hope—well, I hope I'm going to make the right decision. I got an offer on the agency. It's a good one, and. . ." She broke off and took a deep breath. This was possibly the hardest thing she'd ever done, offering her heart like this. "Bob, I think I'll take it. We can move here."

He faced her, and what she saw changed her world. His cheeks were wet with tears.

"You'd do all that—for me?"

She faked a short laugh to cover her own sobs. "It's not all me, Bob. You'd have to leave your law practice. We started our own businesses in Chicago, and let's face it, that's a tough business climate, but we did it. There's no reason we couldn't do it again, here in Prairiedale."

He didn't answer. Instead, his brown eyes pooled with more tears. She'd never seen her husband cry. Never.

She swallowed hard. "We couldn't do it right away, and we don't have to do it at all if you don't want to."

"I don't—I can't—it'd be—I think I. . . Oh, I have no idea

209

how I feel." He managed a shaky grin. "It's so sudden. Are you sure? You want to leave Chicago?"

He'd zeroed right in on the one thing she wasn't sure of. She loved Chicago. Just as Prairiedale was part of his heritage, Chicago was part of hers. She'd grown up there, and part of her soul would always be in the heart of that city.

But she'd always been there. She was ready for a change—she hoped.

⚜

He walked to the front door and paused for a moment before he opened it and let all the memories wash over him. Once again, he was a child, watching a marble careen madly across the uneven kitchen floor. If he concentrated hard enough, he could smell Aunt Greta's brownies, the ones with the white squiggles of frosting on top. And that furry thing running across the living room was their little dog, Fur Bug.

There was nothing to bring him back to the present like realizing that it couldn't be Fur Bug. Fur Bug had long ago gone to puppy heaven.

"Stand back," he ordered Lauren. "There's an animal of some sort in here."

"There are probably all sorts of animals in here," Lauren said, her voice a bit small in the empty house. "I can smell mice."

He turned and grinned. "You can not."

"Well, I can smell something." She moved to the cupboards and opened one. With a little yelp, she jumped back. "Oh, yes indeedy, there are mice here. One was just looking at me. I'm pretty sure he was wearing a gang jacket, too."

"Mice I can deal with. Skunks are a different matter."

210

He entered the living room cautiously, with Lauren close behind him. The furry creature escaped through a hole in the open back door, and he breathed a sigh of relief. It was a cat, a very large calico cat, but at least it wasn't a skunk. A cat he could deal with. Judging from the cat's bulging sides, it was finding plenty to eat. The cat was probably doing them a favor, keeping the mouse population of the house low. Too bad it couldn't open the drawer where Lauren had just found one of the rodents.

The furniture was still there: the old green chair that Uncle Sam had sat in, its cushion still bearing the imprint of his body. The plaid couch with Aunt Greta's smocked pillows piled in the corners.

"If you look under the coffee table there, you'll find my initials," he said to her.

"Robert Fielding, did you carve your initials into your aunt and uncle's table?"

"Nope. Used nail polish and painted them on. Aunt Greta was super about it. She even took a pencil and wrote the date beside it. See?" He upended the table and showed her. "They didn't have any kids of their own, so we got extra-special treatment. I miss them so mu—what is *that*?"

A blaring horn resounded through the farmstead, and Lauren laughed. "Min's here."

≈≈≈

"Should we do it?"

His words broke into her near sleep. She could never really sleep on a plane, not completely and deeply.

She stirred and gripped the box with its precious cargo that she had refused to check through.

"We don't have to move," she replied. "We could buy the property and use it like a vacation home."

He chuckled and leafed through the papers the real estate agent had given him. The poor fellow *had* looked a bit queasy when he'd gotten out of Min's car. "So when everybody else is headed off to the south of France, or to Maui, we can be vacationing instead in lovely Prairiedale, Nebraska?"

She put her head against his shoulder. He was warm, a nice contrast to the chilled air the overhead vent was blasting out. "Uh-huh."

"You never did tell me how you managed to get everybody out there."

Lauren snuggled in even tighter and smiled into the still-clean scent of his shirt. "I used my cell phone at the rest stop. Checked my voice mail, made a few calls, and there you have it. Don't all the high-finance corporations conduct their business at rest stops?"

Chapter 5

L auren pushed a lock of hair off her sweating forehead. "What I wouldn't give for an old-fashioned bobby pin," she moaned.

Bob stepped out from behind the massive refrigerator. "I think we seriously underestimated how much work this was going to be. There has to be a century's worth of dust and dirt and accumulated gunk back here."

"That refrigerator can't be a century old." She crossed her arms and eyed the monstrosity with undisguised animosity. "Can it?"

He laughed. "Let's look at the archaeological evidence." He pushed a pile of debris into a dustpan and brought it to her. "A ball of indeterminate age. A shoestring. A straw—and a paper one, at that. When was the last time you saw a paper straw?"

She poked through the dustpan's contents with a tentative finger and continued the inventory. "This might have been a grape once. Oh, look—a dime. A Liberty dime! An ad for heating oil, I think. No date, but from the looks of the dress that woman's wearing, I'd say late 1950s. And a little green tractor."

"No kidding!" Bob took the last item almost reverently and blew the dust off. "This was mine. This was my favorite toy in the whole world. Fur Bug must have taken it. He was always stealing my miniature vehicles, but usually he ate the tires off and left them in the middle of the hallway. Not the brightest creature in the world."

He looks so happy, she thought as he gently placed the tractor on the windowsill. He looked much younger, much happier. The decision to sell his law practice had been hard, but he'd done it, and she'd sold her agency. And here they were, in the middle of the Nebraska plains, digging through a dustpan.

Life was full of little surprises.

"I'm ready for a break," he announced. "I'll treat you to a PrairieBerry malt at the Dairy Barn."

"I look dreadful, and I'm sure I smell even worse. Can I take a quick shower first?"

"You go first and I'll shower when you're done."

She stood on her tiptoes and kissed him, not worrying even a bit that she probably smelled like a cross between the dustpan and a locker room. "You're my knight in shining armor, letting me go first."

He chucked her slightly on the shoulder. "It's time economics. You've never gone into town without your hair done and all your makeup on, which, let me remind you, you don't need. Haven't you ever heard of gilding the lily?"

"Sure I have, but nobody ever asked the lily how she felt about it, did they?" She flashed him a triumphant smile and vanished into the bathroom.

The water felt great coursing over her aching muscles. She lathered up with lemon-scented body wash and burst into a rousing chorus of "Happy Days Are Here Again"—and the water stopped.

"Everybody's a critic," she grumbled to herself as she groped for a towel and wiped the suds from her eyes. "I know I'm not the greatest singer on earth, but really!"

She clutched the shower curtain and shouted, "Bob!"

There was no answer, so she tried again, "Bob! Bob Fielding, this is not funny!"

When he still didn't reply, she wrapped the oversized towel around her sudsy body and went to the bathroom door and opened it. "Bob, turn the water back on!"

Silence.

Grimly, she pulled her bathrobe on and went out to deal with her husband. "Bob Fielding, you are in big, big trouble," she hollered as she dripped her way into the kitchen. "If you don't like my singing, too bad. You're not exactly Pavarotti yourself."

Through the kitchen window, she saw something that made her stop. Bob was in the yard, his head deep inside the engine compartment of his new John Deere tractor. He couldn't have turned the water off.

She was suddenly aware of an extra sound in the house. Water was running—and it was coming from the cellar.

There was no way she was going to run out there in her robe, still soapy. She'd have to try to fix it herself.

"Oh, I so do not want to do this," she muttered as she went into the entryway. The door to the cellar was cut into the floor, and she had to lean over and pull it open, then hook it to the wall. The sound of splashing emanated from the dark cellar, which was really a pit under the house that had been halfheartedly lined with bricks and broken cement. She'd refused to go into it, knowing that creatures lived down there that were not pleasant.

It probably wasn't a good idea to turn on the light down there. Who knew what shape the electricity was in.

She got the flashlight from the shelf beside her and cautiously played the beam over the cellar. From an overhead pipe at the foot of the stairs, water gushed out in a spectacular arc. "I can fix this. I can fix this," she told herself. It actually felt good, tackling a problem like this. How different was a leaky pipe from a cranky advertising client?

The floor of the cellar was already soaked with water. She hoisted her bathrobe safely above her ankles to keep it dry and waded the few steps to the large handle that had to be the valve to shut the water off.

It was. It even had a hand-lettered sign taped to the open beam beside it: WATER TURN-OFF VALVE. *Excuse me for feeling just a little bit smug,* she thought, *but look at me. A native big-city gal, fixing a leak on my own, instead of calling the building super or a plumber.*

She reached up, unable to stop the smile that insisted on flickering across her lips, and tried to turn the handle. It was stuck in place, so with one mighty wrench, she put her whole body into the effort, and she was rewarded with a metallic screech as the handle's threads loosened.

See? she said to herself. *I can—SNAP—break it.*

The handle was now in her hand, broken off at the pipe's junction, and still the water's cascade continued.

"Well, this didn't go exactly the way I'd planned," she said to no one in particular.

She glared at the spot where the turn-off was supposed to

be. It was not going to defeat her.

With purposeful steps she returned to the entryway and got Bob's brand-new shiny red toolbox and clanked her way back down the stairs. She tried all the silvery tools, from an assortment of screwdrivers—useless—to a series of wrenches. Nothing worked.

I could use a little help here.

She rummaged through the box, trying to remember what she'd seen on all those weekend home fix-it shows Bob liked to watch. A vise grip. Just the ticket. And there was one in the toolbox!

Thank You! Now let it work.

With a loud screech, the nub of the handle turned, and the water slowed to a trickle.

Thank You, thank You, thank You!

Just wait until Bob heard. He'd be delighted to hear she'd solved a problem of rural living in an old farmhouse. She bolted up the stairs, taking the steps two at a time, and flung open the front door.

Someone was standing with him out by the tractor, so she shut the door quickly, not wanting to be seen in her robe. Instead, she peeked through the small window in the door.

As the man talked, Bob listened—she could tell that the man had her husband's total attention by the way he tilted his head—and then he took the fellow's card, they shook hands, and the visitor left.

She watched as Bob leaned back on the tractor and studied the card, and then, with a smile, he pocketed it and walked toward the house. She opened the door as he neared the house.

"I sure hope that was a plumber," she told him.

"Actually, he's a minister. Why do we need a plumber?"

❧

"Those home repair guides had better come in soon," Bob said to Lauren that evening. "They should have been here this week. Did you check the mailbox today?"

"I did, and there was nothing in there except a big black and yellow bug and a flyer for an equipment auction. Be patient. Your books will arrive soon and you can be Johnny Fix-It. In the interim, we'll just keep pouring—no pun intended—money into the local plumber's wallet."

Bob stuck his hands in his pockets as he and Lauren stood on the front porch, watching a particularly fine sunset. The minister's card was still there, and he ran his finger around the edge.

"You know, when you look at a sunset like this, it's hard *not* to believe in God, isn't it?" he asked as his thumb rubbed across the raised cross on the card.

"No kidding. No human being could ever make something that spectacular. Look at the way the peach fades into pink and then magenta and finally becomes that royally rich purple."

"Honey, what do you think about going to church tomorrow? That minister came by just to invite us." He watched her reaction carefully.

Religion was something they hadn't discussed much. He knew she had been raised in a church, and so had he, but both of them had fallen away from the habit of churchgoing when they'd gone to college. They'd been married in a church, and they'd actually attended it a couple of times afterward, but church had become somewhat of a struggle to get to.

"Sure, I'll go."

"I wonder why we stopped going to church back in Chicago."

She laughed and turned to him. Her eyes were touched with the sunset's golds and indigos. "I can tell you in one word. Lattes. Whole Latte Love opened up around the corner from us and we were sunk. There was no way that dressing up— pantyhose for me, a tie for you—and driving through morning traffic was going to beat sleeping in and then walking over to Whole Latte Love."

"There's no Whole Latte Love here. The closest is the Dairy Barn, and it doesn't open until noon." He laughed. "Pastor John told me that church ends at eleven forty-five, so there's plenty of time to get over there for french toast and coffee."

She hugged his arm to her side. "I think it'd be nice to go to church. There's something about living out here that makes me feel close to God."

They stood together as the sun dipped lower, until at last the only colors left were a soft wash of deep amethyst and sapphire— the jewel-hued prairie.

"I've been thinking about God a lot lately," he said. "Coming back here threw me right back to my childhood. We didn't have a church in Prairiedale then. We had to drive over to Calvert Falls. But we did, every Sunday."

"I know what you mean. We never missed a service when I was a kid."

"I think I. . ." His voice broke. "I think I left Him behind."

For a moment she didn't respond. When she did speak, her voice was quiet in the twilight. "When I was little, whenever I pictured God, I saw Grandma's face. She was always the one who was there to hug me when I needed a hug, to be my backbone when I didn't seem to be able to find my own, and even to be honestly stern with me when I was off course."

He pulled her closer and wrapped his arms around her. "She's an extraordinary lady."

Lauren nodded. "She asked me if I'd been going to church. When I said no, she just looked sad." A tear slipped out and caught the last traces of light, like a diamond in the dusk. "I made her sad, Bob. It was like making God sad. Yes, I want to go back to church. I owe it to her—and to Him."

❦

Lauren paused outside the church. It had been built at the end of Main Street, and the modern design seemed at odds with the century-old buildings that lined the business stretch of the street. Yet, at the same time, it bespoke a promise of days to come, days filled with faith and hope.

Other cars pulled into the small parking lot, the drivers looking at them curiously. Her fingers sought Bob's hand, and at the reassuring touch, she relaxed.

This is church. This is the place where people accept you. We don't know anybody here, but church is like home. It'll be okay.

A familiar figure detached from a cluster of people at the front door of the church. "Bob! Lauren!" Caroline waved enthusiastically. "Min's already inside."

Lauren and Bob entered the church in Caroline's wake. As energetic as Min was, Caroline was quietly warm. She was in her glory today, taking them inside and introducing them to the other members of the congregation.

"This is Wyann Lorenz. She works in Calvert Falls at the

220

Ford dealership, so if you need a new car, think of Wyann. And this is Gerald Sollin. Best accountant in the state. Arnold and Bonny Anderson, from Anderson's Drug Store. Maisie Gillette. . ."

Lauren stole a glance at her husband. Bob's smile still seemed genuine, but then he had the capacity to enjoy new experiences fully. She took longer to adapt to new circumstances.

Is this the right place? She couldn't tell if she was talking to herself or to God. Asking God for a sign wasn't something she was comfortable with. Grandma had reminded her often enough that inside her heart were all the signs she'd ever need.

Bob settled right into the service. She edged a bit closer to him and tried to concentrate on the service and the inspiring words of the hymns. At last Pastor John stepped up for his sermon. When he announced the text, Lauren's eyes flew to the stained-glass rose window over the altar where Mary cradled a newborn Jesus as Joseph gazed fondly over her shoulder.

"For this child I prayed."

Chapter 6

The moving van pulled away in a cloud of road dust. "I don't believe I've ever seen anyone as happy as those two were about getting out of here," Bob said to Lauren. He understood why. They'd wedged chairs through impossibly narrow doorways, managed to wrangle a couch around a corner when doing so had seemed physically impossible, and hauled in the coffee table made of a solid granite slice after the dolly had collapsed under its weight.

"Now all we have to do is unpack, put everything away, and clean the house all over again," Lauren said in a chipper voice.

He groaned. "I don't even want to think about it. Just the thought makes me want to take a nap."

His words were only partially in jest. For him, moving was a monstrous task, but Lauren seemed to be energized by it. She had a piece of graph paper in her hand, and with great animation she pointed out her plans. "If we put the bed under those double windows, we can sleep with the breeze on our faces in the summer. Those two darling little end tables will fit perfectly on each side of your blue leather chair. See, I can scoot the lamp over here—well, that's the goldish-colored dot—and if we put our Navajo rug across like this. . ."

He couldn't follow her at all, but it was clear that in her mind the house was laid out in perfect detail, even to which household item went where. "The pillows we got from that fiber artist at the art museum will spill from the end of the couch onto the floor in an inviting 'snuggle up here' effect, and in the middle of it all will be an old doll Sheila and Dwaine sent me from The Older the Better—wearing the christening dress I got from Grandma!"

Her face radiated excitement, and he had to smile in return. Although she'd tried to gloss over it, he knew the move had been hard for her. She was such a high-energy person that suddenly dropping her fourteen-hour days at the advertising agency to leisurely evenings spent driving through the countryside and not so leisurely afternoons devoted to shouldering recalcitrant bureaus into place must have left her reeling. Yet she showed no signs of stress. . .or resentment.

She's doing it all for me. Had he ever felt so loved, so sure of the depth of her feelings?

"Oh, wait 'til you see this!" she bubbled. "I found the niftiest little shop out in the middle of nowhere that sold quilts, if you can believe it. Handmade, breathtakingly gorgeous quilts! There was a little sign nailed to a tree at the end of the driveway, and oh, it was so funny. The sign just said QUILTS, but it was spelled Q-U-L-T-S. So of course I had to stop. Get it? *I* had to stop."

He chuckled. "You comedian."

"Anyway, I left it in the back of my car. Wait a sec. Let me run out and get it."

He watched her as she tore out to the barn area, where they parked her BMW right next to his John Deere tractor. Had he ever been this happy?

Her screech rang through the afternoon air. "Bob!"

His feet seemed to have turned into lead as he ran across the wide farmyard to the barn. Was she hurt? "I'm coming, Lauren!" he called to her. "I'm coming!"

The barn was so dark compared to the bright sunlight that his eyes took a moment to adjust. Overhead an owl hooted in protest.

Lauren was leaned over the BMW, making odd sounds.

"Are you okay?" he panted as he neared her. What *were* those sounds she was making?

Was she crying? Moaning? No, it sounded like she was. . . meowing.

"Look, Bob," she whispered. "Kittens."

He peered into the BMW and saw a wary calico cat curled protectively around a group of newborn kittens. She was undoubtedly the cat he'd seen in the house earlier, and her expansive girth then hadn't been due to her appetite for field mice, but because she was about to give birth.

"She must have just had them," Lauren said, her voice soft with awe. "Have you ever seen anything so beautiful, so precious?"

The mother cat looked up at Lauren with eyes like glowing topaz, and Bob was struck by the perfect trust in the cat's eyes.

Lauren leaned in even closer and straightened the pile of cloth the cat had snuggled into with her kittens.

"I can't believe it. Look at how tiny and perfect they are!"

They were no bigger than field mice, and they blindly

rooted around the curve of their mother's belly.

"How many are there?" he whispered.

"Three. And they're all different. Doesn't she look gorgeous on that quilt?"

"Is that the quilt you just bought today?" He tried not to cringe.

"Sure is," she said. "Isn't it spectacular?"

"Isn't it kind of ruined?"

She shot him a look that would have withered vines. "It's the perfect place to have babies. Catrina has extraordinarily good taste."

"Catrina? Did she make the quilt?"

Lauren laughed. "No. This, my dear, is Catrina. And these are her babies. Tuxedo is the black and white one, the one with the brown stripes is Mocha, and the orange one is Puffer. Aren't they cute?"

"Ahh," he replied. "I see."

Had she ever been more beautiful? A strand of sleek black hair had escaped its ponytail and curled enticingly along her neck. A smear of dirt along her face was mute testimony to her furious cleaning that morning to prepare for the movers' arrival. Even her blue T-shirt had a rip on the bottom where a moving crate had caught the fabric.

The days of seeing her elegantly clad in an expensive suit, her ever-present cell phone at her ear, were apparently happily left behind. Her face was softer now, more relaxed, and he had to say that country life seemed to suit her.

She turned to him and flashed a grin. "Aren't they beautiful? If I were a cat, I'd be having kittens all the time, they're so incredible."

He gave in and bent over the car. Catrina looked up at him, her topaz-colored eyes warm with motherly love, and then returned to tending her slumbering babies.

If it were possible, he told himself, to *see* God's love, it was here, in this car, in this barn, on this prairie.

❦

Lauren carefully divided the last of the chicken. The grocery store in town had an amazingly good broasted chicken in its tiny deli section, and she and Bob had dined on that for dinner.

And now Catrina was about to.

"Honey, I don't think you should do that," Bob said. "She's a barn cat."

"You don't know that," she answered, although she did. Enough times of trying to dress Raggsy had taught her what a barn cat looked like. Catrina had the telltale ragged ears and the snarled underfur of a barn cat. "She's just a cat on her own at the moment, a single mother, and I'm doing all I can to help her."

She knew without looking that he was smiling. She could hear it in his words: "All cats are single, Lauren. I really don't think they get married."

"Maybe so," she replied absently, concentrating on shredding the chicken into small bits, "but it doesn't diminish the fact that she's probably hungry. She can eat this. Then she doesn't have to worry about her babies."

Her words came back to haunt her later, just as she was falling asleep. At some point, Catrina was going to have to get out of the car to answer the kitty call of nature, if not to eat. And during those times, the kittens were vulnerable to anything that might swoop down and snatch them up in taloned claws.

Like that owl she'd heard hooting out there earlier.

Bob was snoring softly, and she quietly slid out of bed and into her bathrobe. Moonlight poured in through the gap in the curtains where the fabric hung unevenly. She made a mental note to fix it in the morning, but for right now it was fine the way it was. The light bathed the floor and made it much easier to find her slippers.

She tiptoed into the kitchen where the pile of boxes from the move were still waiting to be stored, and she selected what she hoped was the ideal size. With the box in hand, she silently crept out of the house and into the farmyard.

The yard light, along with the glow of the full moon, brightened her way. Nevertheless, there was something undeniably creepy about being in the yard in her robe and heading toward the barn with a box. "All I need is an ax, and maybe messier hair, and I'd have a spot in a late-night movie somewhere," she muttered as she hurried toward the barn.

Catrina was wide awake, curled around her sleeping kittens. "Mrrrrp."

"Mrrrrp," Lauren answered. It clearly meant something in cat talk, because Catrina began to purr loudly. "Why you decided to have your babies in a barn is beyond me. Of course, the BMW I understand. You are a feline of exquisite taste. Nevertheless, I'm moving you and your brood inside, into that nice, safe house." Overhead, something big flapped in the rafters, as if confirming its presence.

Lauren picked the quilt up, cat and kittens in position, and placed it all into the box. "Inside we go. Now we've got to be quiet. Bob's asleep."

She walked quickly back to the house, her box of treasures

in her arms. "I'll have to get some dirt out of the back and put it in a box for you," she said to Catrina as she juggled the box and reached for the doorknob. "I'm afraid I'm not prepared with a litter box yet."

As her fingers wrapped around the handle, the door swung open. Bob stood there, his hair sticking out wildly. "I woke up," he said simply, "and you weren't there. I knew you'd gone to get her."

"I couldn't leave her and her babies out there," she said. "There's an owl—"

"Shh," he said, putting his finger on her lips. "I know. I know. Let's put them over here, by the stove. The pilot light should make it just a little bit warmer."

He took the box from her and carried it to the spot between the stove and the counter. Tears sprang into her eyes when she realized that he had already set up food and water dishes. "I've got a shallow box filled with sand by the back entry. After she gets her bearings, I'll take her out there and show her where it is."

"Where did you find sand?"

"There was an old sandbag in the laundry room they'd been using as a doorstop. It's not the best, but it'll do until we can get into town tomorrow and get some of the real stuff." He reached down and stroked Catrina's head. "And we'll see if we can't take this lady and her offspring to a vet."

If there had ever been any doubts in her heart, this evening erased them. Forever.

Chapter 7

Sunlight poured into the kitchen when Bob got up the next morning. Catrina met him near her food dish and wound herself in and out around his ankles, purring heartily. He knelt, and she leaped gracefully into his arms, vibrating enthusiastically.

"You're a wonderful cat," he said to her as he spooned food into her dish.

As soon as she finished her breakfast, the cat jumped back into the box with her babies.

The kittens moved into place within the warm circle of Catrina's body, and Bob couldn't resist stroking each one gently with his fingertip. "They're beautiful children," he told the cat. "Just—"

His words broke off as he realized that Tuxedo, the black and white kitten, wasn't nursing as enthusiastically as the others. He picked up the kitten and studied it. He knew nothing about cats, but this one seemed listless. Its eyes were dull, and it didn't respond to his strokes on its face except with a weak *meow*.

Tears sprang to his eyes. He loved this little cat with every ounce of his being. He held the kitten to his cheek and marveled at how silky the kitten's fur was. He'd never had cats before—only dogs—and this was all a new experience for him, one that he was finding himself enjoying very much. He began to pray: *Dearest Lord, You care for even the tiniest sparrow. You must care for this kitten. Please, please, touch this little creature with Your healing hand.*

The kitten meowed softly, and he leaned to return it to the box. Catrina looked up at him with wide, topaz-colored eyes, and he knew what his responsibility was.

He'd already made an appointment with Dr. Waters, the veterinarian, for the next day, but some things were too important to wait. He paused only a moment before making the call.

⚓

Dr. Waters stood and smiled at Lauren and Bob. "Try not to worry. The mother cat is doing a splendid job of taking care of her kittens, and the two female kittens, the brown and the orange, are in great shape. The black and white spotted one, well, he's just a little one and he isn't quite as insistent about getting his place at her belly. She's got plenty of spots available—he just needs to be pushier. She'll probably see to him herself, but keep an eye on him just the same and give me a call if he seems to be failing."

"He *is* failing," Lauren pointed out. "He's not doing well."

The white-haired veterinarian patted her arm. "I know it seems hard to understand because you love the cats, but you need to trust me on this. I've seen thousands of cats, and I've seen this. Ninety-nine percent of the time, it's nothing."

"But what about the other one percent?" Bob asked, and she hugged his arm in gratitude. He was just as worried as she

230

was. "Maybe Tux is really in danger."

Dr. Waters shook his head. "I'd be very surprised. Very surprised. No, it'll all be okay. The cat doesn't show signs of being very ill. He's just not feeling super at the moment. It could be something she ate that she's passing on to him through her milk. Has her diet changed since she had the kittens?"

Lauren looked at Bob, and they both flushed guiltily. "I gave her some broasted chicken."

"And I bought cat food at the grocery store." Bob cleared his throat. "I suppose she'd been living on field mice before she had the kittens."

Dr. Waters smiled at her. "Didn't feel up to catching her some mice for dinner?"

"Not exactly." Lauren liked Dr. Waters. He was such a nice fellow, and if he thought she and Bob were goofs for being so worried about the cats, he kept his feelings to himself.

"Shouldn't we be giving her food like this?" she asked. "All kidding aside, what am I supposed to do? Is there some special food we can give her?"

"No. I'd cut back on the table scraps, and I'd recommend you give her some dry food for at least half of her feedings. She needs to keep her teeth in shape, and dry food will do that."

"So there's no medicine or anything like that?" Lauren asked.

The vet shrugged and smiled. "Only the best that I know of—prayer."

❧

Bob pulled the sheet up and turned on his side. He flipped over and thumped the pillow. He threw the sheet off and sprawled across the bed.

It was hopeless. He was never going to get to sleep, not when Tuxedo was struggling in the kitchen. He finally got out of bed as quietly as he could and pulled on his robe.

"I'm going with you." Lauren's words broke through the silent darkness and just about scared him silly.

"Give me a heart attack," he muttered.

"Sorry. I couldn't sleep, either. Worried about Tux?"

"Yes."

Lauren pulled the comforter off the bed. "You get the pillows. Let's go."

They set up their makeshift camp in the kitchen, spreading out the comforter beside the box of kittens. Catrina seemed to be happy to see them there, and Lauren said so. "I think she likes having our company."

"Do you suppose we should lower the lights?" he asked. "Maybe it's too bright for them to sleep."

"It might not be a bad idea."

He turned the lights off, and the full moon poured light across the yellow tiles of the kitchen floor. Catrina aligned her babies along her belly, making sure each one was in its position, and with a contented sigh, she closed her eyes.

Bob put his arm around Lauren as they leaned against the wall. "This isn't going to be very comfortable for you," he said as she shifted her position. "Why don't you go on back to bed and I'll stay here and watch them?"

"No. I'm okay." Her uneasy moving around belied her words. "I'll stay here with you. It's not fair for you to do it all."

"We could do shifts," he suggested. "That way we'd each get some sleep."

She snuggled against him and yawned. "I'm fine. I really

am. I'm here for the night. Just. . ." Her words trailed off and a soft snore escaped her lips.

He kissed the top of her head. "Sleep well, honey."

There was no danger that he'd fall asleep. None at all. He'd use this time wisely and do as the veterinarian had suggested. He would pray.

Dearest God, we love these cats. If for no other reason than our love—and I think You'd agree that's a pretty compelling reason—would You please heal this tiny cat? We love him. Make Tux healthy and whole and keep all the cats. . .

He was so tired. He'd finish the prayer later. Right now, he needed a moment, just a moment, to rest his eyes.

Chapter 8

The nursery?" Lauren stared at her husband as if he'd lost total control of his senses. "We can't handle the nursery. We don't know anything about babies."

They stood in the kitchen of their house, still in their church finery, while she held Catrina. The kittens were now a bit over a month old and totally rambunctious. One tried to scale her leg, and she pulled it off, but not before the kitten's claws had destroyed her hose.

Bob poured boiling water over the tea bags draped across their cups and handed one to her. "How hard can it be? We hold them and give them bottles and they sleep."

She didn't want to laugh, but it was nearly impossible to hold it back. "When was the last time you were around a baby?"

"I see babies all the time."

"Uh-huh." She knew what Bob's contact—at least his recent contact—with babies had consisted of. His secretary had recently had a baby and Bob had seen the infant briefly at the hospital afterward.

Lauren returned Catrina to the floor, and together she and Bob walked into the living room, mugs of tea carefully balanced in their hands. The kittens followed them. She sank onto the couch beside the cascading pillows and the doll dressed in Grandma's christening gown. Mocha jumped into her lap while Tuxedo attacked her hair. Puffer rolled around Bob's shoes, working on untying the laces.

Bob took a sip of his tea and put it down quickly. "Oh, hot. Pastor John was in a spot today. He needs somebody to watch the nursery next Sunday and I already said okay. Think of it this way—the parents are just down the hall, and we only have them for an hour or so. If things go absolutely horribly, all we have to do is step out of the nursery and send them back to their parents."

"I suppose that's true. And it's only one Sunday, right?"

"Well, sure, unless we wanted to do more. But it would be good for us. We don't know much about babies."

His thoughts couldn't have been clearer if his head had been made of glass. She ignored the unsaid and picked up the television program guide with an offhand, "Anything good on television tonight?"

He glanced at her, and for a moment she saw an indefinable emotion in his eyes. His gaze held hers and questioned briefly before he answered, "I don't think so. Summer reruns. And there's nothing going on at the church tonight, either. Say, wasn't that a terrific solo today by Randy Gillette? I didn't know he could sing that well. Actually, I didn't know he could sing at all."

They chatted briefly about the service and the people who had been there, including Min, whose spectacular orange hat had been covered with a garden's worth of flowers. "I'm really enjoying the services," Bob said. "It's a nice time apart from the hustle and bustle of the week—well, at least as much as we hustle and bustle out here."

He was right. She had been feeling calmer when she left the little church, as if she'd left some of her burdens at the oaken altar, and she said so. "Things make sense a bit more after church, and my life has an orderliness to it that it didn't before." This was the time to say what had been on her heart. "Do you suppose that I'm getting to believe—that is, believe more? I mean, I always have, but now God is getting to be real for me."

"I know what you mean. And I couldn't explain it if my life depended on it, but why I didn't feel this way in Chicago and I do here—well, it's beyond me."

"We didn't go to church in Chicago," she reminded him. "Well, we did a couple of times, but then we found Whole Latte Love, and we were gone."

He grimaced. "Shallow, huh?"

"Very." She looked down into her mug, letting the shame wash over her. "I guess I thought God would come and find me, and you know, I think He did."

"Here in Nebraska, you mean? Away from the city?"

How could she explain it? All she could do was hope—or pray—that he'd understand. "I found Him in my car."

Bob stared at her, his expression a study of horror and concern. "You found Him in your. . .car? God came to you in a BMW?"

He looked so aghast that she started to laugh. "I didn't mean it that way, but now that I think about it, maybe I did find Him in my car. I really meant Catrina and her kittens. The thought that God could—and would—care so much for

236

such tiny creatures, and furthermore, would move my heart to be His hands—well, that did it."

Bob put his hand on his chest and sighed loudly. "Whew. For a moment there, you had me worried."

"You don't think I'm nuts, do you?" she asked. His answer meant everything to her.

"Not much." He grinned. "Not really."

"I've been to Europe. I've seen impressive cathedrals and historic churches that were filled with the Holy Spirit, but that cat and her kittens touched me in ways stained glass and arched ceilings never did."

The moment that her soul opened was still vivid to her. The look of trust on Catrina's face as she'd let Lauren pick up the sick kitten—that was a kind of faith that reached to the core of her being. She hadn't even known such a thing was possible.

In that moment, God had become visible to her.

She put down her cup and faced Bob. "Then things fell into place. For example, Min and Caroline—how could I ever have lived without them? Bob, I'm so glad I'm here. I feel like a complete person."

"You don't miss Chicago?"

"Oh, of course I wish there were more upscale clothing stores here. And I do miss Whole Latte Love, but I think I'm safer without it. I know my caffeine levels are a lot lower! I miss not having Mom and Dad in town, but thanks to my trusty cell phone and free weekend minutes, we're talking more than ever."

"Ah, technology. I have to agree with you that things certainly are moving along nicely. I feel like God is truly smiling on us. I should be licensed to practice law here pretty soon—it's looking like everything's going to be approved—and when that happens, maybe we can go in together on the old co-op building. Fielding Advertising and Law."

She laughed. "I think we need to work on that name. But I'm really pleased with how well it's going, starting another advertising agency here. I'm doing a bit for Randy Gillette's store—by the way, he said he needs to talk to you about renting the fields from us—and the beauty shop owner has asked me to look into some ways of bringing in more teenagers, so that's making the transition easier."

There was another change in her heart, but she wasn't quite ready to give it voice. She toyed with the edge of the christening gown as she let her thoughts wander.

Someday my child will wear this. The child for whom I prayed. The child for whom I pray. God, this is what I want. I want a child.

⚜

There is absolutely nothing finer than driving a tractor, Bob thought as he rolled out of the barn atop his John Deere. He didn't miss the Lamborghini at all. Not when he could feel power rumbling beneath him like this.

Plus, it was quite a handy vehicle. Thanks to Jeff down at Ags-Trac, he could fallow and till—whatever that meant—in the spring and plow out the driveway in the winter. He even had this nifty front-end loader to do handy things around the farm. The barn was tidily filled with all the implements he'd need—and probably a good number he wouldn't need.

Yes, he could do just about anything with his green tractor.

Right now he was going to put gravel in the driveway. Jeff had known someone who knew someone at a gravel company over to the west of town, and within minutes Bob had agreed to a truckload of gravel.

A truckload of gravel—the thought had given him pause. It was a lot of gravel. Jeff had shaken his head and asked, "Are you sure that'll be enough?"

The problem was that he wasn't sure. And now, facing a pile of gravel, he *really* wasn't sure.

"Well," he said aloud to nobody in particular, "no way to find out but to try!"

He grinned happily. When he'd played here as a child, his toy tractor had been his prized possession. During the summer, he'd plowed evenly tilled fields in the sandbox. In the fall, he'd lifted sticks into neat stacks of miniature lumber, and in the winter, he'd moved snow from the front steps—all with his tractor.

The bucket was as much fun to use as he'd imagined it would be. With delight, he moved gravel from one spot to the other, lifting and dumping, lifting and dumping.

The repetitive motion was calming, and he let his mind wander over the events of the past two months. Tuxedo, the kitten, had recovered completely and was now trying to scale the sides of the box with his siblings. *Thank You, Lord.* Lauren had reassured him that she was adjusting nicely to life in Nebraska, and she seemed happy on the farm. *Thank You, Lord.* And he, too, was comfortable in his new skin as a rural dweller. *Thank You, Lord.*

His life was filled with blessings. He couldn't ask for more— or perhaps he could.

You know what it is, Lord. Certainly You understand. I'm ready. I want to be a father.

❦

Those sure are some cute critters," Min said, admiring the trio of kittens that tumbled together in the kitchen.

Caroline beamed approvingly. "I absolutely agree. I think I like that black and white one the best. He's definitely got some gumption about him."

"He was the one that was sick, wasn't he?" Min rescued her orange hat from Tuxedo's claws. Apparently the mass of silk flowers on it was too much for the kitten to resist. "Looks like he's recovered nicely."

"Did you ever find out what was wrong with him?" Caroline asked, removing Mocha from the couch where she was busily investigating the contents of the woman's purse. "Nothing in there for you, dear, unless you happen to want a stick of gum or a lipstick."

Lauren blushed. "Kind of. Apparently it was the broasted chicken I gave Catrina and the three cans of gourmet cat food that Bob fed her."

"That could do it," Min said. Puffer climbed onto her lap and purred loudly enough for all of them to hear. Lauren suppressed a smile at the image of the rotund cat on the gaunt woman's lap. They were a match made in heaven.

The phone rang. "Excuse me," Lauren said. "I've been waiting for this call."

The problem with the farmhouse was that there was absolutely no privacy for telephone calls. She tried to be discreet, but she knew she was failing. "Yes? You're sure? Absolutely sure?

240

Without a doubt? No kidding? Are you positive?"

Min and Caroline exchanged beaming smiles and nodded knowingly.

"It's about time," Min murmured.

⚜

The kittens played in the sunshine that spilled across the living room floor. They'd outgrown the box and were now busily climbing the furniture and the drapes. Lauren's hands and wrists bore the marks of their feisty teeth and claws.

She and Bob took great delight in the kittens' antics. Could anything be more appealing than three playful kittens cavorting under the watchful eye of a fond mother cat? She couldn't imagine the home without Catrina and her kittens.

"You're a lucky woman," she said to the cat, who sprawled elegantly in the warm sunlight while keeping an eye on her offspring. "May I join you?"

She lay on the floor and the cat purred with satisfaction at her company. Lauren stroked Catrina's sleek fur. "You know, just a couple of months ago, if anyone had said I'd be lying on the floor of a farmhouse, snuggled up with a cat, I'd have said they were insane. But this is wonderful. We should bottle this feeling. We'd make a million bucks."

The radiant warmth of the sun was so relaxing and the regular purring of the cat was so hypnotic that she found herself drifting off to sleep. In the background she heard the kittens climb onto the couch, and she drowsily opened one eye to watch them.

Tuxedo was perched on the top of the couch while Mocha and Puffer played hide-and-seek in the pillows. Suddenly the black and white kitten leaped down and attacked the doll and began to chew on the lace edging of the christening gown.

"Tux, no!" She sprang to her feet and pulled the kitten off the precious dress. "This is an important thing. No claws!" She straightened the lace and breathed a prayer of thanks that the kitten's claws hadn't damaged the gown.

"Hey, honey." Bob came into the room and picked up all the kittens at once. "How's it going, and how's my furry family?"

She stood on tiptoe and gave him a kiss. "We're doing fine. Catrina was just giving me lessons in the joy of sleeping in the sunshine. It's quite a treat."

"I imagine it is." Mocha wiggled free of his grip and jumped to the coffee table, bumping into a vase of daisies. As Lauren tried in vain to stop it from tipping over, Tuxedo made a mighty leap and landed on her head. Puffer slithered down Bob's body, and from the muted "Ow, ow, ow, ow," Lauren knew the kitten's claws had been extended.

Water dripped from the table to the floor, and the kittens skidded through it, smearing it farther across the floor. She laughed as she tried to catch them to dry them off. "These kittens are wild today!"

"Want to repeat what you said to me awhile back?" Bob asked. "You know, that bit about how you'd have babies if you could have kittens?"

She picked up a daisy and stuck it behind his ear. "I was kidding."

"Well, I hope so."

"I mean, I was really kidding. No kittens." She took his hand. "I think maybe you should sit down for this."

They sat together on the couch, and she picked up the doll

clad in her grandmother's christening gown. "I don't think a kitten could wear this," she said. Then she added, "Although Tux tried to eat it a few minutes ago."

As if on cue, the black and white kitten attacked the doll. She gently removed him and placed him on the floor, where he began chewing on her toe. Mocha joined him, and Puffer leaped to the top of the couch and attacked the top of her head, digging in with kitten-sharp claws.

"Are you feeling okay?" Bob asked as she extracted the orange kitten from her hair. "You aren't making much sense."

She took a deep breath and started again. "Three generations of my family have been christened in this dress. I think it's time it was worn again."

He took her hands. "Are you saying what I think you're saying?"

"Wait just a minute, okay?"

She darted into the bedroom and leaned against the bureau as she tried to collect her thoughts. How was she going to do this? She'd run through this scenario a thousand times today, ever since she'd gotten the phone call, and it wasn't going at all according to her plan. The kittens' accident with the daisies had thrown everything off. She'd meant to have the scene private and loving and romantic, not ruled by kittens that insisted on biting her toes or chewing on her hair.

God, just stay with me on this, okay?

She took a deep breath and reentered the living room with a gift-wrapped box. "Here."

"But it's not my birthday. Wait. Why are there baby bottles on this paper?"

"Open it."

He did, and for a moment, he sat motionless, looking into it. Then a single tear dripped into the box.

"Honey, do you remember what Grandma said? She'd send it to me when it was time? Bob, it's time."

"You're sure you want to do this?" he asked, his voice faltering through his tears.

"It's kind of late to go back on it."

He stared at her. "You're—I mean, you—that is, we—"

"Yup. A little Fielding is already on his or her way."

He hugged her, let her go, then hugged her again. "Oh, Lauren, I am so happy!"

Catrina leaped onto Lauren's lap. "Yes, Catrina, you're welcome up here." Lauren gazed into Bob's eyes. "I think Catrina was God's way of bringing me home, home to where I need to be, to who I really am. Do you realize that I was already pregnant when I found her? God used her to prepare me for my own family."

Bob's smile was a bit wobbly. "He did the same for me. He opened my heart."

"And I know one thing for sure. I want your babies—in this house, on this prairie. I want them christened in this dress, in our church, and to sleep under the same Bible verse I did."

Bob lifted the plaque from the box. " 'For this child I prayed.' He answered my prayer, Lauren."

"And mine."

JANET SPAETH

As a child, Janet Spaeth spent many happy hours exploring her grandmother's attic in rural Nebraska and found treasure after treasure there. The dress in this story was, in fact, discovered there. Also, the cat in *This Prairie* really did exist; they met when the cat gave birth in Janet's new Mustang while it was parked in a barn.

Janet treasures her rural heritage and enjoys getting out of the city (although she does appreciate a trip to the mall). She enjoys reading, writing, and spending time with her family—making memories. Her favorite scripture is "For where your treasure is, there your heart will be also" (Matthew 6:21). For Janet, that treasure is her family.

Seeking the Lost

by Pamela Kaye Tracy

Dedication

To Betty Crawford, who made a tough decision
for all the right reasons.

Nobody should seek his own good, but the good of others.
1 CORINTHIANS 10:24

Chapter 1

Y ou do realize," David Webb said, "that Elvis made more than you last year."

Jessica Fleming frowned at her fiancé. If he had a sense of humor, she might have laughed. But David was so serious that even moving furniture was done in a shirt and tie.

He glanced at her, taking his eyes off the road for a moment, and asked for the thousandth time, "What made you decide on teaching as a career? You have the smarts. You could have been a lawyer, a doctor, a—"

Why was he bringing this up now?

"An accountant, like you?"

"Well, yes, or something that pays a decent wage, and it's not too late. You're only twenty-six. I'll support us while you go back to school. It will pay off in the long run."

Two of David's favorite words: *long run*. His other favorites, all groups of two, were *bottom line*, *fiscal year*, and *profit margin*. Sometimes Jessica missed the *old* David, her high school sweetheart. He'd been the heart of their Casper, Wyoming, youth group, a football player, and still a solid A student—the type of boyfriend who thought the teaching profession was a calling, not just a paycheck. Then he'd gone away to college.

She didn't answer his question. He didn't want to hear that columns of numbers never give sticky hugs and gap-toothed smiles.

David aimed the borrowed truck up and onto the slight hill that was Grandmother's bumpy driveway. Then he turned off the ignition and asked, "Is Lydia here?"

"No. Grandma says she has everything she wants."

"She'll get used to the Mountain Springs Retirement Center. My grandmother loves it. It's almost like a dorm for the elderly. And Lydia can't seem to stop talking about that computer class she's taking. What could be better?"

Staying with family, Jessica wanted to say. David saw his parents maybe twice a year, *if* they made the time to fly up from Florida. And while David claimed to enjoy her family, Jessica knew he could just as easily do without them. Sometimes she wondered if he could just as easily do without her.

A truck parked on the street advertised THE OLDER THE BETTER. Good, her cousin's husband was here to help. Newly married, Sheila seemed ecstatically happy. Glancing at her own engagement ring, Jessica wished she felt the same way. Lately, all she felt was lost, sort of like her grandma's two-story Victorian. Dust and covered furniture waited inside instead of Lydia's welcoming presence. Soon, Jessica's favorite place on earth would sport a FOR SALE sign in the front yard, and some family with 2.5 children would gut the fifties decor and perform plastic surgery on a grand ole dame of a house still in prime condition.

It would go on the market in just another month. More than anything else, Jessica wanted to buy it. Grandma had offered them a good price, but according to David, this just wasn't the neighborhood he was looking for. Besides, he'd added, the house was old.

It *was* old. It held irreplaceable memories and didn't look like every other house in a subdivision, which was exactly why Jessica loved it. She pushed open the front door and stepped into a hallway; its bare walls used to boast a cluttering of family photos that were the silent remnants of bygone family gatherings. Grandma's house was supposed to be bustling. There should be smells of supper cooking. The television should be blaring an *I Love Lucy* rerun. Grandma should be shouting, "I'm upstairs!"

Instead, Dwaine Woods yelled, "I'm taping the drawers. Come help!"

"You all right?" David asked softly, sounding almost like the boy she remembered.

"I just get sad coming here."

"It's for the best. Lydia's no longer alone. She'll make friends at Mountain Springs."

"Friends aren't family."

David sighed. "I'm not in the mood to go into this. Let's get the dresser."

It isn't just any old dresser, Jessica thought belligerently. Dwaine claimed it was seventeenth century, but Jessica didn't care if was seventh century or from the Goodwill store seven blocks away. Grandma had told each of the girls they could have one thing from the attic, and the dresser was her first choice. Throughout her childhood, most of the drawers had acted as beds for baby dolls and hiding places for Christmas gifts.

David opened the attic door and sneezed. "Have you hired

someone to come clean?"

"Not yet."

He shook his head, and Jessica got the idea he knew she was dragging her feet. *Change your mind,* her thoughts urged. *Let's set a date and settle down, here.*

"Time to get a move on," David urged.

Dwaine raised an eyebrow. "Hello, David. Why the rush?"

Jessica forced a smile. David wanted to be home and in bed by nine. He started his morning at five, and not even a fiancée took priority over work. Fifteen minutes later, they'd finished taping the drawers to Dwaine's satisfaction and started down the stairs.

Watching them, she said, "Isn't it beautiful?"

"Awkward," David said. He lost his grip and tried to rebalance as one of the drawers slid open. "We should have used more tape."

Jessica watched Dwaine's fingers start to slip, and the drawer—a middle drawer—went from almost open to *really* open. She moved to help. "Wow, I don't think I've ever gotten this drawer to open. It always stuck. We always joked about it holding a secret."

"Looks like there were papers and stuff underneath." David slowly tilted the dresser upward and waited until Dwaine managed a new grip before taking another step.

Jessica gathered the dust, photos, and large envelope that had fallen from the dresser.

Sitting on the bottom step, she thumbed through the photos. "It's my aunt!"

"Which one?" David sat beside her. "I don't recognize her."

"This would be Carol. My mom's youngest sister. She died

before I was born. The family doesn't talk about her much, and I've never seen these before. Aunt Carol is with a guy. He's kinda cute, but I don't remember anybody talking about her having a husband or boyfriend."

Dwaine nudged Jessica over. "Look at that red hair. You look like him."

"I do. You're right." Jessica laughed. Tall, with strong features and big hands, the man dwarfed Carol Dunmore in a stance that Jessica recognized. In a family of vertically challenged brunettes, she had always felt like a bright Amazon among the pygmies.

She stopped laughing a minute later when she slid the adoption papers from the envelope and read the names and saw the signatures.

❦

Haunted churches were rare in the Midwest, and Patrick McDonald wished he hadn't told his publisher about the two he'd heard about in Nebraska. His contract stipulated photos of historic Midwest churches, but the masses who purchased coffee-table books loved the unusual. The so-called haunted Benson Church turned out to be nothing but headstones behind a library. The actual building had burned fifteen years ago.

Opening his briefcase, Patrick removed photos taken a few weeks before the fire. It had been a nice-looking church but nothing special. The still-intact cemetery was a different story. Climbing over the fence, Patrick perused the gravestones. The newest boasted the year of 1973. The oldest looked to read 1883, but it could have been 1888, depending on which eye one closed. Patrick wished he'd pitched gravestones to his publisher. Gravestones came with epitaphs. His favorite so far was "Here lies Ezekial Aikle, age 102. The Good Die Young."

And, then there was the one back in Des Moines that deserved a chapter of its own: "I Told You I Was Sick!"

The one that stopped him and made a lasting impression, especially after all the sermons he'd heard the last few months, read: "Here lies an Atheist; All dressed up; And no place to go."

The library was old, built the same year as the church. Patrick held up one of the better photos to get an idea of the size of the old church. Something about the positioning of the sun, the telephone pole, and the church tugged at a memory. He took out two more photos and compared the landscape.

A few moments later, he remembered. Willie Raymond had been a military photojournalist in the late seventies. He'd died in Afghanistan catching the early faces of evil that would someday rule the Taliban. He had been in the wrong place at the wrong time, and not even the American government knew exactly why he had been killed. His exemplary photos told a political tale of dark intrigue that most people, luckily, never got to see.

But Patrick had seen, and he'd never forget, the brutal truth documented by Raymond's camera. The lost photos had surfaced almost two decades later when Patrick covered a devastating earthquake in Afghanistan. He'd been looking for before and after pictures of the destroyed terrain. Instead, he'd found Willie Raymond's legacy.

Patrick had envied Raymond's talent. Looking at the church photos, Patrick wished he had a source for these photos he'd taken off the Internet. They reminded him of Raymond's work.

Most photographers developed a style. Willie Raymond's had to do with positioning. The man always had some kind of tall object on the right side of the photo. He used it to develop a certain depth to the photo.

Packing up his gear, Patrick figured he could squeeze in both lunch and the other haunted location. This would be his last venture into the paranormal realm. Linnage turned out to be a two-hour drive highlighted by green grass, cornfields, and railroad tracks. Patrick took his eyes off the road long enough to study the map a retired minister—who had done his best to convert Patrick—had drawn for him. The town of Linnage had virtually turned into a ghost town in the fifties when its tractor plant closed down. Soon only farmers remained. It was nothing but boarded-up houses, parking lots, and deserted businesses.

Patrick found the turn he wanted and headed south. The church was right where the map claimed. The ghost stories surrounding it had to do with visitors who experienced a drop in temperature, claimed to see like-new songbooks lying on gleaming pews, and even visited a modern bathroom complete with copper plumbing. Parking the car in a weed-infested parking lot, Patrick figured he wouldn't mind stumbling across a haunted bathroom if it had working plumbing.

White paint peeled from the church's outside walls. Grass grew to Patrick's knees. Two broken steps led to the door that opened to an empty room. Nothing was left, not even window glass. Mice took refuge where believers once worshiped.

The only religious person in Patrick's family had been his grandmother, his mother's mother. She'd taken him to vacation Bible school, and she'd given him a small Bible he'd never read.

She'd died before he finished fifth grade. From childhood, all he remembered about church were snappy songs and pictures of a white-haired man. His dad had believed in giving a child free rein to decide about God. Since his free rein hadn't included ever stepping inside a church building, Patrick had forgotten what it felt like to attend a church service until taking this assignment.

His grandmother was probably smiling in her grave.

Attending church left Patrick with a sore back and in a state of confusion. Sermons that didn't quite make sense were connected to men with names like John the Baptist, Lot, Solomon, Peter, and Jonah. Patrick had heard the names; he just didn't know their history. It seemed that without a character sheet explaining these men's roles in church history, a visitor might as well sleep during the sermon.

Linnage's cemetery was not fenced, and unlike the parking lot, someone kept the grass from overtaking the final resting places of long-forgotten townsfolk. Patrick walked over and stood in front of the tallest monument.

Beloved Father, Beloved Husband.

Patrick had stood in hundreds of cemeteries this year, and lately he wondered what would be written on his tombstone—if anybody took the time to have it engraved.

"Hey, you need something?" A farmer stepped from an old blue truck that probably had been in Linnage back when there was still a gas station.

"I'm taking photos of your church. It's beautiful."

"And not haunted." The farmer stopped before entering the graveyard. "If you're here to see a ghost, you're wasting your time. Fella like you ought to know better."

"I do know better." Patrick took a business card from his pocket and walked over to the man. "I'm photographing old churches across the Midwest and recording their history. I found out about this church from Clarence Webb."

When the man smiled, Patrick knew that farming would be a future book. Every line in the man's face lit up as he waved away the card. "How is Clarence?"

"Fine." Ten minutes later, Patrick was following Manny Otera to his farm just ten miles down the road. When Patrick left the Oteras' place later that evening, after a dinner that was anything but Midwestern—no steak and potatoes; instead, fajitas and beans—he didn't have any new insights about the Linnage church. Instead, he had five photos taken by another visitor sporting a camera. A visitor whose name Manny couldn't recall, but who had later sent Manny some complimentary photos.

Photos that caught the church against a brilliant orange sun; photos that used a tall tree—to the right—to complement the church and give a strong visual impression as to the size and dimensions of a dignified building.

Photos that Patrick suspected had been taken by a dead man.

Chapter 2

Jessica wasn't sure who felt the most disappointed. Maybe *disappointed* wasn't the word; *scared* was more like it. Her parents—that she'd found out the truth. Herself—that she'd found out the truth. Or her fiancé—that she wasn't giving him *all* her attention. Her parents, *adopted* parents, had mentioned words like *forgive*, *forget*, and *fortunate*. David, of course, had gone back to his usual word groupings of two: *stress management*, *unrealistic goals*, and *reasonable timing*. When she'd handed him back his ring, he had one thing to say: *trial separation*. Nothing mattered. Every aspect of her life had changed.

Including her goal to teach summer school.

Instead, Jessica cleaned her classroom, turned in her final grades, and bright and early the first Monday in June, she packed her bags and headed for Loving Heart, Nebraska. It was, after all, only a six-hour drive.

For the first time in her life, she'd made a major decision without her parents' consent or confiding in David. Of course, she thought as she glanced at her naked ring finger, she no longer needed to confide in David. He was out of the picture.

As the miles added up, she kept looking in the mirror,

expecting to see her dad's Ford in pursuit. Truth was, she'd seen her parents yesterday at church, and since she no longer lived at home, he probably wasn't aware yet that she'd taken off.

She'd spent the last few weeks researching William Conner Raymond, her birth father. An obituary on the Internet provided her with information about his hometown but little about *him*. His family was another matter. Raymonds were plentiful in Loving Heart. They owned businesses, sold homes, and had personal Web sites. *Another large family,* Jessica thought as she left Wyoming behind and crossed the Nebraska border. She reasoned that her own large family remained much the same. Lydia was still Grandma. Evelyn, Janet, and Roberta were still her aunts. Sheila, Kimber, and Lauren were still her cousins. It was just that Dad. . .Dad was really her uncle, and Mom—Marlene—was really her aunt. And Aunt Carol, whose grave she'd put flowers on once a year on Memorial Day, was really her mother.

The cell phone buzzed. With one hand, Jessica pressed the power button.

Too bad emotions didn't come with off buttons.

Loving Heart had a four-digit population. She spent a few hours exploring the town and visiting the library. Then, she headed for a decent-looking restaurant. Not that Jessica was hungry. It was more like she needed routine, and it was noon. The Rusty Nail looked like a pizza parlor that had collided with a truckload of Pepto-Bismol. Either The Rusty Nail catered to a mostly female crowd, or the owners of this restaurant had gotten a good deal on pink paint. They'd also gotten a deal on small tables, which they'd packed into a small space.

The sounds of normalcy seemed out of place. How could

people be out for lunch when Jessica's world was falling apart? How could people smile and tease each other? She followed a hostess to a side table and sat down.

A glass of lukewarm water, a table that wobbled like an aged teeter-totter, a waitress who couldn't have been more than twelve years old, and a man at the next table who apparently believed staring to be an acceptable pastime, did nothing to endear Loving Heart, Nebraska, to Jessica. But it was a welcome of sorts. The only welcome she could expect since no one in town knew her.

Yet.

Glancing at her watch, she felt a moment of misgiving. Certainly, she didn't belong all alone cleaning her fork on a flimsy napkin in a town that had once been home to a young man named William Conner Raymond. A man who'd married a woman, fathered a child, and disappeared before the baby bottle needed warming.

Her grandma said he'd died overseas. Her aunts said his family had never tried to contact her. Her uncles said to leave well enough alone. Her parents didn't understand.

And her cousins probably didn't know the story—yet.

The man at the next table interrupted her musings. After all, the tables were so close they could almost touch knees. It was just her luck to take her first solo venture in a strange town, complete with a strange but good-looking man whose intense gaze gave her chills. David used to send her the same kind of hooded looks during fifth-period study hall their senior year. Jessica had gotten chills back then, too. She shoved the memory of her ex-fiancé aside and tried not to notice that the staring man happened to be the only other single diner in the place.

Maybe she should rethink her actions. Maybe then she could swallow the hamburger the waitress had placed in front of her. Instead, she picked up a french fry and took a bite. It tasted like a wad of glue mixed with wet tissue and then lightly salted. She choked.

The inept waitress still hadn't brought Jessica the glass of tea she'd ordered, but the staring man passed over his untouched glass of water. The tables were that close. Jessica took it, without thanking him, and gulped it down. Glue should always be washed down with at least a gallon of liquid.

Plopping down a ten-dollar bill, Jessica stood and slowly walked out of the restaurant. She was careful to avoid the eyes of the man who looked to be enjoying his fries and staring at her. A wrinkled, gray suit jacket hung from his chair, and his white shirt and gray slacks said he'd already put in a full day. He looked like she felt: exhausted.

Before leaving the restaurant, she went to the pay phone and thumbed through the phone book. Opening up to the Rs, she stared at a jagged edge of paper. Great, maybe someone else claiming paternity to Willie Raymond had made off with the R section.

Patrick McDonald thought The Rusty Nail looked like every other small-town restaurant. He handed the cashier his credit card and glanced over when the front door opened and a bad mood blew in. The woman from the next table gave him *that* look. He signed the credit card slip and took his receipt.

"Ma'am," he said.

She didn't acknowledge his greeting. She simply ignored him

ATTIC TREASURES

and asked the cashier if she had an extra telephone directory.

He chuckled, which earned him a dirty look—at least it was a response. So far, Loving Heart and the quest for Willie Raymond seemed just what he needed. This morning's visit to a church and then a cemetery had turned up enough clues to inspire him to want more. He hadn't felt this excited about a story since early in his career, when covering neighborhood drive-by shootings meant one more step in the right direction. He took one more look at the red-haired woman copying down a number from the cashier's telephone book, then he headed for his car.

As he drove back to his hotel, he wondered what had her all in a dither. She reminded him of someone, but he couldn't put his finger on whom. A few minutes later, he was in his room and typing new keywords into an Internet search engine. Information about Willie Raymond was slim. The phone book had listed about twenty families of Raymond, and for a town boasting only seventy-five hundred occupants, he thought that a healthy number.

The female eating by herself and keeping company with a bad mood had the red hair of a Raymond. Maybe that's why he couldn't forget her. And he'd always been partial to redheads—with a name like Patrick McDonald, how could he help it?

Picking up his notes, he decided to go to the Loving Heart library. He'd start there. Find old yearbooks, newspaper articles, and so on. Willie Raymond had been something of a war hero, so information should be available. He copied the address from the phone book and located his newly acquired local map. Before leaving the room, Patrick changed into jeans and a polo shirt and pondered the need for clean clothes. That's what came of spending hours on the road, laundry done on the run, and no home-cooked meals. He'd left Omaha at noon yesterday, exiting the church doors and driving first to York, Nebraska, where he'd shot some photos and then spent the night. This morning he'd logged seven more hours to Loving Heart. Grabbing his camera, he headed out the door.

Just a ten-minute drive from the hotel, the library was in a converted Victorian house. *Cute* was the only adjective that came to mind, and it wasn't a description Patrick was partial to. He'd rather have a cement building with state-of-the-art technology. Patrick parked and headed for a door that opened to what must have once been the living room. Now it housed the checkout desk, three computers, and the magazine rack. A quick exploration told him that the library's renovators had designated each bedroom—one downstairs and three upstairs—for a different genre. The master bedroom, connected to the living room, sheltered mysteries. The other three took care of mainstream fiction, romance, and history. An added-on screened patio housed biographies, cookbooks, and nonfiction. The kitchen was closed to customers—no doubt the break room for employees. The hallway offered a few newspapers and periodicals plus a bathroom that boasted Winnie the Pooh decor. The basement actually gave Patrick pause. Loving Heart had spared no expense in providing its children with up-to-date technology and an expansive collection of books. Best of all, Loving Heart's past was chronicled in black and white across the walls.

Black and white.

Willie Raymond's favorite mode. And Patrick recognized Raymond's touch in many of the photographs. Unfortunately, none were recent, so Patrick had to resist the urge to pry pieces from the wall to try to figure out the date.

The stairs creaked and Patrick turned around, not surprised to find the gray-haired librarian keeping track of him.

"You need some help?" she asked.

"I'm getting the feel of the library before I start my research. I'm a photojournalist. Those pictures on the wall—I'm guessing Willie Raymond took them."

The woman nodded and raised an eyebrow.

"That a problem?" Patrick asked.

"No, I just find it odd that no one has mentioned Willie Raymond in more than a decade, but today brings two curious out-of-towners nosing around."

Chapter 3

Jessica stepped out of the boxlike courthouse and frowned. She'd driven through numerous small towns on her way here, and all of them had quaint courthouses. Not Loving Heart. No, they had a twenty-year-old brick structure without a single ornate decoration—unless one counted the plaque honoring the structure that had burned down twenty years ago. Next to the courthouse, the library hosted a splattering of kids playing on swings while mothers chatted or glanced through magazines.

The library had offered Jessica both feast and famine when it came to information about Willie Raymond. The librarian, a brisk woman with steel-gray hair and sharp eyes, had helped Jessica find plenty of articles, pictures, and yearbooks—all with just minute bits and pieces—and bent the rules to allow Jessica to check items out. Jessica also had walked away with today's newspaper and a rumbling stomach. Nervous anticipation had cheated her out of lunch, and now she was ready to gnaw on the nearest tree.

Three buildings down from the library, on Main Street, she found a café that offered down-home cooking and an older waitress who knew the fine art of providing a customer with plenty of tea. She ordered a meal and spread the newspaper—tabloid, really—out on the table. The ten-page publication, appropriately titled *The Heartbeat*, offered two pages of local chitchat, three pages of classifieds, two pages of business advertisements, one page of comics, one page of church information, and an entertainment page.

The name *Raymond* graced almost every page. Their biggest contribution to the town's economy seemed to be a canoe rental business that carted people to the Niobrara River, dropped them off with an oversized canoe or tube, then hours later picked them up.

On the second page, she homed in on a bed-and-breakfast advertisement. An Opal Raymond was listed as the owner. Taking a pen out of her purse, Jessica circled the ad. Did she dare? Before she could decide, the waitress delivered her food. After taking a few bites, Jessica went back to perusing the ad. The price was right, but it almost seemed too bold. Could she, should she, take a room from a woman who might be a relative? Jessica contemplated while finishing her toast and hash browns.

"Everything all right?" asked the waitress, plopping down a pink guest check.

"Do you know Opal Raymond?"

The waitress grinned as she picked up the empty plates and nodded at the open newspaper. "Sure I do. Probably can't go wrong if you don't mind a revolving door. Everyone loves Opal, and you can't spit without hitting some member of her family."

Armed with directions from the waitress, Jessica left a

respectable tip and pointed her car for the outskirts of town. The house was about five miles from nothing. Opal's driveway was a scenic route of green grass, flowers, and trees that stood like sentries to a stately manor. Parking behind an old, blue Ford truck, Jessica studied the house where maybe a grandmother, aunt, or cousin lived.

The house actually looked welcoming. Its paint had long since forgotten its original color and had settled on a shade of gray favored by the town librarian's hair. Windows looked to be square interruptions in the wall, haphazardly placed, and a darker shade of gray than the rest of the house. For all that, the house had a certain dignity, as if it had seen much and survived even more. A wheelchair ramp offered an alternate route to the front door. Jessica chanced the steps, surprised to find them sturdier than they looked.

A few minutes after twisting the ancient ringer, Jessica knocked. She couldn't hear a thing inside. If no one was home, would she have the courage to return?

She took a step backward, then smiled as the door opened. She'd been expecting white hair, a flowered dress, and ankle socks. Instead, the door was opened by a young woman who looked to be about twenty years old.

"Are you Opal?"

"Yup, I'm Opal." The girl offered a paint-splattered hand, then retracted it and laughed. "I was painting upstairs and didn't hear you at first. Have to get everything done in the summer when I'm not in school, and sometimes I just zone out. That and I like the radio loud. Do I know you?"

"I don't think so." Jessica swallowed, feeling the faint heat of a blush begin. Blushing seemed ridiculous—but it was a safe reaction to seeing another woman of the same height and coloring standing right in front of her.

Opal rubbed her palms on the back of her overalls and held out her hand again. "*Should* I know you?"

"Huh?" Jessica stammered, managing to engage in a limp handshake. First, she'd been disconcerted at finding someone named Opal without gray hair and bifocals, and now Opal had picked up on a connection Jessica wasn't ready to deal with. "I don't think so."

"Well, you've got the Raymond hair and height, I'll say that. I'm surprised you're not a cousin or something. Anyway, how can I help you?"

"I'm here about a room."

"Cool. I painted the first one last week. It's a great room; let me take you up."

It was a great room—except for the color. It had a window seat, a fantastic view, and a sloping roof, and it was an awful shade of lime green.

"Grandma got it in her mind to turn this into a bed-and-breakfast. I can't believe you're here. I just put that advertisement in the paper last week. I didn't figure a bed-and-breakfast would work in Loving Heart, but you're proving me wrong. How long do you plan to stay?"

"I'm not sure."

"Well, it's not like the hordes are knocking down our door. Great, let's get you moved in. What are you doing here in Loving Heart?"

"I'm a schoolteacher and have the summer off. I've read about Loving Heart and thought it would be fun to explore."

Opal raised an eyebrow. "That's a one-day adventure—two

at the most, not a week."

"I've always wanted to live in a small town. I have the time and the money. This is *my* summer to do what I want."

"I guess I can understand that. Where are you from?"

"Casper, Wyoming."

Opal's face did an interesting configuration, every expression suggesting laughter threatening to erupt. "Yeah, Casper, now that's a big city."

Jessica felt her face start to flame.

Opal must have noticed, because she backpedaled. "Follow me down to the kitchen. I'll get you a glass of tea. Then you can fill out the registration card. I think it's brave of you to explore, and all alone, too."

A few minutes later, Opal handed over a house key and went back to painting. Jessica slowly walked to her car, amazed at all she'd accomplished in such a short time. Granted, she hadn't answered any pressing questions yet, but she'd situated herself where the answers surely must be.

And she'd not even been in town twenty-four hours.

She decided not to unload her trunk yet. The sun was beginning its descent and she still had one more place she wanted to visit.

Getting back in her car, she took out the tiny map of the town that the restaurant had provided. Mostly it was a detailed route to the Niobrara River, but the clerk had added directions to the town's cemetery. Jessica had no trouble finding it. The final resting place for Loving Heart's finest was roughly the size of a football field. Statues of angels dotted the four corners and center. An elderly man, with an impressive amount of jet black hair mowed the grass, careful to nudge against the headstones without seeming aggressive. Jessica watched him for a moment, touched that he would care so much for people probably long gone before he'd taken his first healthy cry.

It wasn't that hard to figure out where to start her hunt for Willie Raymond's grave. One section of the cemetery sported a collage of uniquely colored flowers. Jessica figured Opal spent a lot of time here. Oddly enough, Willie Raymond's grave was the only one left unadorned. It was bigger than the rest, off by itself, and the headstone labeled him a war hero.

Jessica went down to her knees. Somewhere under all this dirt lay the remnants of the man who'd fathered her. Touching the stone, she wondered why his grave was neglected when all the others were paid homage to.

She felt her breath catch, and she bit down on her bottom lip to keep from crying. She at least vaguely knew her birth mother's history, grade school antics, and favorite color, and she had been privy to Carol's collection of photographs from birth to almost twenty.

But her birth father, the man who had given Jessica her red hair, height, and ridiculously big feet, she still knew nothing about.

What had he been like? Had he played baseball, like she did? Did he love strawberries? Did he long for romantic movies that made him sigh? Well, probably not that last one. Her ex-fiancé used to have to be bribed into taking her to such movies. Maybe that's why she didn't really miss David—much. Any love she'd had for him died when he'd expressed concern about lost income when she forfeited her summer school job. She'd been holding on to a high school romance. One that hadn't matured well.

Staring down at the piece of earth, all she felt was loss. And that thought finally brought the tears.

"I wouldn't cry," came a deep voice behind her.

She turned, expecting to see the groundskeeper. Instead, the man from the restaurant stood a few feet away. He quickly positioned his camera, and before she could yelp, he took three or four pictures.

"What are you doing?" She stood, wiping the dirt from the legs of her blue jeans and fighting anger. A quick glance around helped her pinpoint where the groundskeeper was, now pulling up a cluster of weeds nearby. At least with the mower turned off, he'd be able to hear her if she screamed.

"Like you, I'm interested in Willie Raymond. But I'm not about to waste any tears over him."

"And why is that?"

"Because I don't believe he's dead."

Chapter 4

S he blinked but didn't say anything. He could see her emotions warring with each other. Should she believe him? Should she kick him in the shin and run? She'd make a great assignment: Redheads of the Midwest. Best of all, based on the way her chin was jutting out, she obviously had some doubts about Willie Raymond.

Her face flushed a shade of vibrant red, and she declared, "I don't believe you."

"There's no body in the coffin." He turned, preparing to whistle, but saw the groundskeeper just a few yards away. "Lionel, is that right?"

"Yup."

From the corner of his eye, Patrick watched Jessica sidle closer to Lionel. Patrick wasn't naïve. It wasn't that she needed to get close to the groundskeeper to hear; she felt she needed to be leery of Patrick.

Lionel looked somewhat amused. "What's your name, young lady?"

By the way she hesitated, Patrick wondered if she'd have given her name if it weren't for the expectant look on Lionel's face.

"Jessica Fleming."

Lionel's eyes lit up and he stuck out his hand. "Pleased to meetcha."

Jessica shook his hand. The man held it a bit longer than was necessary, but she didn't back away, which Patrick had figured she might do. Being a groundskeeper at a cemetery wasn't exactly a cushy job, and the dirt crusting the man's hands hadn't been brushed away.

Patrick put a hand on Jessica's shoulder; she started to move away but instead got caught up in his words. "Lionel, tell us about Willie Raymond."

The old man gave Jessica a hesitant look and finally repeated what he'd told Patrick that morning. "Interesting thing about Willie Raymond. He was what ya might call a no-show."

"A no-show?" Jessica asked.

"Yup, a no-show. There's only dirt residing under Willie's headstone. The government never returned his body. Of course, the family has never given up hope, which is why they don't put out remembrances."

"Are there other plots here without pe—corpses, er, caskets?" Jessica asked.

"Nope. Willie's the only one. He always did expect special treatment."

"You knew him?"

The woman should be a journalist. She'd asked the right questions and gotten more from the man than Patrick had, and he should have figured Lionel as being about the same age as Willie.

"Went to school with him, but that was a long time ago."

Jessica glanced back at Willie's headstone. "Was he married?"

"Maybe briefly, but not long enough so he brought her home to meet the family."

Lionel didn't seem to have much more to say. He excused himself, and soon the lawn mower roared.

"See what I mean?" Patrick took out a business card, handed it to her, and waited for the look of awe.

"Photojournalist," she said, frowning. "Like Willie Raymond. Did *you* know him?"

"I know his work. Let's head for town. I'll buy you dinner. We need to talk."

She looked back at the grave and bit her bottom lip. "Okay."

As he drove away from the cemetery, Patrick noted the groundskeeper dutifully writing down the license plate of both their vehicles. No doubt, just like the librarian, Lionel thought it peculiar that *two* strangers were interested in Willie Raymond.

The diner Jessica picked outperformed The Rusty Nail. His steak was juicy, the baked potato cooked, and the green beans crunchy. The best thing so far about photographing churches in the Midwest had been the food—and the Willie Raymond mystery.

"Jessica, I've—quite by accident—been tailing you most of the morning. You managed to snag the library information I wanted, you rented a room I intended to get, and then we both wound up at Willie Raymond's supposed final resting place at the same time. What are the odds? We're tracking the same guy. Twenty-six years he's been ignored, and suddenly we're both interested. Care to tell me why you're here?"

She shook her head, stabbed some salad, brought the bite to her lips, then put it back down untouched.

"Okay, I'd probably do the exact same thing if I were you,"

Patrick said. "Why should you trust me? I'm going out on a limb here; I'll trust you. I'll tell you why I'm looking for Willie. Then you decide if you want to share why you're looking for him."

She didn't get up and leave, which he took as a good sign. The waitress delivered a hot piece of apple pie with melting vanilla ice cream balanced on top. Patrick took a bite and wished the woman across from him would eat.

"Like I said back at the cemetery—" He took another quick bite before pulling a briefcase from under the table and awkwardly opening it to pull out a folder of photographs, "This is my current assignment. I'm photographing old churches across the Midwest. I take the photos, write the story behind them, and in about two years, my pictures and words will be bound in a coffee-table book."

She didn't nod, shake her head, or speak; she just looked at him—waiting.

"Ahem." He reached back in the briefcase and pulled about an oversized book. "This is one I did about seven years ago. Its focus was twofold. I was covering the earthquakes killing thousands of people in Afghanistan. Plus, as a side job, I was reporting on the U.S. missile strikes. I was there right when the Taliban was first being recognized as legitimate rulers by Pakistan and Saudi Arabia. I was riveted by the stories I found under the surface. Stories going back more than twenty years. In my spare time, I interviewed soldiers, shopkeepers—anyone who would talk with me. Once I distanced myself from the horrors, I did what I always do. I compared and contrasted now to then. For that assignment, I was featuring pictures that had been taken in the late sixties and early seventies to pictures taken, well, by me, seven years ago, present-day. I kept coming across the work of Willie Raymond. He was a fine photographer. Better than me. I remember thinking what a shame it was that he died over there."

She slowly took the book and looked at the back index before turning to the pages featuring Willie's work. He watched her face. Tenderness replaced boredom, and the gentler look became her. She touched the pages almost reverently.

He was missing something here. What was it? It hovered, some idea, some concept, something he needed to grasp.

"I really hadn't thought of Willie much since that assignment. Then I picked up this project covering the history of churches in the Midwest. While doing the preliminary research, I pulled a few recent photos of churches off the Internet. I remember thinking they looked eerily familiar, but I didn't put two and two together right then. I kept photographing more churches and digging up their histories. I spent the first two weeks I was in Nebraska hunting down preachers, old preachers, the older the better."

Most had tried to convert him. He figured he counted as fair game. After all, he'd traveled to their turf. A few had provided small details that might prove useful but more likely not. One had been a jackpot. Jimmy Tate was in his nineties and hadn't tried to convert him. A calm and straightforward man, Jimmy had made Patrick feel at ease. There was something about the man that had made Patrick want to listen—even to scriptures.

"I came across this one old man with lots of photos. Not all of them were of churches. And"—Patrick leaned closer to Jessica—"in his collection, I recognized the work of Willie Raymond."

Jimmy Tate had photos of the first church in Loving Heart. He'd once been the minister. Now he lived with a granddaughter and graded lessons for World Bible School. He'd been a camera buff since childhood. "The boy had an eye," Jimmy had agreed after Patrick recognized Willie's work. "I gave him his first camera, you know."

Patrick had headed for his car and his research, then hurried back inside and opened to a spread. "Do you see what I see?"

Jimmy Tate wasn't a man who moved past first gear. He'd thumbed through the book, nodded, held up his personal photos, and squinted. Then he'd stood up and left Patrick alone. Patrick had been about to pack up when Jimmy returned with two photos in his hand. Together, the two men had placed the photos side by side.

"Yes," Jimmy had agreed. "Willie's work is distinctive. His signature is all over them. I remember when he took this photo at a church picnic. He'd arranged my daughters two or three times. Then he rushed over to the little Marks girl, took her giant stuffed giraffe, and planted it behind where he wanted the shot." In each and every photo, the right side had some sort of towering landmark. Trees seemed to be Willie's favorite. But in a pinch, umbrellas or telephone poles graced the corner. In one photo a basketball hoop watched a gathering of geese.

Patrick had about come out of his skin. Never had a story hit him with such impact. Reaching in his briefcase, he'd brought out the recent church photos he'd downloaded from the Internet. Handing them to Jimmy Tate, he waited for the old man's opinion.

"Yup," Jimmy said. "Willie's work. Where'd you get these?"

Patrick hadn't voiced his suspicions to Jimmy Tate, hadn't pointed out the obvious, but now spreading the pictures in front of Jessica, he bared all. "Willie Raymond supposedly died more than twenty years ago." Separating a picture of a white cathedral with Fourth of July celebrants in front of it, he pointed to a date on a banner. "But he took this two years ago. I'd bet my camera it's Willie's work. Jessica, dead men don't aim cameras. Willie Raymond isn't dead. Now what do you know about him?"

She was tempted to deny she was looking for information about Willie Raymond, but a stack of library books and her interest in a grave marker had already given her away. She hid her shaking hands in her lap and asked, "What does it matter to you whether he's dead or alive?"

Patrick grinned. His eyes glittered in a way that made Jessica want to slide out of the booth and run to her car. He had what her mother called *presence*. Presence was fine if the person exuding it was a friend or family member. It wasn't fine when it came from an overbearing, too good-looking, *disturbing* stranger.

He seemed unaware of her discomfort and rambled on as if she were a typical, everyday confidante. "It'll be a great story: Noted photojournalist thought to be dead is really alive. Whatever it was that made him go into hiding must have been sensational."

Yes, especially since he hid from a daughter.

"I don't think I can help you. He's just, uh. . .someone I've taken an interest in."

278

"Are you related? What branch are you?" Patrick took out a stack of papers. "Willie had two brothers and one sister. Larry, the oldest brother, lives in Florida—no children. Thomas, the baby, lives here, three children: Beth, Opal, and Justin. Then there's a sister, Desiree; she lives here, again three children but all boys: Robert, William, and Timothy. I haven't gone further in my research; maybe you can help me."

Opal was her cousin. Funny, Jessica had figured as much, but hearing it spoken, aloud, even by Patrick McDonald, made it so *real*. Suddenly, Jessica didn't want the book or to be sitting across from Patrick McDonald hearing that not only did she have immediate family, but a birth father who was possibly *alive*.

She slid out of the booth. He could pay for the meal. She hadn't eaten so much as a bite. "Thanks for the meal. Good luck on your search, but I can't help you."

He let her slip away without protesting, even though a dozen questions flickered across his face.

For most of the drive to her lodgings, hers was the only car on the road. Rural Nebraska, at dusk, made Jessica wonder why Hollywood filmed anywhere else. The bright orange sun, hovering over a quaint farmhouse, belonged on a greeting card. The peaceful setting calmed her enough so that after parking her car, she had the courage to grab her suitcase and walk toward the Raymond Bed-and-Breakfast and the people who might have the answers to all her questions.

She'd not, in her wildest dreams, expected what Patrick McDonald had presented. It wasn't too late. She could head home, pretend this had never happened. But then she'd never sleep again. Jessica didn't need to knock, because Opal pushed open the screen door. "Can I help?"

"Nope. I just have this one." Jessica stepped into the kitchen. "Is this where I should come in, or should I use the front door?"

Opal picked up a knife and finished peeling a potato. "We do have a front door, but nobody uses it. Everyone likes the kitchen. Besides, Grandma's always sleeping in the living room. You use that door and you wake her up."

"You wake me up when you come in the kitchen door, too!" The singsong voice didn't sound like it belonged to someone named Grandma.

Opal grinned. "Never a dull moment around here. You want to meet her?"

"Of course she wants to meet me. I'm her landlord."

"No, Grandma," Opal called. "I'm her landlord; this is my house."

"My house first!"

Opal put down the potato peeler and hollered, "My house last!"

The banter between the two women almost brought tears to Jessica's eyes. This should be, could be, happening between her and Grandma Lydia. Well, now that she'd broken up with David—a seemingly not-too-distraught David—she could buy Grandma's house. Okay, not on a teacher's salary, but she could get a second job. And she could paint it, just like Opal was doing. Only Jessica would choose subtler colors.

Jessica blinked away the moisture threatening to overflow and followed Opal through a hallway. The living room had enough knickknacks to support a weeklong garage sale. There was green shag carpeting on the floor and dark brown paneling on the walls. The elderly woman sitting on the couch was as colorful as her granddaughter. A bright red pantsuit was off-set by a pink and orange scarf.

"Grandma Stacy," Opal said, "this is our new renter. Her name is Jessica Fleming. She'll be here for the summer."

Grandma looked up, nodded, pursed her lips, and said, "Jessica Fleming."

"Jessica Louise Fleming."

Grandma shook her head, her liquid blue eyes scrutinizing Jessica for a moment before she said, "What brought you here?"

Jessica had never been overly talkative, and now words eluded her. Stacy, a grandma named Stacy. It didn't seem possible. One thing was for sure: Jessica wanted more time. Things were happening too fast. She'd gone looking for her birth family; she'd definitely found them; and she wanted to get to know them. But an empty coffin lay in the cemetery, and a reporter dogged her every step. Who was Willie Raymond, and why did his family seem not to know she existed?

"Grandma," Opal said gently, saving Jessica from having to answer, "not everyone likes being interrogated. We talked about this. Remember?"

"Nonsense. Everyone has a story to share. Right, child?"

Jessica felt her cheeks flame. "Right," she finally said.

"Let's get you unpacked," Opal said, coming to the rescue.

In the living room, the suitcase hadn't been heavy; but now as Jessica climbed the stairs following Opal to her new room, the suitcase grew heavier—as did her heart.

Oh, this was a bad idea, she thought as she unpacked. A nausea that wouldn't go away accompanied every moment. She'd met a man with more questions than she had—and all of them frightening. She'd met people who *should* know her but didn't.

Had this been Willie Raymond's room? Had he stood at the window and stared off in the distance wondering what his future might be? Two months ago, Jessica's future had included a husband named David. One month ago, her past wasn't a mystery. Now it was a mystery she wanted to solve without the help of that know-it-all reporter.

A flowered armchair beckoned from next to a walk-in closet. Jessica changed into her pajamas and took out her cell phone to call her parents. A fifteen minute conversation did nothing to dispel their worries, probably because Jessica was just as worried. After disconnecting the phone, she plugged it in to charge and emptied her backpack on the bed, pulled out the yearbook from Willie's graduation year, and settled into the soft cushions. She thumbed through the pages. Only three Raymonds had attended Loving Heart High during Willie's senior year. He had been voted "Most Likely to Go the Distance." *Well, that was certainly true.* His younger sister, Desiree, had been having a bad hair experience on photo day. She'd been voted "Future Gossip Columnist." Tomorrow, Jessica would find Desiree. A gossip surely would have the scoop on Willie. The final Raymond was a lowly freshman. Andrew Raymond didn't look old enough to have been voted anything except wet behind the ears.

Taking out a piece of paper, Jessica wrote down all the names of Willie's graduating class. There were more than fifty. The only one she recognized was Lionel Payne. Under his picture—which depicted a young man with lots of black hair—a caption predicted that he'd see the world. He wanted to be a pilot. She wondered if he'd fulfilled that dream or if he'd been a groundskeeper all his life.

As for her birth father, Willie had played baseball. He'd worked on the newspaper. He'd even been in the school play, *Fiddler on the Roof*. He'd played the father. It must have been an interesting play—since her birth father's hair was as red as could be. The fake beard did a good job of hiding the complexion that didn't match a black wig. Come to think of it, this was probably the same picture she'd seen in the hallway earlier. She hadn't given it a close look at the time since the young man in the picture wasn't a redhead.

Jessica put the yearbook in a dresser drawer. Before crawling into bed, she took her Bible and found the story of the prodigal son. Was Willie Raymond the type of son who would foolishly turn his back on family?

I don't believe he's dead. She'd been keeping Patrick McDonald's words in the back of her mind, willing them to go away. It was bad enough to have unanswered questions, but then to find that she wasn't the only one!

Maybe she was the prodigal daughter. Her mom and dad were certainly mourning her leaving. They wouldn't kill a fatted calf if she returned, but they'd order a pizza with her favorite toppings.

This was probably all a wild-goose chase. Willie Raymond was dead and forgotten, his family a part of a mystery she might never solve.

She closed her Bible, keeping her finger in the book of Luke. Like the widow looking for a lost coin, Jessica had a feeling she'd never feel complete until she found what she was looking for.

Chapter 5

Loving Heart High School looked deserted during the summer, but a lone car in the driveway gave away an occupant, and the doorbell brought a secretary who didn't seem too eager to open the door to a stranger. "Can I help you?" she asked.

"I'm Patrick McDonald. I'm doing a piece on Midwest churches."

"Take a wrong turn, did you?" The secretary didn't look the least bit interested. "The church is a mile to the east."

She wasn't wearing a name tag, and her whole attitude told him that asking for her name might be a bad idea. Usually, if he could get them to open up, with a name at least, he was able to get information. He decided to be up front. "Actually, I've found some old photos of neighboring churches. I'm looking for the man who took them. Can you can give me some information about Willie Raymond?"

He'd never seen a face and door attempt to slam shut at the same time. He'd left his camera in the car, but, oh, he wanted it now. He'd put this photo next to the farmer from Linnage and title the page "Faces That Speak." Putting his foot between the door and the doorjamb, he kept her from severing contact.

Obviously, this time, the truth was the wrong choice. "Ma'am, I just ne—"

"Student privacy laws prevent me from sharing information. Good day."

"Excuse me." The voice behind him was soft and lyrical.

Turning around, Patrick almost moved his foot and lost his toehold.

Jessica Fleming stood behind him. She gave Patrick an annoyed look and said, "I've got some of the same questions. I believe the privacy issue is null and void since William Raymond is deceased."

"Willie was a friend of mine." The woman couldn't seem to take her eyes off Jessica. "I'm sure you'll understand if I'd rather not talk about him. But I'll pass on your interest to the principal of Loving Heart High. He's on vacation until Monday."

"Does he live here in town?" Jessica asked. She looked at ease, as if scrutiny by a school secretary wasn't unusual.

"He does, but he's in Omaha right now."

Jessica took a notebook from her purse. "Can you tell me who Desiree Raymond married?"

"She married Mark Sherman. They own the bowling alley. Now move your foot."

Patrick moved his foot and waited until the echo of the slamming door faded away. "The bowling alley is right by my motel."

Jessica busily scribbled in her notebook.

"I'll go there with you," Patrick offered. He'd love to get his hands on her notebook, but the quick peek he managed only assured him that Jessica's future lay in the medical field. Her handwriting was quite illegible. Funny, last night's Internet search identified her as an elementary schoolteacher.

"Why should I go anywhere with you?"

Patrick grinned and nodded. "Because I have answers to some of your questions. Maybe even questions you haven't thought to ask."

"Okay."

Patrick almost laughed. He'd been expecting an argument. "So you admit it. You need me."

"Yes." She flipped the pages of the notebook. "I need you to tell me about the power struggle between Hafizoo. . . Hafizut—"

"Hafizullah Amin?"

"Yes, him and Nur Mohammed Taraki. What happened, and why would Willie Raymond be involved? We were on friendly terms with Afghanistan in 1979. Why was my—why was Willie Raymond over there?"

"Probably investigating the death of Amin. He was executed that year. Where did you get all this information?"

"I interviewed Andrew Raymond this morning."

He'd been on Patrick's list, too.

The school's secretary moved a curtain aside to stare at them. Taking Jessica by the elbow, he guided her toward the cars. "Who else have you spoken with?"

"No one. The exchange we just had with the secretary seems to be typical of all anyone is willing to share."

"Except Andrew?"

"And his cell phone rang while I was there. After he hung up, he excused himself. Said he had an appointment."

"Could be true," Patrick said.

"I was talking to him out in a cornfield. He was busy working. I doubt very much he was at a place where he'd typically crawl out of the tractor and take off."

"You think someone on the phone warned him about you?"

"That's exactly what I think."

"Why?"

"I was hoping you could tell me."

"What makes you think I might know?"

"You're the one who claims Willie Raymond isn't dead."

"Good point. Well, it will be interesting to watch as we try to get information about Willie Raymond from a town that wants to share nothing. Although my gut feeling is that you have a bit more influence with the townspeople than you're willing to share. Yesterday I told you almost everything I knew. Seems to me, you should be willing to do the same. Especially since you want my help."

Vulnerable or not, she had "stubborn" mastered. "I said I'd go to the bowling alley with you, that doesn't mean I have anything to share *with you.*"

"You know, Jessica, there's strength in numbers."

"Unfortunately, you're probably right." She climbed into her car.

He tailed her the whole way, careful not to exceed the speed limit. Not that Jessica had a lead foot. Either she was as suspicious as he, or she was Little Miss Perfect. He suspected the latter and thought it a shame. He'd never had much luck with good girls.

She didn't appear to be the exception.

Glancing in his mirror, he saw only dirt roads behind him, train tracks beside him, and the dust from Jessica's Chevy in front of him. There really wasn't much dust, but then her Chevy wasn't much more than a matchbox car. Ruefully, he grinned. Her car wasn't one that called for attention. But then she didn't seem to be the type who needed attention, although with her looks, he'd bet she got plenty.

His black Ford F-250, on the other hand, shouted *I'm bigger than you are!* Plus, he found that with his male sources, often all he had to do was break the ice with, "It's four-wheel drive and has torque...," and it was amazing how they opened up. Of course, sometimes they opened up more than he expected. His stories often got him into trouble. He'd had experience with small-town justice, and for Jessica's sake, he wished he'd rented a plain brown sedan. Loving Heart didn't really want them there. The police could make their stay uncomfortable.

Funny, the thought of being uncomfortable had never bothered him before. He'd been in jail in Mexico; they didn't like American journalists taking photos of the trafficking of illegals across the border. He'd been in jail in Arizona City; they didn't like journalists capturing the likenesses of plural families for posterity. Being incarcerated had inspired one of his best-selling books. From the turn-of-the-century Yuma Prison to Alcatraz to San Quentin, Patrick had made the rounds covering the history of the prison system.

While the Willie Raymond story didn't appear dangerous on the surface, Patrick knew that fate was a fickle companion. Too much information had gone missing about Raymond. Patrick wasn't sure how Jessica was connected to the Raymond family or why she was suddenly pursuing the same man as he. At the moment, all he knew was that for some reason he felt inclined to do everything in his power to keep Jessica from knowing the indignities of justice gone awry. He wasn't a bit comfortable with the fact that sometime between yesterday and today, he'd become more interested in the redhead than in the story.

❧⧉❧

The Loving Heart Bowling Alley easily rated as one of the most run-down buildings in town. Barn-red paint peeled from a structure that could use an introduction to nails and shingles. A brown dog lay in front of the open front door. There were four cars in the parking lot. Jessica doubted if all their parts combined would equal one working vehicle.

She parked by the sign that advertised SUMMER SPECIAL: CANOE RENTAL $25.00 PER PERSON. Patrick pulled in beside her. He drove an ugly, giant truck that dwarfed her little Chevy. He climbed down from the vehicle and waited for her. She wasn't sure she wanted to follow him, but it did feel good to have someone by her side.

Without a word, they walked into the bowling alley and through a maze of video games, pool tables, and boating paraphernalia. Nervousness made her dig her fingernails into her palms. Finding the truth about her father was getting harder instead of easier. By this time, she had expected to know his history, favorite food, favorite sports team, favorite restaurant, and favorite hobby—besides photography.

Instead, she'd met Patrick McDonald, who claimed Willie Raymond was alive, and now there was more reason than shock value to keep her parentage a secret. And much of the blame belonged to the man in front of her.

He really was an interesting-looking guy. Brown hair curled against the collar of his polo shirt. Tan chinos proved that the wrinkled look wasn't all that bad. Brown work boots covered his feet. Taller than David, he seemed like an uncomfortable Jimmy Stewart maneuvering in a world where doorways and ceiling beams were designed for the Jessicas of the world.

He didn't seem bothered by the mess. Jessica couldn't help but stop to stare. There were only five lanes, and judging by the haphazard placement of pins and balls, they hadn't been used in a while. Probably the Shermans ran the bowling alley in the winter and switched to canoeing in the summer.

"Desiree Sherman?" Patrick asked.

Without answering, the woman reached for a form and said, "You'll only have time for the two-hour ride. The final pickup is at six."

"We're not here for a canoe ride," Jessica said.

Desiree Sherman looked up. Red hair mimicked acrobatic endeavors and defied the barrettes that so bravely tried to control it. They had not only height in common, but a sprinkling of freckles that skipped across their noses. Jessica almost stopped breathing. This is what she would look like in twenty years.

"What do you want?" Desiree said. "The safe answer would be canoe rates and pickup times."

"Why is that?" Jessica asked.

Desiree pushed an errant curl away from her eyes and frowned at Jessica. "Looks to me like today you're visiting the Raymonds in ABC order. I figured you'd get to me sooner or later."

290

Suddenly Jessica wanted time to regroup before taking on this woman—an aunt who obviously knew who Jessica was but wasn't willing to admit it in so many words. "I've never been canoeing."

"And in those clothes, you aren't going today." Desiree shook her head as if Jessica's sanity was in question.

Patrick had been silent during the interchange, but now he looked at Jessica as if he'd just noticed her and she were a prized possession. Looking down, she knew she'd dressed sensibly—but not for canoeing, of course—in black slacks and a loose black-and-white, short-sleeved shirt. Black sandals covered her feet, and a black box purse held her identification and notebook.

"I didn't mean for today. We want to make reservations for tomorrow morning."

Desiree took out a card and wrote. "Jessica Fleming, 222 East Mocking Bird, 555-1538. I'll bet my mother's beside herself having you stay there. We open at seven."

"That would be fine." Jessica walked to the counter and leaned against it. Her heart was beating so loudly she couldn't believe the others couldn't hear it. "Why did you say that about your mother? That she's beside herself?"

Desiree didn't even blink, and Jessica knew the words hadn't been a slip.

"Only a few of us know about you," Desiree said slowly, "but for everyone involved, it's better that you just disappear. Please go back to your family."

"What are you talking about?" Patrick asked. He looked at Jessica, the question directed at her, as if she'd spoken the words.

Jessica swallowed, her eyes filling with tears. "Disappear? Like my father? Tell me why and I will."

"I can't. But believe me, it's what your father would have wanted. If you have any feelings at all for him, you'll respect his wishes."

"It's hard to respect the wishes of someone you didn't know existed! With that being the case, how can I have feelings for him?"

"You're here, aren't you?"

Chapter 6

"You have nothing to share!" Patrick wasn't about to lose track of this woman, even as she flew out of the building. Never had he felt such anger—or was it disappointment?

"I didn't lie," Jessica protested, skidding to a halt. "I said I had nothing to share *with you*."

Patrick stopped so fast he almost tripped over his own feet. "When I told you Willie Raymond, *your father*, was alive, you didn't even blink. How can that be?"

She had her car door open.

He managed to grab the top, stopping her from flight. "I spent weeks researching *your father*. There's no mention of you! Who were you adopted by? What was your birth mother's name?"

"I'm not telling you. Leave me alone and let go of my door."

He let go because he wasn't sure if the fear in her eyes was due to him or due to her father. No matter, he didn't like her frantic movements. "Jessica, I'm the only one in this town who wants to know the truth as badly as you do. We can still help each other."

"I don't need help."

"Yes, you do. This is not something you should deal with alone."

She sagged against the car door. It took him two steps to get to her, and this time she didn't fight. He could feel her body shuddering against him as she fought the tears. She nestled her head against his shoulder, and he was lost. And angry! At himself! Why now? Why this woman? Where were these feelings coming from? It didn't pay to get personally involved with a source. And this could be the story of the century for him.

Gently, he pushed her away. "Why are you doing this alone? Where is your family? Why aren't they helping?"

She bit her lower lip. "Why? They don't know I'm here. And every time I mention Willie Raymond to them, they tell me the same thing: It's better I don't know and that the Raymonds severed all ties with me."

"How would they know to say that?"

"I'm not sure, completely. My whole family knew Willie Raymond, and it was Carol's sister who adopted me. For some reason, my grandfather convinced the family not to tell me the truth. Everyone begged me to leave this alone."

"What happened to your mother?"

"She died right after I was born. Complications of childbirth."

"What was her name?"

"Carol. I guess Carol Raymond."

"Impossible," Patrick said. "What was her—her maiden name?"

"Dunmore."

"Jessica, Willie couldn't have been married to your mother. He was never married. I have his military records. He listed his mother as his beneficiary."

"I have the marriage license," Jessica said slowly, "and quite a few pictures."

❧

Even if the marriage license was fake—which he doubted— the wedding photos she'd pulled out of the trunk of her car were enough to convince him.

"Jessica, do you know what this means?"

"No, but I'm sure you have a theory." Jessica picked up a black-and-white photo from the pile of papers he'd placed in front of her. It had been taken by Willie Raymond, but she didn't know that—probably wouldn't believe that. She wasn't as jaded as he was. If anything, she was probably the most innocent woman he'd met in a long time. She hadn't been willing to compare notes in his motel room, and it was broad daylight, so they'd sequestered themselves in what served as the breakfast nook of his motel. Since it was well after noon, they had table space and privacy to spare.

She glanced up, and he almost gasped. Talk about a photo opportunity. The sun cast a shimmering light that surrounded her like a body halo. She had kicked off her shoes, tucked one leg under the other, and spread everything on the table in order of date. That didn't surprise him since the papers she'd handed him had been in messily labeled folders. She, apparently, was even more skilled than he at getting information from the Internet.

She impressed him—and it scared him to death.

Taking another folder from his bag, he pulled out the few military documents he'd managed to acquire about Raymond's time in the service. "Someone made their marriage license disappear from both public and military records. Someone wanted Willie's past, as well as Willie, to disappear."

"He didn't disappear; he died."

"I tell you, he's not dead. Look at these photos." Patrick took the photo from her hand and spread it out next to about ten others, arranging them in the order they were probably taken: starting with town picnics from before Jessica was born, moving on to the Afghanistan year, and ending with the recent church photos. "This first one was taken here in Loving Heart before he even met your mother. This gruesome one he took in 1979. And these he probably shot about three years ago in Linnage, Nebraska. I've studied Raymond's work extensively. He took all of them."

"Oh, how can you tell?" Doubt dripped from every word.

He pulled the other chair around so he was sitting next to her. "Look." Carefully he explained the attention taken with the light, with the positioning of the camera, and with the arrangement of objects. When he finished, she didn't believe him. He could tell by the way she raised her eyebrow. Although she was too polite to call him a liar.

"Jessica, the man's alive, and only a few people know what really happened. Otherwise, why would his family be either ignorant of you or dead set against accepting you?"

"I don't think the family is dead set against me. We've only met one person who acted like they knew I existed." She set down a photo she'd been examining. "I've bungled this. I should have told them the truth from the moment I arrived in town.

After all, Willie *was* married to my birth mother."

"If Willie died overseas, there'd be no reason to keep you a secret; no reason for a marriage license to disappear. You'd be entitled to survivor benefits. You know that. You're not stupid."

"I might be stupid for trusting you."

He shut up because she was right. She shouldn't trust him. He'd never had any qualms before while pursuing a story, but this one. . . Something told him this one would make or break him, and it was all her fault—for making him care.

They were sitting close; the smell of her perfume was a tangible fruity scent he could live with for the rest of his life. But he didn't have a life, he had a career, with a potential award-winning story. It was what he'd always wanted.

"Jessica, you dig into research and books as if you were born to it. I'll bet you've been a bookworm all your life. Am I right?"

"Yes."

"Do you read mysteries?"

"All the time."

"Then tell me, in a good mystery, whenever there's no body, what does that mean?"

She shook her head. "This isn't fiction. This is real. Willie Raymond was a real man. Not a figment of someone's imagination."

"Come on, Jessica. I've got you thinking. There's no body. What does that mean?"

"The dead person is really alive and is the murderer."

"Except your father wasn't a murderer. Although I think he pretended to be murdered."

"Why?" Jessica asked.

"He was military, and he saw or possibly even took a photo of something that got him into trouble." Patrick reached for one of the Afghanistan pictures. "I wonder what he saw."

"Saw?" Jessica looked numb, and pale, and mad, if all three were possible at the same time.

Patrick stood up and paced the small room. "If he got in trouble in the military, he'd be dishonorably discharged or court-martialed. There's no record of that. There'd be no reason for his marriage license to disappear and for you to be kept a secret."

Color came back to her face, and with it, righteous indignation. She stood up, ready to denounce him and leave. He respected her for it.

Yes, this story could very well make him, but more likely it would break him. Because for the first time, he felt the urge to protect the source at all costs. Oh, he'd always protected his sources, but never by compromising—by burying—the story.

Patrick continued. "I think he saw something, probably had a hand in making the Taliban angry, and he disappeared in order to stay alive. You're a secret because it keeps *you* alive."

"Oh, come on." She grabbed her purse from the table. "No wonder you're a journalist. What an imagination."

"Yes, I have an imagination, and you'd be surprised by how often I'm right. But more important, do you have any other explanations for what we've discovered?"

"No, I don't, but that doesn't make you right."

"I agree. We need to dig some more."

She shook her head. Her words were almost a whisper. "I think I do better alone."

"I think *alone* is the last thing you need."

She took a step but didn't leave. There were words, he knew, that would convince her to stay, but he couldn't find them. Finally, he managed, "We have a date tomorrow."

She turned back, wariness in her eyes. "You're kidding."

"I'll meet you at the canoe place at eight sharp."

"Oh, puh-leeze."

"When Desiree talks, we'll need to sift through the truth. I have more contacts than you."

"And that should make me trust you?"

"I'm not asking for trust."

She stepped into the hallway. "Good, because I'm not giving it."

She didn't tarry, almost afraid Patrick would convince her to stay and force her to face more obstacles, more truths about the man who had given her red hair and height and who *wasn't* buried in the Loving Heart Cemetery. Goose bumps prickled her arms. All this was happening because papers had been hidden in her favorite antique—her grandmother's dresser—and Jessica just had to stumble across them.

Patrick McDonald's argument was that they needed to work together because he had more contacts. Yeah, right. Well, she had contacts, too. Contacts who hadn't lied but who'd only told her what they thought she should know. It was time to make a phone call and push past what she *should* know and find out what she *needed* to know.

In Casper she always went to talk with Grandma, but in a pinch, the phone would do. Pulling into the library's parking lot, she looked for a secluded area. Picnic tables dotted the green lawn. A few children played at the nearby park as the sun continued its downward curve. Their noise didn't bother her. Why should noise, children, everyday politics, and the lack of sleep bother her? She had other things that bothered her more.

Hard to believe she'd been in Loving Heart just two days—two jam-packed days. Maybe now that she knew so much, she could convince Grandma to talk. Finding a secluded picnic table, she settled in and dialed Lydia Dunmore's cell phone. Grandma didn't like new gadgets, but once she realized that owning this particular little gadget—which rang at inopportune times and often cut out in mid conversation—meant more contact with the grandkids, she'd embraced the idea wholeheartedly.

"Hello, Grandma," Jessica chirped after Lydia answered. Holding the phone away from her ear, she grimaced. *Great,* she thought, *I sound like a dying quail.*

"You sound funny," Lydia greeted. "Everything all right?"

Funny how Grandma always picks up on moods. When Jessica and her cousins had been young, Grandma had always seemed to know which one needed hugs the most. Today, Jessica certainly felt the need for one. "I'm in Loving Heart. Grandma, tell me everything you know. Please."

Lydia didn't answer right away. Finally, after Jessica left the picnic table and started pacing, Grandma said, "Jessica, we went over this already. Carol fell in love, married without our permission, and the boy died before we had a chance to get to know him."

"That much I believe. Grandma, it's what you're not telling me that will keep me in Loving Heart and maybe in trouble—"

"Trouble!" Lydia's voice rose.

Jessica winced. Everyone kept reminding her Grandma was not the woman she used to be. That's why she shouldn't live alone. That's why the family had looked for assisted living. For the first time, Jessica thought about *old*. Grandma shouldn't be excited.

Stupid papers.

"Grandma, there's no body buried in Willie Raymond's grave. Most of the family doesn't know I exist, and the only one who admits to knowing who I am told me to go away. Grandma, why do I have a copy of Willie and Carol's marriage license when the military has no paperwork documenting a marriage? Could Carol have lied to you?"

"No, they were married. Evelyn was the witness, and Carol would never lie to us."

"Grandma, there's a reporter here. He's hunting for Willie Raymond, too. He says Willie's not dead."

Silence. The kind that could be cut with a knife. Jessica felt the phone grow hot against her ear, so she switched sides and waited.

And waited.

"Stay away from this reporter," Lydia finally said.

"Why?"

"Come home."

"Why?"

"Because we love you and want you to be safe. We always have."

"Grandma, there's a girl here, my age. I'm renting a room from her, and you know what? She looks like me. Red hair, tall, freckles. . . I think she's my cousin. She lives with her grandmother, Stacy Raymond. Does that name mean anything to you?"

More silence, so Jessica continued. "It's amazing. I've been studying the Raymond family portraits in the hallway of her home, and I see my nose. I see my smile. And I *have* to know."

"Oh, I didn't think it would go this far."

"How far?"

"I thought you'd get there, realize William Raymond was dead, and come home. Well, your grandfather always said I was a dreamer. Have you talked with this reporter?"

"Yes. He says that Willie Raymond was in Afghanistan and probably saw something he shouldn't have. He's really a photojournalist, and his name is Patrick McDonald. He thinks that Willie isn't dead but is in some kind of witness protection program."

"Does this reporter know who you are?"

"Yes."

"You told him!"

"No, a woman named Desiree Sherman told him."

"Desiree? You've spoken to Desiree?"

"Do you know her?"

"Not personally, but a long time ago"—Lydia's voice softened—"more than twenty years ago, when you were a baby, I spoke to her on the phone. Once. What has she told you, and why did she tell this reporter who you were?"

"She didn't tell me anything except that I should go home, and I don't think she realized he was a reporter. I'm pretty sure she thought he was my boyfriend."

"You need to avoid him."

"Why, Grandma?"

"Child—"

"Why, Grandma?"

"Because you're right. Willie Raymond didn't die overseas. He went into hiding. And to save you, he even hid from you."

Chapter 7

Lydia Dunmore had plenty to say—so much so that later, when Jessica finally made it back to the Raymonds' house, dusk's gray tentacles brushed the cornfields with an invisible finger. Jessica could imagine God spelling words amid the crop. Maybe He'd write, *I love you.* Maybe He'd write, *I gave my Son for you.* Maybe He'd write, *Prodigal child, go home.*

She sat in the car for a few minutes, weighing her options and talking to God. She'd neglected Him since arriving in Loving Heart. She'd been on a mission, and perhaps if she had trusted in her Father, her stomach wouldn't be churning now.

Grandma Lydia always said Jessica worried too much. Trust in God, Grandma Lydia had said after finally spilling all. *All* took about ten minutes. Not much to go on, but enough to know that Willie was alive, but probably not in Loving Heart.

After she hung up the phone, her first instinct was to pack and disappear immediately, but Patrick McDonald would follow her back to Casper and gnaw at the threads of a twenty-six-year-old secret. She couldn't allow those threads to break until she knew what they concealed. Somehow she had to get

Patrick off Willie Raymond's scent.

Even if it meant she also lost the chance to meet the man who'd fathered her.

Opal's car was gone when Jessica pulled her Chevy into the driveway. The solitary living room light cast a welcoming glow, which meant that Stacy Raymond was home. If Opal were home, every light would be burning. Yup, Stacy and Grandma were cut from the same cloth. They'd never leave a light burning in a room they didn't occupy.

Taking the key from her purse, Jessica took a deep breath and headed for the front door. Switching on the kitchen light, she wondered why Opal and Stacy didn't have a dog. Everyone should have a dog—especially if they were related to a spy.

"That you, Jessica?" Stacy called.

"Yes."

"You have a good day?"

"Yes."

"Can you lend me twenty dollars?"

"Yes—what?"

"Caught you." Stacy Raymond was curled in the corner of the couch crocheting a burgundy, gray, and beige afghan. The television was on loud and some late-night judge was reprimanding a woman for lending money to her deadbeat ex-boyfriend.

"Silly shows," Stacy said. "I watch them for laughs. Do you watch much?"

"No, not really. Back home I'm either grading papers or out with. . ."

"With?"

"I broke up with my fiancé right before I came here."

305

"Then why is he here with you?"

"He's not."

The afghan settled on Stacy's lap as the crochet needle stilled. "Then who is the man you spend all your time with? We thought he was your fiancé."

"He's not with me; he just happened to arrive about the same time I did. His name is Patrick McDonald. He's a photojournalist."

Stacy paled, not an easy feat for a fair-skinned woman. "Oh. You'll need to excuse me. I have to make a phone call."

"Who will you call?" Jessica asked. "Desiree? Opal? *Willie?*"

The afghan slipped to the ground. "I don't know whether to scold you or hug you."

Jessica picked up the afghan and folded it onto a chair before carefully sitting down. "I just got off the phone with my grandmother, Lydia Dunmore. Do you know her?"

"Yes, and I wondered why she let you come here."

"She didn't let me. Everyone tried to stop me, but after I found the papers—"

"What papers?"

"The adoption papers."

"They didn't tell you that you were adopted?"

Jessica's throat closed and she couldn't swallow. She could feel her teeth clenching so tightly that her jaw hurt.

Stacy reached down and took a hank of yarn and a needle. "You know how to crochet?"

Jessica shook her head.

"My father taught me," Stacy said. "Your great-grandfather."

Jessica swallowed, finally able to breath. "Great-grand*father?*"

Stacy laughed. "And who says the new generation isn't

gender biased. My father would come in from working in the fields all day, and we'd eat. Then, just before bedtime, we'd all head out to the front porch, and he'd crochet and talk to me and my mother. It was our favorite time. He's the one who passed on the red hair and freckles."

"They didn't tell me I was adopted," Jessica said slowly. "I was getting married next summer. My fiancé bought a house, and we were moving this old dresser. Grandma said I could have it. It was my treasure from the attic. The papers fell out of a drawer."

"I'm not going to say I'm sorry that you're here. Worried, yes; sorry, no. I've dreamed about meeting you. Of course, for some reason, I still pictured you as a child. All Willie got was the birth picture. I have a copy of it, and even that's hidden."

"Grandma says Willie's not dead. Do you know where he is?"

"I do, and he knows you're here. He's just not sure what to do about it. How much do you know?"

"I know he went in the witness protection program and for my safety his marriage to Carol was erased. Surely the danger has passed. It's been more than twenty-five years."

"We were getting to the point where we thought it had, and then September eleventh happened. If the danger were truly past, Willie Raymond would own this farm and you'd be a grandchild I could openly buy a Christmas present for. If the danger was past, the thought of a photojournalist being in town wouldn't frighten me."

"It frightens me, too."

Stacy shook her head, reached over, and put her hand on top of Jessica's. "You are more beautiful than I imagined. My son is a brave man, and he sacrificed fatherhood so you could live a happy, safe life. He knows you're here, and he wants you to return to the parents who raised you. When—and if—he thinks it's possible, he'll contact you."

"What about Patrick McDonald?"

"I'll let Willie know what's going on. He'll figure something out."

"Stacy, I truly do believe Patrick McDonald will not only uncover Willie's whereabouts, but also put Willie in danger. That's the reason I came to talk to you. Otherwise, I'd respect Willie's wishes and leave tonight. I'm meeting Patrick in the morning. Before we get everyone all riled up, let me keep my date with him and see if I can convince him to leave this whole situation alone."

"You think you can do that?"

"I think there's a chance."

❧❦❧

The bowling alley's parking lot was fairly full when Patrick pulled in at eight the next morning. Jessica's car was next to a junker up on four cement blocks. Knowing that she arrived before he did worried him. Maybe she'd managed to get Desiree to talk. And he doubted Jessica would share information. Pushing past a lazy dog, he entered the bowling alley to find Jessica sitting on top of a pool table, swinging her legs nervously and reading an old magazine.

She looked a bit different. Her lime-green one-piece bathing suit was covered by an open, bright pink shirt bearing green polka dots. Her shorts were yellow, as were her flimsy sandals. Her hair was tied back with a green scrunchie.

"I'm wearing Opal's clothes," she explained. "She insisted."

"Is she a redhead, too?"

"How did you know?"

"It just figures."

He needed to meet this Opal and get a photo.

Jessica grinned, but that didn't erase the fatigue from her eyes, and he wondered what she'd done after leaving him last night. Obviously she hadn't slept much.

A line of people were filling out canoe rental forms and talking excitedly about their upcoming adventure. Jessica slid off the pool table and joined the line. "Desiree's pretty good about avoiding eye contact. She definitely doesn't want to talk."

And for some reason, neither did he. At least not with Desiree. It had been a long time since he'd looked forward to something unrelated to work. And, yes, he knew this venture had started out work related, but looking at Jessica's golden skin and bouncing ponytail, he knew that work was the last thing on his mind. There was something appealing about the thought of being alone in a canoe with her for several hours.

When it was their turn, Desiree frowned and turned their paperwork over to a teenager who'd been busy selling other customers waterproof key rings and potato chips.

"Two, four, or six hours?" the teenager asked.

"Two," Jessica said.

"Six," Patrick said.

"I'll put down four," the kid said.

Taking advantage of Jessica's annoyance, Patrick answered the rest of the questions and turned over his credit card.

"What's your name?" Jessica asked the teenager as he copied down information.

"William Sherman."

"William Conner Sherman?"

"How'd you know?" He looked surprised.

"I take it every generation has a William Conner?"

"Here's a map," Desiree interrupted before her son could answer. She moved back to the counter. "Drive to this spot, and a bus will pick you up. Then the bus will drop you off at Point Three. Your car will be at Point Seven. Make sure you watch the signs. You'll probably see some other canoes pulled up on the side. Just leave your canoe."

"Should I know you?" William Conner asked Jessica.

"No," Desiree said firmly. "Thank you for your business. Good day."

Jessica nodded. Patrick got the idea she'd accomplished whatever she was after. He'd love to know what. Four hours in a canoe should give him time to wear her down.

"Let's take my truck," he suggested. "I've driven the roads. They're pretty rough."

She nodded and headed for the passenger side of his truck. Climbing in, she pushed aside the cooler he'd bought last night.

"I packed water, chips, and stuff," he explained.

"Good idea."

"You pack anything?"

She reached in a pocket and pulled out a small tube. "Sunblock."

"A definite redhead necessity."

"Definitely."

Jessica studied the map Desiree had shoved at them, and her nose wrinkled. "I've never been canoeing," she finally said.

"I've never even been on a boat, except a few times when I went fishing with my grandfather."

"You'll have fun. I promise."

Almost an hour later, they'd been equipped with a canoe, two paddles, two life jackets, and a reminder about where to exit the Niobrara.

He'd put Jessica at the front, partially because it made things easier on her, but mostly because it made things easier on him—or at least on his eyes. She frowned when she got her sandals wet. Then she explored with the paddle, dipping it first on the right, then on the left, until she felt comfortable with how it moved the canoe. Around them were other canoes and a few large inner tubes, some holding as many as five people. A radio played classic rock.

It just might turn out to be a perfect day, Patrick mused. For the first time in years, he didn't long for his camera. He intended to just live today. Once Jessica was settled, he pushed away from the bank. "So why did you ask the kid his name? And how did you figure he was in a long line of William Conners?"

"Last night I studied the portraits and photos hanging in Stacy's hallway. She has a habit of writing names and events at the bottom. I noticed four William Conners. Since I'll never meet my birth father, I'm trying to get an idea of what he was like when he was young."

"You'll meet him. I'm convinced."

"No, I'm done searching. Finding him can only cause heartache. Besides, I'm starting to believe he is dead."

Her words were forced, and he knew she wanted him to assure her he'd also drop his detective work.

When he didn't reply, she started ignoring him—as if silence would convince him. Luckily, he enjoyed just watching her. She seemed content to paddle on just one side of the boat. He wished he could see her face and memorize the concentration he figured pinched her forehead.

A gentle touch might soothe her.

Or a gentle touch while on a canoe might land them both in the river. He deftly guided the canoe so they didn't hit the bridge support. The Niobrara quickly absorbed his attention. Steep sandstone canyons flanked the calm river. Up ahead, Patrick could see tall oak, ponderosa, and paper birch trees. In a few hours they'd hit Smith Falls, the biggest waterfall in Nebraska. It felt like a vacation. Not since he was a child, visiting his grandmother, could he remember taking a vacation.

It wasn't possible that in just three days, one woman had had such an effect on him. He needed to focus, get back to business. A noisy bird broke the hypnotic pull of the peaceful river, and Patrick cleared his throat and said, "Even though you are no longer interested, would you care to share whatever else you uncovered last night?"

"I called my grandma. She says Willie Raymond is dead and I should come home."

"And you believe her?"

"I always listen to my grandma."

"That's not what I asked. I asked if you believed her."

"I believe her."

"No, you don't."

"I do. I'm going home tomorrow. I wish you would do the same."

"I don't have a home."

"But I do, and you're threatening it."

Now her words bothered him, more than he wanted to admit. But there were still details to uncover, things he wanted to know. "What else did your grandmother say?"

"Never trust a photojournalist. Seems Willie Raymond left a legacy."

He couldn't see her face, but he heard the ire in her tone. Resting the paddle on his lap, he snagged two bottles of water from the cooler and passed one up to her. She took it with one hand and laid her paddle in the bottom of the boat with the other. Then she took off her sandals, arranged the extra life jacket as padding against the middle canoe seat, and in what looked like an impossibly awkward movement, settled down so she was looking up at the sky instead of straight ahead and paddling. She closed her eyes, and although he had more questions than answers, he decided to just let her be for a moment. A moment turned into an hour.

When she finally sat up, she stretched and started trying to yank herself into a seated position. She had one leg in the air when it occurred to him to warn her, remind her that she wasn't on land and to be careful. Before he could get the words out, the canoe hit an underwater protrusion, skidded a bit, stopped, and swerved left. Her leg kicked for a moment, then both hands lost their grip and down she went. Luckily, still in the canoe. Unluckily, her head hit the seat with a clunk that made him wince.

He struggled to get the canoe away from the rock. "You okay?"

"No!"

He chuckled, because if she could speak, obviously the pain

was external. "About time you started being sociable."

She sat up. Retrieving her paddle, she glanced at the offending rock and helped him move forward.

Letting her take over for a moment, he opened the cooler and pulled out a floppy hat. "When the motel manager heard we were canoeing today, she lent me these." He tossed her a black Gilligan hat and took the Atlanta Braves cap for himself.

"What do you think?" he asked, putting it on.

"It's not you."

She was right. He never wore headgear, not even baseball caps, and at one time he'd covered the major league.

She looked, um, interesting. The hat was at least two sizes too big and fell over her forehead, almost obscuring her eyes.

He smiled, trying not to wish for his camera and wanting this day to last forever.

She started to smile back, and for a moment he felt a connection. Then she looked down and lifted one foot. "Hey!"

"Hay is for horses and—"

"The canoe is leaking."

"Canoes always gather a bit of water."

"This is more than a bit."

His tennis shoes *were* a bit damp, now that he thought about it. Looking down, he saw the water swishing and then the cooler moved. Yup, it was a bit much.

"What do we do?"

She didn't sound concerned. He liked that. It meant she trusted him.

"Don't worry," he said. "We have a few minutes before we go down with the ship. Keep up with me."

Digging in with the paddles, they rowed up to a few other

canoes, and he shouted, "Hey, what do you do if your canoe is leaking?"

Laughter greeted him. A few minutes later, they knew that faulty canoes were an everyday occurrence. Basically, the advice was, "If you can make it, there's a sandbar up ahead, or if you think you can't, pull over now." Patrick decided on now. He studied the bank and wasn't too thrilled with his choices. No matter where he looked, they'd be climbing through plants, weeds, and overgrown shrubbery.

"Put your shoes back on," he advised.

He picked an area that didn't have a forbidding sandstone wall. They dragged the canoe a safe distance inland. Unwelcoming foliage pricked his legs. He looked at Jessica. An hour earlier, she'd been annoyed when her sandals were sullied. Now she didn't seem to mind a sweat-stained T-shirt and a silly hat that had ruined a good hair day.

She'd never looked more appealing.

His father had always claimed that women were trouble.

If that were the case, then Patrick was in trouble.

Big trouble.

Chapter 8

With one hand, Patrick managed the cooler. He'd hiked rougher terrain than this; Jessica obviously had not. Her colorful sandals were not meant for hiking. Every time she stumbled, he managed to steady her. He convinced her to merely slow down when she wanted to stop. He told funny anecdotes about his career, trying to help the miles pass quickly.

She lathered more sunblock on and stepped over green plants with stickers just waiting for her bare legs. Looking around, she drank the last of the water and asked, "Are there rattlesnakes?"

"As a rule, no, but then rules are made to be broken. I doubt if we have to worry. Snakes avoid people. We're making plenty of noise."

Slapping at a mosquito, she also brushed away the foliage that tickled near her ankles. If she'd let him, he'd pick her up and carry her the rest of the distance. But he figured she'd bristle if he tried. "There's a camp just ahead. We can get something to eat, cool off, and figure out what to do next."

"I'd like to know what you plan to do next."

"Probably look for a phone and—"

"No, after I leave Loving Heart."

"Jessica, you know my plans."

"Plans can be changed."

"Not this time."

"Not even when what you discover will hurt someone you lo—care about?"

She almost said *love*, and Patrick almost stopped in his tracks. Three days and he felt like he'd known this woman all her life. And somehow she knew him, his feelings, because when she almost said *love*, she meant the love he felt for her.

She knew.

He did stop, and she walked right into him. "I know how to be careful. No one will get hurt."

"You can't guarantee that."

"I'm not leaving until I have what I want."

She looked ready to protest more, but before she could find the right words, a rough wooden building came into view. It had splintered picnic tables and portable restrooms. He stopped talking and started walking faster. The way his luck was running today, she just might be able to convince him to drop the search.

Because she knew he was falling in love with her.

Impossible, not in three days.

And he'd learned about love from his father.

Love was fickle.

The Willie Raymond story was tangible—a safe bet.

Patrick couldn't get to the snack shop soon enough. The woman behind the counter served them overpriced hamburgers and chips before asking them if they needed to use the phone to call Desiree.

"You want to keep canoeing, or do you want to call it a day?" Patrick asked.

Jessica checked her watch. She picked up her meal and said, "Thanks, but go ahead and call Desiree. Church is in just five hours. I want to get back, shower, and all."

"You'd rather go to church than keep canoeing this gorgeous river?" Patrick asked.

"Of course."

"Look, Jessica. No one's going to know if you miss church. Your family—"

"I don't attend church because of my family; I attend church because of God."

"I'm trying to understand," Patrick said as he followed Jessica to the picnic table. "You mean to tell me you'd really give up an idyllic day to attend church."

"I always go to church."

"Because your family expects it."

"No, because God expects it."

"Have you ever attended the church here in Loving Heart?"

"No."

"It's a small church. Only about fifty people attend, and many of them are Raymonds. You know, the people who may or may not be your family. The people who either act like they don't know you or act like they want you to disappear."

"It doesn't matter. God knows me, and He doesn't want me to disappear. I'm not attending church because I have to but because I want to."

❦

"You want to go to church?" Patrick honestly sounded confused.

Jessica felt sorry for him. How sad not to *want* to go to church.

An old truck pulled in beside the camp, and Desiree's son poked his head out the window. "You guys stranded?"

"That was quick," Jessica said.

Patrick tossed the remnants of their lunch away and grabbed the cooler. "Probably someone with a cell phone called ahead before we ever got the chance."

William Conner Sherman IV, or was it V? had a canoe strapped to the top of his truck. "You game to try again?" Typical teenager fashion, he didn't get out of the vehicle, just yelled.

"No. Take us back to my car," Jessica hollered.

"Get in."

Only on television did three people fit comfortably in the front of a pickup. Jessica felt squashed between the two over-sized men. William Sherman—who made it clear he was simply Will—was more a man than a teen, or at least he took up the same amount of space as a man.

Patrick had some problems of his own. He didn't seem to have a comfortable place for his left arm, so he rested it along the seat behind her neck and shoulders. Every bump the truck hit brought his arm closer, until his fingers caressed her shoulder.

"So who are you anyway?" Will asked.

Jessica tried not to slump. She was uncomfortable, not only because of proximity and small space, but because of her awareness of Patrick's touch and the fact that she liked it a lot more than the circumstances dictated. "What did your mom tell you?"

"Nothing. She'd stepped out when the call came in about your canoe. I left my little brother in charge while I came to get you. He can't drive yet."

"Desiree's not going to be too happy about this," Patrick said.

"Mom's been pretty grouchy for about three days. I guess that's how long you've been here, huh?"

"You'll have to ask her, Will. It's not up to me to tell you."

"She's going to be unhappy no matter what."

"Probably—"

"My little brother accidentally backed into your car. He's only got a learner's permit. Mom's out trying to find a new fender for you. She's hoping there's not much damage."

❧

If Patrick had his camera now, Desiree would definitely grace the cover of his *Redheads of the Midwest*. Her lips were nonexistent, so thin was their straight line of anger.

Will pulled into the parking lot. Desiree took one look at the trio, shook her head, and threw her hands up in the air. "I give up. What did you tell him?"

"Nothing."

"It's true, Mom. She said you had to tell me."

Jessica gave Patrick a gentle nudge. "Why don't you and Will go inside. I'm sure there's an accident report or something to fill out."

"Not a chance."

Two redheads glared at him.

"Dude," Will said, "you might as well. They ain't talking while we're here."

Following the teenager inside, Patrick found a window and watched Jessica go over and stand next to Desiree.

"So will you tell me what's going on?" Will asked.

"I wish I could."

"I hate being the kid." Will took the stool behind the counter and picked up a magazine with an off-road vehicle on the cover.

Jessica and Desiree seemed to be having a decent conversation. Both redheads used their hands while they conversed, and after a few moments, Desiree no longer had clenched fists. As soon as he had a chance, Patrick determined he would master lipreading. Suddenly they both looked at him as if they knew right where he was standing. They studied him for a minute, then Desiree nodded. They hugged—*hugged?*—and headed back for the building.

"Settle up over the car?" Patrick asked after they entered.

"Yup," Jessica said. "It was just a scratch."

"But my husband's convinced he can hammer the dent out. She's leaving the car here for the evening. You can give her a ride to my mom's, right?"

Great, a ten-minute conversation and very little had been about the car. That meant Patrick has missed sensationalism at its best.

Chapter 9

He knew the way to Stacy Raymond's, so he didn't ask for directions. He'd researched Willie thoroughly but, stealing a glance at the woman beside him, obviously not thoroughly enough. He'd missed all the juicy stuff.

"Patrick, what would it take to make you forget this story?"

Her question surprised him, although if their roles were reversed, he'd be asking the same one.

"Why should I?"

"Is it money? What would a breaking story like this pay?"

"It's not about money. You're asking me to turn my back on the best story I've ever come across."

She nodded and stared out the window.

It annoyed him that he was tempted. Attraction—no way was he thinking the word *love*—was definitely a conflict of interest.

Attraction? It already felt like so much more.

Impossible; it had only been three days.

It was. . .*like*, definitely *like*.

Time to focus on what was real, what he could count on: his career. He posed a question—one he'd asked many times but she had yet to answer. "Why don't you tell me what's going on, and then I'll decide."

"Are you kidding?" She jerked her head in his direction so quickly he was surprised she didn't cry whiplash. As it was, the oversized Gilligan hat fell off. She picked it up and put it back on.

"Earlier you were telling me there's nothing more to know. You hinted that Willie Raymond really was dead. Now you're asking me to leave it alone just because you've asked me to. I've come too far to back off now."

"Even if what you find hurts people?"

"People always expect the worst, Jessica. When this is all over and done, everyone involved will probably give a big sigh of relief."

She didn't respond.

"Is Willie still alive? Do you know where he is?"

Still no response.

"Does Stacy Raymond know who you are?"

Continued silence came from the passenger side. He wasn't getting anywhere with her. Luckily, the Raymond farm was right ahead.

He'd done a coffee-table book on farms a few years back. The Raymond house probably dated back about a hundred years. He imagined that the original spread had shriveled as urban sprawl infringed on farmland.

"Who's in a wheelchair?" he asked when he saw the ramp.
"Stacy."

Life just kept throwing him curves with this story.

"Come in and meet her," Jessica urged.

He'd had no intention of doing otherwise. He followed

Jessica into the house. The incredible Opal, who lent such stylish clothes, was making homemade spaghetti sauce at the kitchen table. She lived up to his expectations. Yellow overalls—decorated with green, big-eyed worms—a purple-and-red-striped shirt, and platform tennis shoes made up her ensemble. She was Jessica, only without all the angst.

Patrick started to shake her hand, but since he didn't care for cheese, green onion, butter, and tomato paste smeared over his arm, he settled for a nod. "You must be Opal. I'm Patrick McDonald."

Opal reached toward a hand towel, but before she could snag one, someone hollered from another room. "Come to the living room!"

"That would be my grandmother," Opal said. "I think she's been half expecting you both. She made me dust the living room *twice*."

Patrick followed Jessica into a living room that overwhelmed him with its collision of history and present day. A cabinet filled with wedding paraphernalia was against one wall. Two antique sewing machines flanked a modern television. A grandfather clock chimed the wrong time. And Stacy Raymond sat in the midst of it all, looking at him as if he were the big bad wolf standing next to Goldilocks.

"She knows who *you* are," he said out of the corner of his mouth.

"Since I arrived," Jessica said in a normal voice.

"She knows who *I* am?" He kept talking out of the corner of his mouth.

"Stacy, I haven't been able to convince him to go away. Tell him Willie Raymond is dead. Tell him."

"Uncle Willie died more than twenty-five years ago." Opal came in the room and handed Stacy a glass of lemonade. "Why are you bringing him up?"

"I'm doing a human interest story on him," Patrick said.

"Oh, because of the war and all. That's cool." Opal nodded. "You guys want some lemonade or something?"

Freshly squeezed lemonade tasted pretty good on a warm afternoon. Especially to a man who'd canoed, hiked, and then walked into the home territory of the most unique story he'd ever pursued. Opal went back to finish dinner. Jessica joined Stacy on the couch, and soon both of them were looking at him as if he should be doing the talking. He needed to ask questions, but their faces denied answers before the words could be uttered. He finished his drink and took it back to the kitchen. On the way back, he paused in the hallway by the stairs. Soon he was studying all the photos gathered there.

"I'll show you Willie." Jessica snuck up behind him. With the help of Stacy's labels, Jessica chronicled from birth to off to war, stopping to smile at both Willie's first date and his lead in the high school's production of *Fiddler on the Roof*. "Now please drop this adventure. For me," she said softly.

The words hung in the air, and he almost said yes.

Then she touched a photo. Her finger traced Willie's red hair as she murmured, "He looks like me."

"You look like him, and why does that surprise you?"

"I was raised in a family where I'm the only redhead. Plus, I'm about a foot taller than everyone, even the men. I always wondered why. Finding the adoption papers surprised me, but I wasn't shocked. You know what I mean?"

He did and didn't. She was telling him she'd felt somewhat

displaced in a family that obviously adored her. She didn't know what displaced meant. Patrick's mother had died when he was two. He'd been raised by a father who shed wives like winter coats. Patrick's father had never purchased a birthday card. Oh, a few of the stepmothers had been willing, but they'd not lasted long. He had no brothers, no sisters, and his only aunt had lived overseas and stopped sending birthday cards when Patrick turned twelve. His grandmother, the one who had attended church, was the only who had added personal messages to the cards. She'd died when Patrick turned ten.

It embarrassed Patrick to remember he'd kept the cards.

Families—a coffee-table book he had no inclination to attempt. Looking back at the pictures on the wall, the idea of family almost assaulted him. He could see a few family photos that Willie had taken. The ever-present visual marker on the right was evident.

Taking one last look, Patrick stalled in front of the *Fiddler on the Roof* photo. Willie Raymond with black hair.

He couldn't give her what she wanted. He couldn't tell her he'd give up the quest to find Willie Raymond.

❧❦❧

Patrick had been optimistic putting church attendance at fifty, Jessica thought as she followed Opal down the aisle. Heads turned, and a few people gasped. Jessica knew then that she should have skipped church. Stacy had been of two minds about her attendance—figuring if they acted like they had nothing to hide, no one would get suspicious. Plus, Stacy reasoned, Jessica had been all over town, from the restaurants to the library to the cemetery.

Coming to Loving Heart had been a mistake. She'd put Willie, his family, her family, oh, pretty much everyone, in danger. Too late now, though. They'd wheeled Stacy to a special chair behind the last pew and already the woman was surrounded by friends.

Settling in, Jessica put her purse on the floor and picked up a songbook. A deep burgundy, it looked exactly like the ones in her home church. A quick peek showed the same songs. Opal turned and laughed at something happening behind her. Quite a few people moseyed over to be introduced and ask about family ties. Desiree didn't walk over, but Jessica understood why. Sitting next to Opal was one thing; they could blame their similarities on youth. But with Desiree, the similarities would lean toward a mother/daughter image.

Jessica met Opal's parents. By the looks in their eyes, she knew they knew who she was. Finally, a song leader stepped behind the podium and the service began. Her home congregation in Casper boasted over two hundred members. Songs were displayed via presentation software on a huge screen up front. Jessica suddenly realized how a large space absorbed sound. The small, Loving Heart church was alive with sound. It echoed from the walls and surrounded her with, could it be. . .comfort?

She was just starting to relax when Opal whispered, "Look."

Turning, Jessica watched as Patrick McDonald walked in the door, late, and with an older gentleman Jessica couldn't recall meeting. Behind them came Lionel Payne, the cemetery's groundskeeper. Jessica couldn't tell if the three men were together, but Lionel veered off and sat with the librarian Jessica had met on Monday.

Jessica's heart sank. She'd been so hopeful that he'd rethink her request and leave the Raymonds alone. Instead, it looked like he'd found reinforcements.

He wasn't the man she wanted him to be.

"Who's the older man?" Jessica whispered.

"That's Jimmy Tate. He used to preach here. What's he doing with your friend?"

Jessica started to deny that Patrick was her friend, but she stopped.

How could someone become a friend in just three days? Friends didn't try to convince you to destroy tender family ties. Friends didn't make your cheeks flush red from just eye contact.

"I don't know what's going on," Jessica whispered back.

"Things have sure been hopping since you showed up. I think—"

The sound of a father clearing his throat, letting a daughter know she'd been too conversationally active in church, quieted both women. *Just like home.*

Jessica needed to go home.

Oh, sure, she wanted to know her birth father, especially now that she knew why he'd stayed away. She wanted to know Opal, become best friends, share memories—but not until it was safe.

She needed to go home, before her disappointment in Patrick McDonald spilled over in tears that might never end.

She was more disappointed in him after just three days than she had been in David after an engagement of three years.

Finally, the preacher stood behind the podium and asked the congregation to open to 1 Corinthians 10:24. " 'Nobody should seek his own good, but the good of others,'" he read.

Could it be? Could the answer really be as simple as a scripture? Was Patrick listening, *really* listening? Jessica closed her eyes and listened to the Word. It took a few minutes of just letting the woes of the world slip away, but finally Jessica felt peace. She had two families. No, three, if you counted her church family. Right now she needed to deal with her present family—a mom and dad who were worried, a grandmother who wanted her to come home—and the other family would be in her future. Bowing, she prayed while the minister continued.

"Let go and let God," Grandma Lydia always said, right after she scolded Jessica for worrying too much.

"You're right, Grandma," Jessica whispered.

"What?" Opal asked, stealing a glance back at her father.

"I just figured out where I'm supposed to be."

"Wow," said Opal. "Most people never figure that out."

❦

Two weeks later, Jessica stood in the foyer of her home church. "How can you stand it?" her cousin Sheila asked as they walked toward the auditorium.

"Stand what?"

"Watching David with his new girlfriend. You dated him forever."

Jessica looked over to where David was introducing his new girlfriend to some members of the singles group. "It's fine. We've broken up. I have no hold on him."

"You'll get back together."

"No." Jessica was firm. "We won't. If I thought that, it would bother me to see him with Marie."

Two weeks ago it might have bothered her. But so much had changed. Most of the family hadn't even realized she'd gone to Loving Heart and had an adventure, and for safety's sake, she didn't tell them. Grandma Lydia and Jessica's parents had sat her down one night and shared the whole story, what they knew, and why everyone, especially Grandpa, had so wanted Carol's marriage and Jessica's birthright a secret.

There really hadn't been much to add to what Lydia had shared earlier on the phone. The best thing about knowing the truth had been the photographs and the stories about Carol. Suddenly the family was more open about the sister who had tragically died young. Jessica felt as though she could almost feel Carol's approval and love.

Sheila was still talking. "Dwaine says you're trying to buy Grandma's house. I think that's great! It needs to stay in the family. How will you afford it, though?"

"Well, for one thing, Grandma might come live with me. She likes the retirement center, but she liked her house more. Plus, we're talking about turning it into a bed-and-breakfast, open only in the summer while I'm off school."

"A bed-and-breakfast? You don't know anything about running a bed-and-breakfast."

"I know more than you might think." Jessica smiled, thinking about Opal, crazy colored paint, and crocheting. She'd only stayed in Loving Heart three days, but she'd actually learned quite a bit.

Only three days and I miss it, she thought.

Or, maybe I miss him.

Patrick.

The family had been so overprotective, trying to shield her

from the fact that David was seeing someone new. Truthfully, it didn't bother her a bit. When she looked at him, she missed him, sure, but only because he was comfortable, like a favorite pair of shoes.

Patrick wasn't comfortable. He was difficult and challenging and interesting, and Jessica wondered if she'd ever see him again.

She also wondered whether he was still pursuing Willie Raymond.

One of the teenagers went up front and tapped on the microphone. The words to the first song appeared on the screen, and those tarrying from either arriving late or a penchant for conversation hurried to their seats. Jessica followed her cousin to their usual pew. Dwaine scooted over, and soon their voices were lifted in praise. Jessica loved Sundays. She listened to the announcements, making note of who needed prayers. She sang songs, wishing her voice was as lyrical as Sheila's. Finally, it was time for the scripture reading. Reaching for her Bible, she waited for the scripture to be announced.

"First Corinthians 10:34: 'Nobody should seek his own good, but the good of others.' "

It was her favorite scripture. It had brought her home to the comfort of her family.

She was just starting to relax when Sheila whispered, "Look."

Two gentlemen entered the church and looked around. Arriving late wasn't a good idea. It always meant a center spot where one had to crawl over legs and hope the need to leave early didn't arise because then one would have to crawl over them again.

"Now that's a good-looking man," Sheila said, giving Dwaine a wink.

"Shh," he said.

Patrick was a good-looking man. And what was he doing in Casper?

More to the point, what was he doing in Casper with Lionel Payne at his side?

Chapter 10

After months of photographing old churches, it felt foreign to be in a modern structure. The size, design, and smells were all different. Looking around, Patrick wondered how he'd find Jessica in this crowd. Beside him, Jessica's father stood on tiptoes. Patrick didn't know who was looking forward to the reunion more, him or Lionel—er, make that Willie.

Patrick had wanted to hunt Jessica down with the truth when he'd finally wrung it from Willie, but they had to be sure it was safe. Patrick had uncovered the best story of his career, and if he were lucky, he'd be able to write about it and publish the pictures when he and Jessica were in their eighties and touring the United States in their RV.

Where was she?

He felt impatient just to see her again and not because of Willie. Willie was Patrick's first gift to her, because he'd gladly give her anything she asked for. He'd spent three days with her and two weeks away from her. He knew which he preferred.

The congregation stood, and that's when Patrick saw her. She was moving toward them. She wore an emerald green silk skirt and a white blouse. Her hair was loose and she didn't have that pinched look that had seemed a permanent fixture back in Loving Heart.

They stepped into the foyer, and Patrick tried to fade into the background as Willie embraced his daughter.

"I'm William Conner Raymond," Willie finally said, reaching for her hand.

Watching this gracious woman embrace her birth father, Patrick was sure if given the choice between telling the story live on television and starting a family and life with Jessica Fleming, he'd choose Jessica—if only she'd take him.

It looked like she was listening to her birth father. Willie clutched both her hands and spoke softly. Tears ran down Jessica's cheeks. Patrick started to go to her, but just in time he recognized them for what they were—tears of joy over finding her father.

Finding Willie Raymond.

Patrick stepped back, giving them time and wondering how much Willie intended to tell her.

Unlike most people protected by the government, Willie had not been a criminal testifying against his peers. He'd been an army corporal who'd angered a key figure in the Taliban: a key figure whose rise to power had kept Willie from resuming his true identity for far too long.

In most cases, the government kept tabs on its witnesses for maybe two years. Willie had followed protocol—after all, in the military he'd been conditioned to follow rules. He'd taken a new name and new Social Security card, and he'd lived in Hawaii for the two years, but the minute he'd felt free, he'd been unable to stay away from Afghanistan and the terror he saw building there. There was still work to be done, pictures to be taken, truth to be told.

He'd not been a comfort to his dying wife, he'd forfeited a relationship with his daughter, he'd been estranged from his family, and if there was any justice in the world, the least he could expect would be to make a difference in Afghanistan, a country that had a life expectancy of forty-six and dismal living conditions.

Time and time again, Willie had worked with the government. His new identity had kept Jessica safe, but it had made for a lonely decade, a decade in which Willie Raymond had done lots of good for others—and found God.

When Lionel Payne—a good friend and one of the few who knew the truth—died, Willie went to the authorities and set about taking over Lionel's identity. Neither Willie nor Lionel had been back to their hometown since the late seventies. Being back in Loving Heart, being with his mother and siblings, made Willie appreciate life, but it never lessened his fear that Jessica might be targeted, so he kept his secret.

With the 9/11 attacks, Willie's enemy fell, but by then Jessica was a grown woman—who might resent him. Plus, it was easier to stay Lionel Payne than it was to resume life as Willie Raymond. After all, Lionel was married—to the town's librarian. Lionel had a good and *safe* job. Lionel had long stopped looking over his shoulder.

When Patrick cornered him, Lionel decided to take the plunge, but first he wanted to do a little research. It took a week to ascertain that the captured Abrahim Abdel-Malik was the same Malik whom Willie had angered. Patrick and Willie had traveled to Washington and spoke with officials and waded through red tape. Then they'd gone to Afghanistan—not a wise move, but a necessary one. It took another week to discover that Malik had no sons or brothers bent on a decade's worth of revenge.

After twenty-six years, Willie severed his ties from the witness protection program, but instead of fading into the relative comfort of anonymity, Willie became Willie again.

And now they were back in America, standing in the back foyer of a church in Casper, Wyoming, so Willie could get to know his daughter.

Tentatively, Willie took a step toward Jessica, reaching out and touching her hair. "I'll stop dying my hair soon," Willie said.

Patrick waited, giving them time, but conversation stalled. Two people stared at each other, feeling both awkward and in awe.

"The black hair is what gave him away," Patrick finally told Jessica. "I figured it out after seeing that photo of Willie in *Fiddler on the Roof* in the hallway at Stacy and Opal's bed-and-breakfast."

"How?" Jessica asked. She didn't seem to grasp that he'd given her what she wanted. Her father. He'd found her father.

"It was partially your fault. You and that silly black Gilligan hat. Once I saw the photo of Willie portraying dairyman Tevye, his red hair hidden by that ridiculous black wig, I remembered how you looked, the shape of your face, your eyes, and for some reason it took me to Lionel—the groundskeeper we met that first day."

"Lionel was a friend of mine," Willie said. "He died overseas ten years after I went into hiding. He didn't have much family left, just his mother. With her permission, I stepped into his shoes. Strangest thing that could ever happen. After having no family connections for a decade, I got some of my life back."

"Lunch is going to be entertaining today." Grandma Lydia joined them in the foyer and put her hand on Jessica's shoulder. "Good morning, William. People are starting to look back here, and I'm thinking today might not be the day for their questions. Why don't we enjoy the rest of the church service and then figure out what to do afterward?"

"Fine by me," Willie agreed.

Lydia took Willie's arm and looked back at Patrick. "And you must be the photojournalist who's changed my granddaughter's life. Our family doesn't have much luck with photojournalists, you know."

"I'm thinking your luck is about to change," Patrick said.

❧❦❧

Not many restaurants could handle a party of twenty-five on short notice, so a pancake house had to suffice. Looking down the long table, Jessica watched as her family stole looks at her and Willie, and then at her and Patrick McDonald. Willie couldn't seem to stop looking at her and smiling.

Her dad kept coughing and drinking more tea. Funny, she'd only thought about how finding out that she was adopted would affect her. But truthfully, it seemed to be affecting her parents more. They were trying so hard to be jovial and accepting. Her dad was having the toughest time.

"So when did you get saved, Willie?" Lydia asked.

"While I was in the Federal Witness Protection Program.

I spent years in and out of Afghanistan under an assumed name—nothing like losing everything to make you think about your soul."

"I'm sure your mother was relieved."

"She didn't find out for two years."

"You were raised in the church," Lydia said. "Why'd it take you so long?"

"Stubborn, I guess."

"Now you," Lydia said, turning to Patrick, "were not raised in the church. Right?"

"Right."

"Do you know the Lord?"

"I'm getting to know Him," Patrick said.

"You found God in just two weeks?" Jessica sounded surprised. "You couldn't believe that I *wanted* to go to church that Wednesday night. What brought about the change?"

Willie chuckled.

"Your fa—um." Patrick looked from Willie to the man who'd raised Jessica and made a hasty correction. "Um, Willie believes in traveling light. He went to Afghanistan with only one change of clothes and a Bible."

"I was in a hurry to pack," Willie defended himself.

"By the end of those five days of travel, I knew if we ever traveled again, I'd be in charge of his packing, but I also knew I'd be packing both his Bible and mine."

"Oh, I can't take all the credit," Willie said. "The boy's own grandmother planted the seed—even gave him a Bible which he still owns. Jimmy Tate got him thinking about God again. Then you came along and confused him. It just took me and the Bible to straighten him out."

"I confused you? How?" Jessica asked.

Never had twenty-five members of the Dunmore family managed to be quiet at the same time. But they were now as they waited to hear Patrick's answer.

"I think it might take a lifetime to answer that question."

"Oh." Jessica squirmed. "We barely—"

"I realize that," Patrick said. "I'm starting my new book, *Redheads of the Midwest*. I'm going to make Casper my home base. Then, I think my next book—thanks to something your grandma said a minute ago—might be *Attic Treasures*." He reached across the table and took Jessica's hand. "Again, I think I'll find all I need here, in more ways than one."

"I like that idea," Jessica said quietly.

"Here! Here!" said both her father and Willie as they held up their iced tea glasses.

"Looks like everybody likes the idea," said Grandma.

Epilogue

Four months later

Lydia Dunmore settled back in her favorite rocking chair and smiled as she surveyed her living room.

Yes, her living room, still.

She'd never been happier.

Home, she was *home* again.

From her vantage point, she could see and hear Jessica on the phone. The bed-and-breakfast opened in five months and already they were receiving calls asking for reservations. They had Patrick McDonald to thank for their grand-opening success. He had connections from here to China, and apparently photojournalists liked to take vacations in obscure locations—like Casper, Wyoming.

Jessica and Patrick weren't engaged yet, but the family all knew it was just a matter of time.

Time enough for Jessica to settle into her new home and career and for Patrick to settle in with his newfound faith.

Lydia closed her eyes. She'd often napped in this chair, but today all the girls were here. . . .

Crash!

Lydia's eyes flew open. She started to get up, but before she could move, Sheila came running around the corner.

"If she's dropped the vintage Syphon study lamp, I'm going to thump her!" Sheila exclaimed.

"You shouldn't thump cousins or pregnant women," Lydia advised. "And what's a Syphon study lamp?"

"Dwaine spent two days locating that lamp!" Sheila took the stairs two at a time and was out of sight before Lydia could remind her that lamps were replaceable. A few moments later, Lydia heard the hum of Sheila's and Lauren's words.

Sheila and her husband had both embraced the idea of a bed-and-breakfast with enthusiasm. They'd promptly started giving advice about what personal touches such an establishment needed. Sheila poured through magazines, and Dwaine located antiques and bartered prices.

Watching Sheila and Dwaine together, so loving and committed, made Lydia long for her husband. He'd been gone almost three years now.

He'd loved the girls as much as she had.

Lydia sighed. It was so good to have all four granddaughters in the house again. When they heard Jessica's idea about a bed-and-breakfast, they had insisted on investing not only money, but their time. Oh, the memories they brought back.

And the new memories they were making.

But memories weren't all they were making!

Lauren, who denied that she missed her job in Chicago, had taken over the renovations. She was making walls appear and disappear. First with a deft mark of her drafting pencil, and then with the help of her husband and his trusty sledgehammer.

Since buying that farm, Bob had become quite handy with tools. He now used his new skills on the old Victorian home. He built a closet in the den, giving them one more bedroom. He'd put up shelves and bookcases, enclosed the back patio, and even managed to install a window seat in the living room. Lydia loved that window seat. Soon Lauren would need the rocking chair, and Lydia thought the window seat would give her the perfect perch when taking photographs of her new great-granddaughter.

She could hardly wait.

Closing her eyes, she tried yet again to catch the midday nap she seemed to enjoy more and more as the years went by, but the earlier crash had put all her senses on alert, and now the pounding of Bob's hammer seemed to gain intensity with every whack.

Funny how close it sounded when Bob was all the way in the backyard. Lydia stood and wandered to the back door. The arch Bob was working on would be permanent. Lauren had imagined a nice garden area for their guests.

But the arch's first job would be to highlight Kimber and Jake when they exchanged their vows in just six short weeks. They were getting married in Lydia's backyard and then honeymooning at Niagara Falls. Their guests would be the first to occupy the newly renovated rooms at Grandma's Attic Bed-and-Breakfast—free of charge, of course.

Come to think of it, Kimber had certainly kept a low profile this morning. Where was the girl? Lydia left the kitchen and headed for the family room. Yup, she should have guessed. Kimber sat at the computer desk, maps of the area opened beside her and her fingers flying over the computer keys. She and Jake had scouted all the nearby lakes and streams. They planned to promote Grandma's Attic Bed-and-Breakfast as a premiere fishing location weekend vacation spot. Kimber's years in college had produced a young woman who could put together a stellar brochure.

Kimber seemed so carefree lately. Such a joy to watch. She and Jake had taken much of Charles's old fishing gear, and now the newly enclosed back porch was decorated in a "lazy day at the lake" motif.

Since Kimber had returned some of her attic treasure, Lydia had the two quilts wrapped up in wedding paper.

My girls, Lydia thought.

The doorbell sounded. Kimber didn't move, so involved was she in her graphic design. Upstairs, it didn't sound as if Sheila and Lauren were anywhere near finished with their discussion, and Jessica still held on to the phone.

No rest for the weary, Lydia decided. She felt needed, and that was the best feeling in the world.

Of course, she remembered as she opened the door and found Bill there waiting to take her to lunch, there was one even better feeling—the feeling of being loved.

It was a feeling both she and her granddaughters were thankful to the Lord for. Now, because Lydia would be staying in her beloved old house, she could someday pass along to her great-grandchildren even more wonderful attic treasures.

PAMELA KAYE TRACY

Pamela Kaye Tracy lives in Scottsdale, Arizona, with a newly acquired husband (yup, somewhat a newlywed) and two confused cats ("Hey, we had her to ourselves for thirteen years. Where'd this guy come from?"). She was raised in Omaha, Nebraska, and started writing while earning a BA in Journalism at Texas Tech University.

Her first novel, *It Only Takes a Spark*, was published in 1999. Since then she's published seven more writings. *Promises and Prayers for Teachers*, a 2004 release, was her first nonfiction book.

Pamela is an English professor who, besides writing, teaching, and taking care of her family, often speaks at various writers' organizations in the Phoenix area. She belongs to Romance Writers of America, The Society of Southwestern Writers, and The Arizona Authors' Association. Her biggest dream of the moment is to change her status of newlywed to newlymom. In February 2005, that dream should come true.